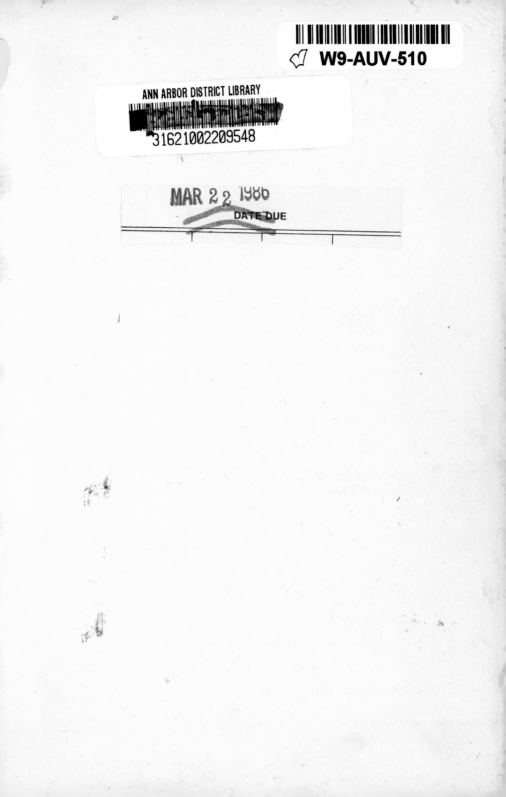

ALSO BY JULIO CORTÁZAR

The Winners
Hopscotch
End of the Game
Cronopios and Famas
62: A Model Kit
All Fires the Fire and Other Stories
A Manual for Manuel

A
CHANGE
OF
LIGHT
AND
OTHER
STORIES

A CHANGE OF LIGHT

AND OTHER STORIES

JULIO CORTÁZAR

*TRANSLATED FROM
THE SPANISH BY
GREGORY RABASSA*

*ALFRED A. KNOPF
NEW YORK 1980*

Translation Copyright © 1976, 1978, 1979, 1980 by Alfred A. Knopf, Inc.
All rights reserved under International and Pan-American Copyright
Conventions. Published in the United States by Alfred A. Knopf,
Inc., New York, and simultaneously in Canada by Random House of
Canada Limited, Toronto. Distributed by Random House, Inc., New York.
The following stories were originally published in Spanish in Octaedro,
by Alianza Editorial, Madrid. © by Julio Cortázar, © Edición Castellana,
Alianza Editorial, S.A., 1974: "Summer," "Liliana Weeping," "Severo's
Phases," "Manuscript Found in a Pocket," "Footsteps in the Footprints,"
"There but Where, How," and "Throat of a Black Kitten."

All other stories were originally published in Spanish in Alguien que
anda por ahí, by Ediciones Alfaguera, Spain. © by Ediciones
Alfaguera, S.A., 1978.

This English translation of "In the Name of Bobby" was printed in
The New Yorker.

English translations of other stories have appeared in Chicago Review,
Kenyon Review, New England Review, *and* World Literature Today
(formerly Books Abroad*).*

Library of Congress Cataloging in Publication Data
Cortázar, Julio.
A change of light and other stories.
Translation of author's Octaedro and Alguien que anda
por ahí.
I. Title. II. Cortázar, Julio. Octaedro. English.
1980. III. Cortázar, Julio. Alguien que anda por ahí.
English. 1980.
PZ3.C81929Ch 1980 [PQ7797.C7145] 863
80–7656
ISBN 0–394–50721–5

Manufactured in the United States of America
First Edition

CONTENTS

SUMMER   3

IN THE NAME OF BOBBY   15

LILIANA WEEPING   27

A PLACE NAMED KINDBERG   39

SECOND TIME AROUND   53

SEVERO'S PHASES   63

BUTTERBALL'S NIGHT   75

TRADE WINDS   91

MANUSCRIPT FOUND IN A POCKET   103

APOCALYPSE AT SOLENTINAME   119

FOOTSTEPS IN THE FOOTPRINTS   129

ENCOUNTER WITHIN A RED CIRCLE   153

THE FACES OF THE MEDAL   163

SOMEONE WALKING AROUND   181

THE FERRY, OR ANOTHER
TRIP TO VENICE   189

THERE BUT WHERE, HOW   235

A CHANGE OF LIGHT   247

THROAT OF A BLACK KITTEN   259

A
CHANGE
OF
LIGHT
AND
OTHER
STORIES

SUMMER

In the late afternoon Florencio went down to the cabin with his little girl, taking the back road full of holes and loose stones that only Mariano and Zulma were up to following in their Jeep. Zulma opened the door for them, and Florencio thought that her eyes looked as if she had been peeling onions. Mariano appeared from the other room; he told them to come in, but Florencio only wanted to ask them to take care of the little girl until the next morning because he had to go to the coast on an urgent matter and there was nobody in the village he could ask to do him this favor. Of course, said Zulma, leave her, don't worry, we'll set up a bed for her here downstairs. Come on in and have a drink, Mariano in-

sisted, it'll only take five minutes, but Florencio had left his
car in the village square, he had to take off right away; he
thanked them and kissed his little girl, who had already
spotted the stack of magazines on the bench. When the door
closed, Zulma and Mariano looked at each other almost ques-
tioningly, as if everything had happened too fast. Mariano
shrugged his shoulders and returned to his workshop, where
he was gluing an old chair; Zulma asked the little girl if she
was hungry, she suggested she play with the magazines, in the
closet there was a ball and a net for catching butterflies; the
little girl said thank you and began to look at the magazines;
Zulma watched her a moment while she prepared the arti-
chokes for dinner that evening and thought she could let her
play by herself.

Dusk fell early in the south now; they barely had a month left
before returning to the capital and getting into that other life
during the winter which, in any case, was only a continuation
of this one, distantly together, amicably friends, respecting
and performing the many trivial, delicate, conventional ceremonies of a couple, as now, when Mariano needed one of the
burners to heat the glue jar and Zulma took the pot of potatoes off saying she'd finish cooking them later, and Mariano
said thanks because the chair was almost ready and it would
be better to do all the gluing in one application, but he had
to heat the jar first, of course. The little girl was leafing
through the magazines at the end of the large room that was
used both as a kitchen and as a living room. Mariano looked
in the pantry for some candy to give her; it was time to go out
into the garden to have a drink as they watched night fall
upon the hills. There was never anybody on the road; the
first house in the village could barely be seen at the highest

point; in front of them the slope kept on descending to the
bottom of the valley, which was already in the shadows. Go
ahead and pour, I'll be right there, said Zulma. Everything
was done in cyclical fashion, each thing in its time and a time
for each thing, except for the little girl, who had suddenly
disturbed the pattern just a bit; a stool and a glass of milk for
her, a stroke of her hair, and praise for how well she was
behaving. The cigarettes, the swallows clustering above the
cabin; everything went along repeating itself, fitting into the
right slot, the chair must be almost dry by now, stuck together like that new day which had nothing new about it.
The insignificant difference was the little girl that afternoon,
as sometimes the mailman would draw them out of their solitude for a moment at midday with a letter for Mariano or
Zulma that the addressee would receive and put away without saying a word. One more month of foreseeable repeti-
tions, like rehearsals, and the Jeep loaded to the top would
take them back to the apartment in the capital, to the life that
was only different in form, Zulma's group or Mariano's artist
friends, afternoons in the stores for her and evenings in the
cafés for Mariano, a coming-and-going separately although
they always got together to perform the linking ceremonies,
the morning kiss, the neutral programs in common, as now
when Mariano offered her another drink and Zulma accepted
with her eyes lost in the most distant hills, which were tinted
already in deep violet.

What would you like to have for supper, little one? Me?
Anything you say, ma'am. She probably doesn't like arti-
chokes, said Mariano. Yes, I like them, said the little girl,
with oil and vinegar, but only a little salt because it burns.
They laughed; they would make a special vinaigrette dress-
ing for her. And boiled eggs, how do you like them? With a
teaspoon, said the little girl. And only a little salt, because it

burns, teased Mariano. Salt burns a lot, said the little girl, I give my doll her mashed potatoes without salt, today I didn't bring her because my daddy was in a hurry and wouldn't let me. It's going to be a lovely night, thought Zulma out loud, see how clear the air is toward the north. Yes, it won't be too hot, said Mariano, bringing the chairs into the downstairs room and turning on the lamps next to the picture window that faced the valley. Automatically he also turned on the radio. Nixon is going to Peking, how about that, said Mariano. There's nothing sacred, said Zulma, and they both laughed at the same time. The little girl was into the magazines and marking the comic strip pages as though she planned to reread them.

Night arrived in between the insecticide Mariano was spraying in the bedroom upstairs and the fragrance of an onion Zulma cut while humming along with a pop tune on the radio. Midway through supper the little girl began to doze over the boiled egg; they joked with her, they prodded her to finish; Mariano had already prepared the cot for her with an inflatable mattress in the farthest corner of the kitchen so they wouldn't bother her if they stayed a while in the room downstairs listening to records or reading. The little girl ate her peach and admitted she was sleepy. Go to bed, sweetie, said Zulma, don't forget if you have to tinkle, you only have to go upstairs, we'll leave the stairway light on. The little girl, half-asleep, gave them each a kiss on the cheek, but before she lay down she selected a magazine and placed it under the pillow. They're unbelievable, said Mariano, such an unattainable world and to think it once was ours, everybody's. Perhaps it's not so different, said Zulma, clearing the table, you too have your compulsions, the bottle of cologne on the left and the razor on the right, and as for me, forget it. But they weren't compulsions, thought Mariano, rather a re-

sponse to death and nothingness, fixing things and times, es-
tablishing rituals and passages in opposition to chaos, which
was full of holes and smudges. Only now he no longer said it
aloud, more and more there seemed to be less of a need to
talk to Zulma, and Zulma didn't say anything either that
might prompt an exchange of ideas. Take the coffeepot, I've
already set the cups on the stool by the chimney. Check to see
if there's any sugar left in the bowl, there's a new package in
the pantry. I can't find the corkscrew, this bottle of rum has a
good color, don't you think? Yes, a lovely color. Since you're
going up, bring the cigarettes I left on the dresser. This rum
is really good stuff. It's hot, don't you think so? Yes, it's stif-
ling, we'd better not open the windows, the place will fill
with moths and mosquitoes.

When Zulma heard the first sound, Mariano was looking
among the stack of records for a Beethoven sonata which he
hadn't listened to that summer. He stood still with his hand
in the air, he looked at Zulma. A noise as if on the stone steps
of the garden, but nobody came to the cabin at that hour,
nobody ever came at night. From the kitchen he switched on
the light that illuminated the nearest part of the garden, saw
no one and turned it off. Probably a dog looking around for
something to eat, said Zulma. It sounded strange, almost like
a snort, said Mariano. An enormous white blur lashed against
the window. Zulma muffled a scream, Mariano, with his back
toward her, turned around too late, the pane reflected only
the pictures and furniture in the room. He had no time to ask
anything, the snort resounded near the north wall; a whinny
that was smothered just like Zulma's scream, her hands up to
her mouth and pressing against the back wall, staring at the
window. It's a horse, said Mariano, I hear his hooves, he's

galloping through the garden. His mane, his lips, almost as if
they were bleeding, an enormous white head was grazing the
window; the horse barely looked at them, the white blotch
was erased on the right, they heard his hooves again, an
abrupt silence coming from the side of the stone steps, the
neighing, the flight. But there are no horses in these parts,
said Mariano, who had grabbed the bottle of rum by the neck
before realizing it and now put it back on the stool. He wants
to come in, said Zulma, glued to the rear wall. Of course
not, what a foolish idea, he probably escaped from some herd
in the valley and headed for the light. I tell you, he wants to
come in, he's rabid and wants to get inside. Horses don't get
rabies, as far as I know, said Mariano, I think he's gone, I'll
take a look from the upstairs window. No, please, stay here, I
can still hear him, he's on the terrace steps, he's stomping on
the plants, he'll be back, and what if he breaks the window
and gets in? Don't be silly, what do you mean he'll break the
window, said Mariano weakly, maybe if we turn off the lights
he'll go away. I don't know, I don't know, said Zulma, sliding
down until she was sitting on the stool, I heard how he whin-
nied, he's there upstairs. They heard the hooves coming
down the steps, the irritated heavy snort against the door,
Mariano thought he felt something like pressure on the door,
a repeated rubbing, and Zulma ran to him screaming hysterically. He cast her off, not violently, extended his hand
toward the light switch; in the dark (the only light still on
was in the kitchen, where the little girl was sleeping), the
neighing and the hooves became louder, but the horse was no
longer in front of the door; he could be heard going back and
forth in the garden. Mariano ran to turn out the kitchen light
without even looking toward the corner where they had put
the little girl to bed; he returned to put his arms around
Zulma, who was sobbing. He caressed her hair and face, ask-

ing her to be quiet so he could listen better. In the window
the horse rubbed his head against the large pane, not too
forcefully, the white blotch appeared transparent in the darkness; they sensed the horse looking inside, as though searching for something, but he could not see them any longer, and
yet there he still was, whinnying and puffing, bolting
abruptly from side to side. Zulma's body slipped through
Mariano's arms and he helped her sit on the stool again,
propping her up against the wall. Don't move, don't say anything, he's leaving now, you'll see. He wants to come in,
Zulma said feebly, I know he wants to come in, and what if he
breaks the window, what's going to happen if he kicks it in?
Shh, said Mariano, please shut up. He's going to come in,
muttered Zulma. And I don't even have a shotgun, said Mariano, I'd blast five shots into his head, the son of a bitch. He's
not there anymore, said Zulma, rising suddenly, I hear him
up there, if he sees the terrace door he might come in. It's
shut tight, don't be afraid, remember in the dark he's not
about to enter a house where he couldn't even move around,
he's not that dumb. Oh yes, said Zulma, he wants to come in,
he'll crush us against the walls, I know he wants to come in.
Shh, repeated Mariano, who also was thinking about it, and
could do nothing but wait with his back soaked in cold
perspiration. Once again the hooves echoed upon the flag-
stone steps, and suddenly silence, the distant crickets, a bird
high in a walnut tree.

Without turning on the light, now that the window let
the night's vague clarity enter, Mariano filled a glass with
rum and held it against Zulma's lips, forcing her to drink
even though her teeth hit the glass and the liquor spilled on
her blouse; then holding the bottle by the neck he took a long
swig and went to the kitchen to check on the little girl. With
her hand under the pillow as if clutching the precious maga-

zine, incredibly she was asleep and had heard nothing, she hardly seemed to be there, while in the big room Zulma's sobbing broke every so often into a smothered hiccough, almost a shout. It's all over, it's over, said Mariano, sitting up against her and shaking her gently, it was nothing but a scare. He'll be back, said Zulma, her eyes nailed to the window. No, he's probably far off by now, no doubt he escaped from some herd down below. No horse does that, said Zulma, no horse tries to enter a house like that. It's strange, I'll grant you that, said Mariano, maybe we'd better take a look outside, I have the lantern right here. But Zulma had pressed herself against the wall, the idea of opening the door, of going out toward the white shadow that might be near, waiting under the trees, ready to charge. Look, if we don't check to see if he's gone, nobody will sleep tonight, said Mariano. Let's give him a little more time; meanwhile you go to bed, and I'll give you a tranquilizer; an extra dose, poor kid, you've certainly earned it.

Zulma ended up by accepting passively; without turning on the lights, they went toward the stairs and with his hand Mariano motioned toward the little girl asleep, but Zulma scarcely looked at her, she was climbing the stairs reeling, Mariano had to hold her as they entered the bedroom because she was about to bump into the doorframe. From the window that faced the eaves they looked at the stone steps, the highest terrace of the garden. You see, he's gone, said Mariano, fixing Zulma's pillow, watching her undress mechanically, staring at the window. He made her drink the drops, dabbed cologne on her neck and hands, gently lifted the sheet up to Zulma's shoulders as she closed her eyes and trembled. He wiped her cheeks, waited a moment, and went downstairs to look for the lantern; carrying it unlit in one hand and an ax in the other, little by little he opened the door of the large room and went out to the lower terrace, where he could get full view of the entire side of the house facing eastward; the night was identical to so many other summer nights, the crickets chirped in the distance, a frog let fall two alternating drops of sound. Not needing the lantern, Mariano saw the trampled lilac bush, the huge prints in the pansy bed, the flowerpot overturned at the bottom of the steps; so it wasn't an hallucination, and, of course, it was better that it not be; in the morning he would go with Florencio to check on the herds in the valley, they weren't going to get the upper hand so easily. Before going in he set the flowerpot straight, went up to the front trees and listened for a long while to the crickets and the frog; when he looked toward the house, Zulma was standing at the bedroom window, naked, motionless.

The little girl had not moved; Mariano went upstairs without making any noise and began to smoke a cigarette next to Zulma. You see, he's gone, now we can sleep in peace, tomorrow we'll see. Little by little he led her toward the bed, undressed, stretched out on his back still smoking. Go to sleep, everything is all right, it was only an absurd fright. He stroked her hair, his fingers slid down to her shoulder, grazing her breasts lightly. Zulma turned on her side, her back toward him, not speaking; this too was like so many other summer nights.

Getting to sleep should have been difficult, but no sooner had Mariano put out his cigarette than he dropped off suddenly;

the window was still open and no doubt mosquitoes would enter, but sleep came first, with no dreams, total nothingness from which he emerged at some moment driven by an indescribable panic, the pressure of Zulma's fingers on one shoulder, the panting. Almost without realizing it, he was now listening to the night, the perfect silence punctuated by the crickets. Go to sleep, Zulma, it's nothing, you must have been dreaming. Insisting she agree with him, that she lie down again, her back turned to him now that she had suddenly withdrawn her hand and was sitting up rigid, looking toward the closed door. He got up at the same time as Zulma, helpless to stop her from opening the door and going to the top of the stairs, clinging to her and asking himself vaguely if it wouldn't be better to slap her, to bring her back to bed by force, to break such petrified remoteness. In the middle of the staircase Zulma stopped, taking hold of the banister. You know why the little girl is there? With a voice that must have still belonged to the nightmare. The little girl? Two more steps, now almost in the bend that led to the kitchen. Zulma, please. And her voice cracking, almost in falsetto: she's there to let him in, I tell you she's going to let him in. Zulma, don't make me do something I'll regret. And her voice, almost triumphant, still rising in tone, look, just look if you don't believe me; the bed's empty, the magazine on the floor. With a start Mariano headed for Zulma, he sprang toward the light switch. The little girl looked at them, her pink pajamas against the door that faced the large room, her face drowsy. What are you doing up at this hour, said Mariano wrapping a dish towel around his waist. The little girl looked at Zulma naked, somewhere between being asleep and embarrassed she looked at her as if wanting to go back to bed, on the brink of tears. I got up to tinkle, she said. And you went out to the garden when we had told you to go upstairs to the bathroom.

The little girl began to pout, her hands comically lost in the
pockets of her pajamas. It's okay, go to bed, said Mariano,
stroking her hair. He covered her, and placed the magazine
under the pillow for her; the little girl turned toward the
wall, a finger in her mouth as if to console herself. Go ahead
up, said Mariano, you see there's nothing wrong, don't stand
there like a sleepwalker. He saw Zulma take a couple of steps
toward the door of the large room, he blocked her path;
everything was fine now, damn it. But don't you realize she's
opened the door for him, said Zulma with that voice which
wasn't hers. Stop the nonsense, Zulma. Go see if it's not so, or
let me go. Mariano's hand closed around her trembling forearm. Get upstairs right now, pushing her till he had led her
to the foot of the steps, looking as he went by at the little girl,
who hadn't moved, she must be asleep by now. On the first
step Zulma screamed and tried to escape, but the stairway was
narrow and Mariano kept shoving her with his whole body;
the towel unfastened and fell to the bottom of the stairs.
Holding on to her by the shoulders, he hurled her upward to
the landing and flung her into the bedroom, shutting the
door behind him. She's going to let him in, Zulma repeated,
the door is open and he'll get in. Lie down, said Mariano. I'm
telling you the door is open. It doesn't matter if he comes in
or not, let him come in if he wants to, I don't give a damn
now whether he comes in or not. He caught Zulma's hands as
they tried to repel him, from behind he pushed against the
bed, they fell together, Zulma sobbing and begging, power-
less to move under the weight of a body that pressed her
nearer and nearer, that bent her to a will murmured mouth
to mouth, wildly amidst tears and obscenities. I don't want to,
I don't want to, I don't want to ever again, I don't want to,
but it was too late now, her strength and pride yielding to that
leveling weight, returning her to an impossible past, to

the summers without letters and without horses. Later in the night—it was beginning to get light—Mariano dressed in silence and went down to the kitchen; the little girl was sleeping with her finger in her mouth, the door of the big room was open. Zulma had been right, the little girl had opened the door but the horse hadn't entered the house. Unless, he thought, lighting his first cigarette and looking at the blue ridge of the hills, unless Zulma had been right about that too and the horse had entered the house, but how could they prove it if they had not heard him, if everything was in order, if the clock would continue to measure the morning and later Florencio would come to get the little girl, probably around twelve the mailman would arrive whistling from afar, leaving for them on the garden table the letters that he or Zulma would pick up without saying anything, shortly before deciding by mutual consent what was best to prepare for lunch.

—*Translated from the Spanish
by Clementine Rabassa*

I N
T H E
N A M E
O F
B O B B Y

Yesterday was his eighth birthday. We had a fine party for
him, and Bobby was happy with the windup train, the soccer
ball, and the cake with candles. My sister had been afraid that
at precisely this time he would come home from school with
bad grades, but it was just the opposite; he'd done better in
arithmetic and reading, and there was no reason to take his
toys away—quite the contrary. We told him to invite his
friends, and he had Beto and Juanita; Mario Panzani came,
too, but he didn't stay long, because his father was ill. My
sister let them play in the yard until dusk, and Bobby broke
in the ball, even though we were both afraid that he would
knock over our plants in his enthusiasm. When it was time

for orangeade and the cake with candles, we all sang "Happy
Birthday" to him in a chorus and laughed a lot, because
everybody was happy, especially Bobby, and it seemed to me
to be a waste of time keeping an eye on what there was nothing to keep an eye on. Just the same, I kept an eye on Bobby
when he was distracted, trying to catch sight of the look that
my sister doesn't seem to notice but that upsets me so much.

This time he looked at her that way only once, just as my
sister was lighting the candles, scarcely a second before he
lowered his eyes and, like the well-brought-up child he is,
said, "The cake is very nice, Mama," and Juanita approved,
too, and Mario Panzani. I had laid out the long knife for
Bobby to cut the cake with, and at that moment especially I
kept an eye on him from the other end of the table, but
Bobby was so happy with the cake that he hardly looked at
my sister again and concentrated on the task of cutting small,
equal pieces and passing them around. "You first, Mama,"
Bobby said, giving her a slice, and then Juanita and me, because ladies first. They immediately went out into the yard to
continue playing, except for Mario Panzani, but first Bobby
told my sister again that the cake was delicious, and he ran
over to me and jumped up and put his arms around my neck
and gave me one of his wet kisses. "The train is wonderful,
Auntie," he said, and that night he climbed up onto my lap
to confide his great secret in me: "I'm eight years old now,
you know, Auntie."

We went to bed rather late, but it was Saturday and
Bobby could loll about like us until late in the morning. I
was the last one to go to bed, and first I busied myself tidying
up the dining room and putting the chairs in place. The
children had played Going to Jerusalem and other games,
which had turned the house upside down. I put away the
long knife, and before going to bed I saw that my sister was

already sleeping the sleep of the just. I went to Bobby's little room and looked at him; he was face down, as he had always liked to be since he was an infant, and had already thrown the blankets to the floor and had one leg buried in the pillow. If I had a son, I would let him sleep that way, too, but why think about such things? I went to bed and didn't feel like reading. I may have done the wrong thing, because sleep didn't come to me and I went through what I usually do at that hour when you lose your will and ideas leap out from all sides and seem to be true—everything you think about is suddenly true and almost always horrible and there's no way to shake it off, not even by praying. I drank some water and sugar and waited, counting down from three hundred, backward, which is harder and makes sleep come. Just as I was about to fall asleep, I was seized by doubts about whether I'd put the knife away or whether it was still on the table. It was silly, because I'd put everything away and I remembered that I'd put the knife in the bottom drawer of the cupboard, but just the same I got up and, of course, it was there in the drawer, mixed in with the other kitchen utensils. I don't know why, but I got a kind of urge to keep it in my bedroom. I even took it out for a moment, but that was already too much. I looked at myself in the mirror and made a face. That didn't make things any better, and then I poured myself a drink of anisette, even though it was imprudent, with my liver and all, and I sipped it in bed to help sleep come. From time to time my sister's snoring could be heard, and Bobby, as always, was talking or moaning.

Just as I was falling aleep everything came back suddenly—the first time Bobby asked my sister why she was mean to him and my sister, who is a saint, everybody says so, stood looking at him as if it were a joke, and even laughed. But I, who was preparing the maté, remember that Bobby

hadn't laughed. On the contrary, he was upset, and wanted to
know; at that time he must have already been seven and he
always asked strange questions, like all children. I remember
the day he asked me why trees were different from us and I in
turn asked him why and Bobby said, "But, Auntie, they cover
themselves in summer and uncover themselves in winter,"
and I stood there openmouthed, because, really, that child;
they're all like that, but after all . . . And now my sister was
looking at him puzzled; she had never been mean to him, she
told him—just strict a few times when he'd misbehaved or
had been ill and had to do things he didn't like. Juanita's
mother and Mario Panzani's mother were also strict with
their children when it was necessary. But Bobby kept on
looking at her sadly and explained that it wasn't during the
day—that she was mean at night, when he was asleep. The
two of us were flabbergasted, and I think that it was I who
began to explain to him that no one is to blame for what
happens in dreams, that it must have been a nightmare and
that was all, there was no need to worry. That day Bobby
didn't insist—he always accepted our explanations and he
wasn't a difficult child—but a few days later he awoke weeping and shouting and when I got to his bed he hugged me and
wouldn't speak. He just cried and cried, another nightmare
surely, but at noontime he suddenly remembered and asked
my sister again why she was so mean to him when he was
alseep. This time my sister hugged him to her breast, told
him that he was too big now not to know the difference, and
that if he kept on insisting about that she was going to talk to
Dr. Kaplan, because he probably had worms or appendicitis
and something would have to be done. I felt that Bobby was
going to start crying and hastened to explain to him again
about nightmares—he had to realize that nobody loved him
as much as his mother, not even I, who loved him so much—

and Bobby listened very seriously, drying a tear, and said of
course he knew and got out of his chair to go kiss my sister,
who didn't know what to do and remained thoughtful, looking into space. That afternoon I went to look for him in the
yard and asked him to tell me, his aunt, because he could
confide everything in me the same as with his mother, and if
he didn't want to tell her, he could tell me. You could see
that he didn't want to talk—it was too much for him—but
finally he said something like at night it was all different; he
spoke about some sort of black cloth that he couldn't get his
hands or feet out of. Anyone can have nightmares like that,
but it was a shame that Bobby should only have them about
my sister, who made so many sacrifices for him. I told him
that, and I repeated it, and he, of course, agreed.

Right after that my sister came down with pleurisy and I
had to take care of things. Bobby was no trouble for me,
because, small as he was, he could handle almost everything
by himself. I remember that he would come in to see my
sister and stay by the side of her bed without speaking, waiting for her to smile at him or to stroke his hair, and then he
would go quietly out into the yard and play or into the living
room to read. I didn't even have to tell him not to play the
piano during that time, even though he would have liked to
very much. The first time I saw that he was sad I explained to
him that his mother was better now and that one of these days
she would get up for a while to take some sun. Bobby put on a
strange expression and looked at me out of the corner of his
eye; I don't know, the idea suddenly came to me and I asked
him if he was having his nightmares again. He began to weep
very quietly, hiding his face; then he said he was—why was
his mother that way with him? That time I realized that he

was afraid; when I lowered his hands to dry his face I could see the fear, and it was hard for me to act indifferent and explain to him once more that they were only dreams. "Don't say anything to her," I told him. "Remember, she's still weak and it might have some effect on her." Bobby nodded in silence—he had so much trust in me—but later on I came to think that he had taken me too literally, because not even when my sister was convalescing did he talk about it again. I could sense it in him on some mornings when I would see him come out of his room with that lost expression, and also because he spent all of his time with me, hovering about in the kitchen. One or two times I couldn't take it anymore and spoke to him in the yard or when I was bathing him, and he was always the same, making an effort not to cry, swallowing his words, because his mother was that way with him at night, but he wouldn't go beyond that, he was weeping too much. I explained again to Bobby, who understood quite well, that I didn't want my sister to find out, because she was still weak from the pleurisy and it might affect her too much, but on the other hand he could tell me anything. He would soon see that when he got a little older he'd stop having those nightmares; it would be better, though, if he didn't eat so much bread at night. I was going to ask Dr. Kaplan if he might not need a laxative, so he could sleep without any bad dreams, but I didn't, of course; it was difficult to talk about something like that with Dr. Kaplan, who had such a busy practice and wasn't about to waste his time. I don't know if I did the right thing or not, but little by little Bobby stopped worrying me so much. Sometimes I would see him in the morning with that slightly lost air and I would say to myself, probably again, and then I would wait for him to come and confide in me, but Bobby would start to sketch or go to school without saying anything to me and would come home happy, and he was stronger and healthier each day and got the best grades.

The last time was during the February heat wave; my sister was completely recovered and we lived life as usual. I don't know if she was aware that something was wrong, but I didn't want to say anything to her, because I know her and I know that she's too sensitive, especially when it's a question of Bobby, even though I can remember when Bobby was small and my sister was still suffering from the shock of the divorce and all that—how hard it was for her to bear up when Bobby would cry or do some bit of mischief, and I had to take him out into the yard and wait for everything to calm down; that's what we aunts are for. Actually, I think that my sister didn't realize that sometimes Bobby would get up as if he were returning from a long trip, with a lost face that lasted until breakfast; when we were alone I always waited for her to say something, but she didn't, and I thought it was bad to remind her of something that could only make her suffer. I imagined, rather, that one of those times Bobby would ask her again why she was mean to him, but Bobby also must have thought that he didn't have the right to do something like that; it was possible that he remembered my request and thought that he would never have to talk about that to my sister anymore. Occasionally I would get the feeling that I was the one who was inventing it all, and would be certain that Bobby was no longer dreaming anything bad about his mother—he would have told me at once in order to console himself. But afterward I would see on him that face from certain mornings and start to worry again. I decided it would be better for my sister not to be aware of anything, not even the first time that Bobby gave her the look. I was ironing and from the door of the pantry he looked at my sister in the kitchen, and I don't know how something like that can be explained except that the iron almost put a hole in my blue nightgown—I lifted it off just in time. Bobby was still looking at my sister that way as she rolled dough to make meat tarts. When I asked him what he wanted, just for the sake of saying something to him, he was startled and said he didn't want anything, that it was too hot outside to play ball. I don't know what tone I used to ask the question, but he repeated the explanation as if to convince me and went off to sketch in the parlor. My sister said that Bobby was quite dirty and she was going to give him a bath that afternoon—big as he was, he always forgot to wash his feet and behind his ears. In the end I was the one who bathed him, because my sister still got tired in the afternoon, and while I was soaping him in the bathtub and he was play-ing with the plastic duck that he refused to let go of, I got up the courage to ask him if he was sleeping better these days.

"More or less," he told me after a moment dedicated to making the duck swim.

"What do you mean, more or less? Are you dreaming ugly things or not?"

"The other night I did," Bobby said, sinking the duck and holding it under the water.

"Did you tell your mother?"

"No, not her. She—"

He didn't give me time for anything; soaped up and all, he threw himself on top of me and hugged me, weeping, trembling, making me miserable while I tried to push him off, and his body slipped between my fingers until be dropped into a sitting position in the bathtub and covered his face with his hands, weeping and shouting. My sister came running and thought Bobby had slipped and hurt himself somewhere, but he said no with his head, stopped crying with

an effort that wrinkled up his face, and stood up in the bathtub so that we could see that nothing had happened to him—
refusing to speak, naked, soapy, and so alone with his held-in
weeping that neither my sister nor I could calm him down,
even though we brought towels and caresses and promises.

After that I always looked for a chance to build up Bobby's
confidence without his realizing that I was trying to make
him talk, but weeks passed and he never tried to tell me anything. When I spotted something in his face now, he would
go away immediately or embrace me and ask for some candy
or permission to go to the corner with Juanita and Mario
Panzani. He never asked my sister for anything; he was very
attentive toward her, as she was basically still in rather delicate health, and she didn't worry too much about taking care
of him, because I was always there first, and Bobby would
accept anything from me, even what was most disagreeable,
when it was necessary. So my sister never came to be aware of
what I had seen immediately—his way of looking at her like
that for a moment, of remaining in the doorway looking at
her until I became aware of it and then he would quickly
lower his eyes or start running or jumping. The business of
the knife was just by chance. I was changing the paper on the
pantry shelves and had taken all the dishes down; I didn't
realize that Bobby had come in until I turned around to cut
another strip of paper and saw him looking at the long knife.
He became distracted right away or didn't want me to notice,
but I already knew that way of looking he had, and, I don't
know, it's stupid to think such things, but it all came over me
like a chill, almost an icy wind in that overheated pantry. I
was unable to say anything to him, but at night I thought of
how Bobby had stopped asking my sister why she was mean to

him; only at times would he look at her as he had looked at the long knife—that different look. It might have been just chance, of course, but I didn't like it during the following week when I saw the same face on him precisely at the moment I was cutting the bread with the long knife and my sister was explaining to Bobby that it was time now for him to learn to shine his own shoes. "Yes, Mama," Bobby said, paying attention only to what I was doing to the bread, accompanying every movement of the knife with his eyes and swaying in his chair, almost as if he were cutting the bread himself; he was probably thinking about the shoes and moving as if he were shining them—my sister certainly thought that, because Bobby was so obedient and so good.

At night I wondered whether I shouldn't talk to my sister, but what was I going to tell her, since nothing was happening and Bobby was getting the best grades in his class and things like that. Except that I couldn't sleep, because suddenly everything came together again; it was like a mass that grew thicker and then the fear, impossible to know of what, because Bobby and my sister were already asleep and they could be heard moving or sighing from time to time—they were sleeping so well, much better than I, lying there thinking all night long. And, of course, I finally sought out Bobby in the garden after I saw him look at my sister that way again, and I asked him to help me transplant a mastic and we talked about lots of things and he confided in me that Juanita had a sister who was engaged.

"Naturally. She's big now," I told him. "Look, go get me the long knife from the kitchen so we can cut these raffias."

He ran off as always, because there was no one better than he for doing what I wanted, and I remained looking toward the house waiting for him to come back, thinking I really should have asked him about the dreams before sending him for the knife, just to be sure. When he came back, walking very slowly, as if wading through the siesta-time atmosphere in order to take longer, I saw that he had picked out one of the short knives, even though I had left the long one in plain view, because I wanted to be sure that he would see it as soon as he opened the cupboard drawer.

"This one is no good," I told him. It was hard for me to speak; it was stupid with someone as small and innocent as Bobby, but I couldn't look him in the eye. I only felt the shove when he threw himself into my arms, letting go of the knife, and pressing himself against me, pressing himself so much against me and weeping. I think that at that moment I saw something that must have been his last nightmare. I couldn't ask him, but I think that I saw what he had dreamt the last time before he stopped having the nightmares, and yet there was that way of looking at my sister, of looking at the long knife.

L I L I A N A
W E E P I N G

At least it's better that it's Ramos and not some other doctor; with him there was always a pact, I knew that when the moment arrived he'd tell me or at least would let me understand without telling me everything. It's been hard on the poor guy: fifteen years of friendship and nights of poker and weekends in the country, the usual problem; but that's the way it is, at the moment of truth and between men that's worth more than office lies, colored like the pills or the pink liquid that enters my veins drop by drop.

For three or four days, without his telling me, I know that he's going to see to it that there isn't that thing they call the death agony, letting the dog die slowly, what for; I can trust him, the last pills will still be green or red but inside there'll be something else, the big sleep that I thank him for already while he stays with me, Ramos, looking at me from the foot of the bed, a little lost because the truth has emptied him out, poor guy. Don't say anything to Liliana, why should we make her weep before it's necessary, don't you think? Alfredo, yes, you can tell Alfredo, so he can arrange for time off to take care of Liliana and Mama. Yeah, and tell the nurse not to bug me when I'm writing, it's the only thing that makes me forget the pain, apart from your eminent pharmacopoeia, of course. Oh, and have them bring me coffee when I want it, this hospital takes things so seriously.

It's true that writing calms me from time to time, maybe that's why there's so much correspondence from those condemned to die, who can say. It even amuses me to imagine in writing those things that are only thought of when something is caught in your throat, not to mention the lachrymals; I can see myself through the words as if I were someone else, I can think anything as long as I write it down immediately, a professional deformation or something that begins as a softening in the meninges. I only stop when Liliana comes, I'm not so nice with the others; since they don't want me to talk much, I let them tell me if it's cold outside or if Nixon is going to beat McGovern, with the pencil in my hand I let them talk and even Alfredo realizes it and tells me just to go right on, to act as if he weren't there, he has the newspaper and he'll stay a while longer. But my wife deserves better than that, her I listen to and smile at and it hurts me less, I accept that slightly damp kiss that comes back time and again although it tires me a little more every day when they shave me and I must hurt her mouth, poor dear. It has to be said that Liliana's courage is my greatest consolation, seeing myself dead already in her eyes would take away from me that remnant of

strength with which I can talk to her and return some one of
her kisses, so that I keep on writing as soon as she's left and
the routine of injections and sympathetic little words begins.
No one dares get involved with my notebook, I know I can
keep it under my pillow or on the night table, it's my whim,
we have to let him because of Dr. Ramos, we have to let him,
poor thing, it's a distraction for him.

So it means Monday or Tuesday, and the little place in
the crypt Wednesday or Thursday. In the middle of summer
Chacarita is going to be an oven and the boys are going to
have a bad time of it, I can see Pincho with those twill jackets
and shoulder pads that are a source of such amusement for
Acosta, who, for his part, will have to dude up even if it
hurts, the king of the campground putting on a coat and tie
in order to go with me, it's going to be wild. And Fernandito,
the trio complete, and Ramos too, of course, right to the end,
and Alfredo taking Liliana by the arm and Mama, weeping
with them. And it will be real, I know how much they love
me, how they're going to miss me; they won't go the way we
went to Fats Tresa's funeral, partisan obligation and a few
shared vacations, doing our duty rapidly with the family and
cutting out back to life and forgetting. Of course, they'll have
a fierce hunger, especially Acosta, who's got no match as a
glutton; even though it pains them and they curse this absurdity of dying young and in the middle of one's career,
there's the reaction that we've all known, the pleasure of
going back and getting on the subway or into the car, of
taking a shower and eating with hunger and shame at the
same time, how can we deny the hunger that follows staying
up nights, the smell of flowers at the wake and the interminable cigarettes and strolls along the sidewalk, a kind of
recovery that's always felt at those moments and which I
never denied because it would have been hypocritical. I like

to think that Fernandito,. Pincho, and Acosta will go to a
barbecue place together, sure that they'll go together because
we did it when it was Fats Tresa, friends have to go on for a
while, drink a quart of wine, and get rid of some innards;
God damn it, I can see them now, Fernandito will be the first
to crack a joke and swallow it along the way with half a sau-
sage, sorry but too late already, and Acosta will look at him
out of the corner of his eye, but Pincho will already have let
out a laugh, it's something that he can't help, and then
Acosta, who's as good as gold, will say to himself that there's
no reason for him to pass as an example in front of the boys
and he'll laugh too before lighting a cigarette. And they'll
talk about me for a long time, each one will remember so
many things, the life that brought us four together, although,
as always, full of gaps, moments that we all didn't share and
which will pop up in Acosta's or Pincho's memory, so many
years and fights and love affairs, the gang. It's going to be
hard for them to separate after lunch because that's when the
other thing comes back, the time to go back home, the last,
definitive burial. It will be different for Alfredo and not because he doesn't belong to the gang, quite the contrary. Alfredo's going to take care of Liliana and Mama and not even
Acosta or the rest can do that, life goes on creating special
contacts among friends, they've always come to the house but
Alfredo is something else, the closeness that was always good
for me, his pleasure in staying for a long time chatting with
Mama about plants and medicines, how he liked to take
Pocho to the zoo or the circus, the serviceable old bachelor, a
package of petits four and gin rummy when Mama wasn't
feeling well, his timid and clear confidence with Liliana, the
friend of friends who now will have to spend those two days
swallowing his tears, probably taking Pocho to his country
place and coming back at once to be with Mama and Liliana

until the end. After all, he's going to have to be the man of
the house and bear up under all the complications, starting
with those of the funeral arrangements, this had to happen
just when the old man is traveling in Mexico or Panama, who
knows if he'll get back in time to stand the eleven o'clock heat
in Chacarita, poor old man, so it will be Alfredo who will
take Liliana because I don't think they'll let Mama go, Liliana on his arm, feeling her trembling against his own trembling, whispering to her everything I probably whispered to
Fats Tresa's wife, the useless necessary rhetoric that isn't
consolation or a lie or even coherent phrases, a simple being
there, which is so much.

For them, too, the worst part will be the return, before
that there's the ceremony and the flowers, there's still contact
with that inconceivable thing covered with handles and gilt,
the halt in front of the crypt, the operation neatly executed
by those in the trade, but afterward it's the return automobile and especially the house, entering the house again, knowing that the day is going to stagnate without telephone or
hospital, without the voice of Ramos stretching out hope for
Liliana, Alfredo will make coffee and tell her that Pocho is
happy in the country, that he likes the ponies and plays with
the farmboys, he'll have to look after Mama and Liliana but
Alfredo knows every corner of the house and of course he'll
stay there lying awake on the couch in my study, right there
where once we laid out Fernandito, the victim of a poker
game in which he hadn't had a single good hand, not to mention the five compensatory cognacs. Liliana has been sleeping
alone for so many weeks that maybe the fatigue will get the
better of her, Alfredo won't forget to give Liliana and Mama
sedatives. Aunt Zulema will be there passing out manzanilla
and linden tea, Liliana will let herself slip into sleep little by
little in that silence of the house which Alfredo will have

conscientiously locked up before going to stretch out on the couch and light another of the cigarettes that he doesn't dare smoke in front of Mama because of the smoke that makes her cough.

In the end there's that good part: Liliana and Mama won't be so alone or in that even worse loneliness which is the invasion of the house of mourning by distant relatives; there will be Aunt Zulema, who's always lived on the upper floor, and Alfredo, who also has been among us as if he weren't there, the friend with his own key; during the first hours perhaps it will be less hard to feel the irrevocable absence than to bear up under a troop of embraces and verbal wreaths, Alfredo will take care of maintaining distances, Ramos will come for a while to see Mama and Liliana, he'll help them sleep and will leave some pills with Aunt Zulema. At some moment there will be the silence of the darkened house, only the church clock, a distant horn, because the neighborhood is quiet. It's nice thinking that it's going to be like that, that abandoning herself little by little to a stupor without images Liliana is going to stretch out with her slow cat movements, one hand lost under the pillow wet with tears and cologne, the other beside her mouth in a juvenile recurrence before sleep. Imagining her like that is so good, Liliana sleeping, Liliana at the end of the black tunnel, feeling vaguely that today is ending and becoming yesterday, that the light in the curtains will no longer be the same one that beat full on her breast while Aunt Zulema opened the boxes from which the blackness was emerging in the form of clothing and veils strewn over the bed and mingled with an angry weeping, one last, useless protest against what still had to come. Now the light from the window would arrive before anyone, before the memories dissolved in sleep and which only in confusion would open a path in the final drowsiness. Alone,

knowing that she was really alone in that bed and in that
room, on that day which was beginning in a different direction, Liliana would be able to weep, hugging the pillow
without their coming to calm her, letting herself use up the
weeping until the end, and only much later, with a half-sleep
of deception holding her back in the nest of the sheets, the
hollow of the day would begin to be filled with coffee, with
opened curtains, with Aunt Zulema, with Pocho's voice telephoning from the farm with news about the sunflowers and
the horses, a catfish caught after a fierce struggle, a splinter in
his hand but nothing serious, they had given him one of Don
Contreras' remedies, he was the best for such things. And
Alfredo, waiting in the living room with the newspaper in his
hand, telling her that Mama had slept well and that Ramos
would come at twelve o'clock, proposing that she go see
Pocho in the afternoon, with that sun it would be worth traveling to the farm, and it was one of those times they could
even take Mama, the country air would do her good, maybe
spend the weekend on the farm, and why not everybody, with
Pocho, who would be so happy having them there. Accepting
or not was all the same, they all knew it and waited for the
answers that things and the passage of the morning were giving, going passively in to lunch or commenting on the textile
strike, asking for more coffee and answering the telephone,
which they would have to disconnect some time, the telegram
from the father-in-law abroad, a noisy collision on the corner,
shouts and whistles, the city out there, two thirty, going with
Mama and Alfredo to the farm because one of these times the
splinter in his hand, you never knew with children, Alfredo
behind the wheel, calming them, Don Contreras was better
than a doctor for things like that, the streets of Ramos Mejía
and the sun like boiling syrup until they took refuge in the
great whitewashed rooms, maté at five o'clock, and Pocho

with his catfish that was beginning to smell, but so beautiful, so big, what a fight to get it out of the brook, Mama, it almost cut my line, I swear, look at the teeth. Like leafing through an album or seeing a movie, the images and the words one after the other filling the vacuum, now you'll see what Carmen's roasts are like, ma'am, light and so delicious, a green salad and that's it, that's all we need, with this heat it's best not to eat too much, I brought the insecticide because of the mosquitoes this time of day. And Alfredo silent there, but Pocho, his hand patting Pocho, you're the fishing champ, old boy, tomorrow we'll go out early and one of these times, they told me there was a peasant who caught one weighing five pounds. Here under the eaves it's nice, Mama can sleep a while in the rocker if she wants, Don Contreras was right, you haven't got a thing in your hand anymore, show us how you can ride the piebald pony, look, Mama, look at me when I gallop, why don't you come fishing with us tomorrow, I'll show you how, you'll see, Friday with a red sun and the catfish, the race between Pocho and Don Contreras' boy, the stew at noon and Mama slowly helping husk the corn, telling Carmen's daughter that she had that stubborn cough, siesta in the naked rooms that smelled of summer, the darkness against the rather rough sheets, sunset under the eaves and the bonfire against the mosquitoes, the never manifest nearness of Alfredo, the way of being there and taking care of Pocho, seeing that everything was comfortable, even the silence that his voice always broke in time, his hand offering a soft drink, a handkerchief, turning on the radio to hear the news, the strikes and Nixon, it was foreseeable, what a country.

The weekend and hardly a mark from the splinter on Pocho's hand, they returned to Buenos Aires very early on Monday to avoid the heat, Alfredo dropped them at the house so he could go meet the father-in-law, Ramos was also at the airport in Ezeiza, and Fernandito, who helped during those hours of meeting because it was good to have other friends at the house, Acosta at nine with his daughter who could play with Pocho in Aunt Zulema's apartment, everything was becoming more muffled, going backward but in a different way, with Liliana making herself think more about the old people than about herself, controlling herself, and Alfredo among them with Acosta and Fernandito, turning the straight shots aside, crossing over to help Liliana, to convince the old man to get some rest after a trip like that, friends coming and going until only Alfredo and Aunt Zulema, the house quiet, Liliana accepting a pill, letting herself be put to bed without having faltered one single time, falling asleep almost at once as after something fulfilled to the very last. In the morning it was Pocho running into the living room, the old man dragging his slippers, the first telephone call, almost always Clotilde or Ramos, Mama complaining of the heat or the humidity, talking about lunch with Aunt Zulema, at six o'clock Alfredo, sometimes Pincho with his sister or Acosta so that Pocho could play with his daughter, the colleagues from the lab who scolded Liliana, she had to go back to work and not stay cooped up at home, she should do it for them, they were short of chemists and Liliana was needed, she should come for half a day in any case, until she felt in better spirits; Alfredo took her the first time, Liliana didn't feel like driving, then she didn't want to be a bother and she took out the car, sometimes she went out with Pocho in the afternoon, took him to the zoo or the movies, at the lab they were grateful that she was giving them a hand with the new vaccines, an epidemic on the coast, staying late at work, getting to like it, a team race against the clock, twenty cases of ampuls to Rosario, we did it, a job, Pocho at school and Alfredo protesting, they're teaching these kids a different type of math, he asks me all kinds of questions that turn me off, and the old folks with their dominoes, everything was different in our day, Alfredo, they taught us penmanship and look at the handwriting this boy has, where are we going to end up. The silent recompense of looking at Liliana lost on a couch, a simple glance over the newspaper and seeing her smile, a silent accomplice, saying the old folks were right, smiling at him from afar, almost like a little girl. But for the first time a real smile, from within, like when they went to the circus with Pocho, who'd done better at school, and they took him for some ice cream, for a stroll along the docks. The big cold was starting, Alfredo came to the house less frequently because there were union problems and he had to go out to the provinces, sometimes Acosta came with his daughter and on Sundays Pincho or Fernandito, it didn't matter anymore, everybody had so much to do and the days were short, Liliana would come back late from the lab and give a hand to Pocho, lost in decimals and the Amazon basin, in the end and always Alfredo, the little gifts for the old folks, that never mentioned tranquillity of sitting down with him by the now late fire and talking in a low voice about the problems of the country, Mama's health, Alfredo's hand resting on Liliana's arm, you're getting too tired, your face doesn't look good, the thankful smile denying it, one day we'll go to the farm, this cold can't last for our lifetime, nothing could last for a lifetime even though Liliana would slowly withdraw her arm and look for the cigarettes on the table, the words almost without meaning, the eyes meeting in a different way until the hand again, slipping along the arm, the heads coming together and the long silence, the kiss on the cheek.

There was nothing to say, it had happened that way and there was nothing to say. Leaning over to light the cigarette that was trembling between her lips, simply waiting without speaking, perhaps knowing that there would be no words, that Liliana would make an effort to swallow the smoke and would let it out with a moan, that she would begin to weep deeply, from another time, without moving her face away from Alfredo's face, without denying and weeping silently, only for him now, because of all the other things that he would understand. It was useless to murmur things so well known, Liliana weeping was the end, the edge from which a different way of life was going to begin. If calming her, if returning her to tranquillity would have been as simple as writing it with the words lining themselves up in a notebook like congealed seconds, small sketches of time to help the interminable passage of the afternoon, if only it were that, but night arrives and so too Ramos, incredibly, Ramos' face looking at the tests just taken, feeling for my pulse, then another Ramos, incapable of hiding, pulling off the sheets to look at me naked, feeling my side, with an incomprehensible order to the nurse, a slow, incredulous recognition at which I am present as if from afar, almost amused, knowing that it can't be, that Ramos is mistaken and that it isn't true, and that the only thing true was the other thing, that the time remaining hadn't been hidden from me, and Ramos' laugh, his way of touching me as if he couldn't admit it, his absurd hope, nobody's going to believe this from me, old man, and I, forcing myself to recognize that it's probably that way, that who can say after all, looking at Ramos, who's getting up and laughing again and giving orders with a voice that I had never heard from him in that drowsy penumbra, having to convince myself little by little, yes, so I'm going to have to ask him, as soon as the nurse leaves, I'll have to ask him to wait a bit, to wait at least until it's daylight before telling Liliana, before pulling her out of that dream in which for the first time she's no longer alone, out of those arms that hold her tight while she sleeps.

A

P L A C E

N A M E D

K I N D B E R G

Named Kindberg, ingenuously translated as child mountain
or called gentle mountain, friendly mountain, something or
other like that, a town which they reach at night coming in
out of a rain that washes itself wrathfully against the wind-
shield, an old hotel with deep hallways where everything has
been prepared for forgetting what's still out there beating
and scratching, the place, at last, where one can change, tast-
ing good shelter; and soup in a large silver tureen, white
wine, breaking the bread and giving the first piece to Lina,
who takes it in the palm of her hand as if it were an homage,
and it is, and then she blows on it, who knows why, but in
that way seeing Lina's bangs rise up a little and tremble as if

the blowing on the hand and the bread were about to raise
the curtain in a tiny theater, almost as if from that moment
on Marcelo could see Lina's thoughts come out onstage,
Lina's images and memories as she sips savory soup still
smiling.

But no, the smooth animated forehead doesn't change, at
first it's just the voice that goes along dropping bits of person
that make up a first approximation of Lina: Chilean, for example, and a theme hummed from Archie Shepp, her nails a
little chewed but all shiny against clothes that were dirty
from hitchhiking and sleeping in barns or youth hostels.
Youth, Lina laughs, sipping her soup like a little bear, of
course you couldn't imagine: fossils, just imagine, walking
corpses like in that horror movie by Romero.

Marcelo is about to ask her what Romero, the first he's
heard of such a Romero, but better let her talk, it amuses him
to be a witness to that happiness over a hot meal, as over his
contentment with a room with a fireplace that waits and
crackles, the protective bourgeois bubble of traveler's checks
and no problems, the rain exploding outside there against the
bubble as that afternoon it had on Lina's white face by the
side of the road as she came out of the woods at dusk, what a
place to hitchhike but there she was, some more soup, little
bear, eat it for me because you have to be saved from an
attack of angina, her hair still damp but the fireplace crack-
ling now waiting there in the room with the big Hapsburg bed,
with mirrors to the floor, with small tables and decorations
and curtains and why were you there in the rain, tell me,
your mother would have spanked you.

Corpses, Lina repeats, better to go on alone, of course
if it rains but don't worry my raincoat is really rainproof,
only my hair and legs a little, that's all, an aspirin just in case.
And between the empty bread basket and the nice full new

one that the teddy bear is already sacking and what delicious
butter, and what do you do, why do you travel around in that
great big car, and you why, oh and you're Argentine? A double acceptance that fate does things well, the predictable
memory that if Marcelo hadn't stopped twelve miles back to
have a drink the little bear settled in a different car now or
still in the woods, I sell prefabricated materials, it's something that makes you travel a lot but this time I'm wandering
around between two meetings. Teddy bear attentive and almost serious, what's all that prefabricated stuff, a boring subject right off, but what can he do, he can't tell her that he's a
lion tamer or movie director or Paul McCartney: the salt.
That brusque way of a bird or an insect even though little
bear bangs dancing around him, Archie Shepp's recurrent
refrain, so you've got the records, but how, oh well. Catching
on, Marcelo thinks ironically of how normal it would have
been for him not to have had the Archie Shepp records and
it's idiotic because in reality of course he has them and sometimes he listens to them with Marlene in Brussels but he just
doesn't know how to live them like Lina, who suddenly hums
a piece between two bites, her smile full of free jazz and a
mouthful of goulash and damp little hitchhiking bear, I
never had such good luck, you were good. Good and conse-
quential, Marcelo intones his concertina Gardel revenge, but
the ball goes out of bounds, it's a different generation, it's a
little Shepp bear, no more tango, eh?

Of course the tickling still remains, almost a kind of bit-
tersweet cramp with the arrival in Kindberg, the hotel parking place in the enormous ancient shed, the old woman lighting their way with a period lantern, Marcelo valise and
briefcase, Lina knapsack and slogging, the invitation to dine
accepted before Kindberg, so we can talk a little, the night
and the rain shrapnel, not good going on, better for us to stop

in Kindberg and for me to invite you to dine with me, oh yes great, that way you can dry your clothes, the best thing is to stay over here until morning, it's raining, it's pouring, the old man is snoring, oh yes, Lina said, and then the parking shed, the resonant Gothic galleries to the desk, how nice and warm this hotel, what luck, the last drop of water on her bangs, the knapsack hanging teddy bear girl scout with good uncle, I'm going to get the rooms now so you can dry out a little before dinner. And the tickling, almost a cramp down there, Lina looking at him all bangs, the rooms what foolishness, just ask for one. And he no, looking at her but the tickle disagree-agreeable, so she's a hooker, so she's a delight, so little bear soup fireplace, so another one and what luck, old man, she's quite pretty. But then seeing her take another pair of blue jeans and the black sweater out of her knapsack, turning her back to him gabbling what a fireplace, it smells, perfumed fire, looking for aspirins for her in the bottom of his suitcase among vitamins and deodorants and after-shave and how far are you going, I don't know, I've got a letter to some hippies in Copenhagen, some sketches that Cecilia gave me in Santi-ago, she told me they're great types, the satin screen and Lina hanging up her wet clothes, indescribably emptying out her knapsack onto the gilded arabesqued franzjosef table: James Baldwin Kleenex buttons dark glasses cardboard boxes Pablo Neruda sanitary napkins map of Germany, I'm hungry, Mar-celo, I like your name it sounds good and I'm hungry, so let's go eat, forget the shower you've had enough of a one already, you can arrange that knapsack afterward, Lina raising her head quickly, looking at him: I never arrange anything, what for, the knapsack is like me and this trip and politics, all mixed up and what difference does it make. Snot-nose, Mar-celo thought, cramp, almost tickle (give her the aspirins at coffee time, more rapid effect) but she was bothered by those verbal distances, those you're-so-young-how-can-you-travel-around-alone-like-thats, in the middle of soup she'd laughed: youth, fossils, just imagine, walking corpses like in the movie by Romero. And the goulash and little by little from the heat and the teddy bear content again and the wine, the tickle in the stomach giving way to a kind of joy, a peace, she speaking nonsense, continuing to explain to him her vision of a world that must have been his some time back although he was no longer up to remembering, looking at him from the theater formed by her bangs, suddenly serious and as if worried and then brusquely Shepp, saying how nice to be like that, feeling dry and inside the bubble and how once in Avignon hitch-hiking in a wind that tore the tiles off the roofs I saw a bird fly into a tree, fall like a handkerchief just imagine, the pepper please.

So (they took away the empty platter) you intend to go on to Denmark just the same, but have you got any money or what? Of course I'm going on, aren't you going to eat your lettuce, give it to me then, I'm still hungry, a way of folding the leaves with her fork and chewing them slowly humming Shepp to them from time to time a silvery bubble plop on her damp lips, pretty well-shaped mouth ending just where it should, those Renaissance drawings, Florence in autumn with Marlene, those mouths that pederast geniuses loved so much, sinuous sensual subtle, etc., this riesling sixty-four is going to your head, listening to her between bites and humming I don't know how I got through philosophy in Santiago, I'd like to read a lot of things, it's now that I've got to start reading. Predictable, poor little bear so content with her lettuce and her plan to swallow Spinoza in six months mixed with Allen Ginsburg and Shepp again; how many clichés would she parade out until the coffee came (don't forget to give her the aspirin, if she starts sneezing on me it'll be a problem, little snot-nose with wet hair face all sticky bangs the rain lashing her by the side of the road) but parallel between Shepp and the end of the goulash everything was kind of spinning in a short while, changing, they were the same phrases and Spinoza or Copenhagen and at the same time different, Lina there across from him breaking the bread drinking the wine looking at him content, far away and near at the same time, changing with the spinning of the night, although far away and near wasn't an explanation, something else, something like a show, Lina showing him something that wasn't herself but what then, please tell me. And two slices along the grain of the Gruyére, why don't you have some, Marcelo, it's delicious, you didn't eat anything, silly, a fine gentleman like you, because you are a gentleman, right, nothing but cigarettes, rettes, rettes, rettes, without eating anything, listen, and a little more wine, you'd like some, wouldn't you, because with this cheese, you can imagine, you have to wash it down a little, come on, eat some: more bread, it's incredible the way I eat bread, they always predicted that I'd get fat, just what you hear, it's true that I've got a bit of a belly already, it doesn't look it but it's there, I swear, Shepp.

Useless to expect her to talk about anything sensible and why expect it (because you're a gentleman, right?), teddy bear among the flowers of the dessert looking dazzled and at the same time with calculating eyes at the tea cart full of tarts compotes meringues, a bit of a belly, yes, they'd always predicted she'd get fat, *sic*, this one with more cream, and why don't you like Copenhagen, Marcelo? But Marcelo hadn't said that he didn't like Copenhagen, just a little absurd that business of traveling in the middle of a rainstorm and weeks to discover most probably that the hippies were already wandering around California, but you don't realize that it doesn't matter, I told you I don't know them, I'm bringing

them some sketches that Cecilia and Marcos gave me in Santiago and a little record by the Mothers of Invention, do you
think they have a record player here so I can play it for you,
probably too late and too Kindberg, don't forget, still if they
were gypsy violins but those Mothers, wow, the very idea, and
Lina laughing with lots of cream and a bit of a belly under a
black sweater, the two of them laughing thinking about the
Mothers howling in Kindberg, the innkeeper's face and the
heat there that for some time now had replaced the tickling
in the stomach, wondering whether she'd play hard to get,
whether in the end the legendary sword in the bed, in any
case the rolled-up pillow and one on either side moral barrier
modern sword, Shepp, that's it, you're starting to sneeze, take
some aspirin coffee will be right along, I'm going to order
some cognac it activates the salicylic, I learned it from a good
source. And really he hadn't said he didn't like Copenhagen
but the little bear seemed to understand the tone of his voice
more than his words, like him with that teacher he'd fallen in
love with at the age of twelve, what did words matter in the
face of that cooing, that thing that was born out of the voice
like a desire for heat, to be wrapped up and stroked on the
skin, so many years later psychoanalysis: anguish, bah, nostalgia for the primordial uterus, everything since the word go
after all was floating on the waters, read the Bible, fifty thousand pesos to be cured of dizzy spells and now that snot-nosed
girl who in a way was plucking out pieces of him, Shepp, but
of course, if you swallow it dry it's sure to stick in your throat,
silly. And she stirring, suddenly raising a pair of intense eyes
and looking at him with a new respect, of course if she was
beginning to pull his leg she'd pay double for it, but no,
really, Marcelo, I like it when you get so doctor and so papa,
don't be angry, I always say what I shouldn't, don't be angry,
but I'm not angry, silly, yes, you did get a little angry because

I called you doctor and papa, it wasn't in that sense but precisely because it looks so good on you when you talk about aspirin and just think you remembered to get it and bring it, I'd already forgotten, Shepp, you see how I need you, and you're a little comical because you look at me so doctor, don't be angry, Marcelo, how delicious this cognac is with the coffee, how good for sleeping, you know that. And yes, on the highway since seven in the morning, three cars and a truck, pretty good all told except for the storm at the end but then Marcelo and Kindberg and the cognac, Shepp. And to leave her hand very still, palm up on the tablecloth covered with crumbs when he stroked it lightly to tell her no, that he wasn't angry because now he knew that it was true, that he really had moved her with that minimal care, the pill that he'd taken out of his pocket with detailed instructions, plenty of water so it won't stick in her throat, coffee and cognac; friends all of a sudden, but really so, and that fire must have been getting the room even warmer, the maid must have turned down the bed already as no doubt always in Kindberg, a kind of ancient ceremony, welcome to the tired traveler, to foolish teddy bears who wanted to get soaked all the way to Copenhagen and afterward but what did afterward matter, Marcelo, I already told you I don't want to be tied down, donwanna-donwanna, Copenhagen is like a man you find and leave (ah), a day that passes, I don't believe in the future, my balls swell up with the future, and he too his Uncle Roberto transformed into a loving tyrant to take care of Marcelito, who'd lost his father and still so little poor thing, you've got to think about tomorrow, m'boy, Uncle Roberto's ridiculous retirement, what's needed is a strong government, the young people of today only think about having fun, God damn it, in my day on the other hand, and the teddy bear leaving her hand for him on the tablecloth and why that suction, that going back to a Buenos Aires of the thirties or forties, better Copenhagen, yeah, better Copenhagen and the hippies and the rain beside the road, but he'd never hitchhiked, practically never, once or twice before going to the university, then he'd had enough to get by on, for the tailor, and still he could have done it that time the guys were planning to sail on a windjammer that took three months to get to Rotterdam, cargo and stopovers and six hundred pesos in all or something like that, giving the crew a hand, having fun, of course we're going, at the Café Rubí on Plaza Once, of course we're going, Monk, you've got to get up the six hundred clams, it wasn't easy, your salary going for cigarettes and a girl from time to time, one day the get-togethers end, there was no more talk about the windjammer, you've got to think about the future, m'boy, Shepp. Ah, again; come on, you've got to get some rest, Lina. Yes, doctor, but just one more little minute, you don't know how good this supply of warm cognac is for me, taste it, yes, see how nice and warm it is. And something he should have said without knowing what while he remembered the Rubí because Lina again and with that way of guessing his voice, what his voice was really saying more than what it was saying which was always idiotic and aspirin and you have to get some rest or why go on to Copenhagen for example when now, with that little hot white hand under his, everything could be called Copenhagen, everything could have been called windjammer if six hundred pesos, if balls, if poetry. And Lina looking at him and then quickly lowering her eyes as if all that was there on the table, among the crumbs, the trash of time already, as if he had spoken of all that instead of come on, you've got to get some rest, without mustering the courage for the more logical plural, come on, let's go to bed, and Lina, who was licking her chops and remembering some horses (or were they cows, he only heard her at the end of the sentence), some horses running across the field as if something had suddenly frightened them: two white horses and one sorrel, on my aunt and uncle's farm you don't know what it was like to gallop into the wind in the afternoon, come back late and tired and of course the scolding, tomboy, right away, wait till I finish this little drink and then, right away, looking at him with her bangs all blown as if on horseback at the farm, snorting because the cognac was so strong, he had to be an idiot to make problems when it had been she in the long, dark hallway, she splashing and happy and two rooms what foolishness, ask for just one, assuming of course all the meaning of that economizing, knowing and probably used to it and expecting it at the end of every episode, but and what if it wasn't like that in the end because it didn't seem like that, if in the end surprises, the sword in the middle of the bed, if in the end suddenly on the couch in the corner, of course then he, a gentleman, don't forget the coverlet, I never saw such a wide staircase, this certainly must have been a palace, there were counts who gave parties with candelabra and things, and the doors, look at that door, but it's ours, painted with stags and shepherds, it can't be. And the fire, the red fleeing salamanders and the open white enormous bed and the curtains smothering the windows, oh how delicious, how good, Marcelo, what a sleep we're going to have, wait at least till I show you the record, it's got a wild cover, you're going to love it, I've got it here at the bottom with my letters and maps, I can't have lost it, Shepp. You can show it to me tomorrow, you're really catching cold, get undressed fast, it'll be better with the lights out, that way we can see the fire, oh yes, Marcelo, look at the coals, all those cats together, look at the sparks, it's nice in the dark, it's a pity to go to sleep, and he hanging his jacket on the back of a chair, going over to the teddy bear huddled by the fireplace, taking off his shoes beside her, crouching down to sit facing the fire, watching the light and shadows run across her loose hair, helping her take her blouse off, looking for the catch on her bra, his mouth against her naked shoulder now, his hands searching among the sparks, snot-nosed little girl, silly little bear, at some moment both of them naked now standing in front of the fire and kissing, the bed cold, white and suddenly nothing now, a total fire running over his skin, Lina's mouth on his hair, on his chest, her hands on his back, the bodies letting themselves be borne off and known and only a moan, an anxious breathing and having to ask her because that did have to be asked, before the fire and sleep he had to ask her, Lina, you're not doing this out of thanks are you, and the hands lost on his back coming up like whiplashes to his face, his throat, squeezing it furiously, inoffensively, sweetly and furiously, tiny and wrathfully dug in, a moan of protest and denial, a rage too in her voice, how can you, how can you, Marcelo, and if that's it, then yes, everything fine like that, I'm sorry, love, I'm sorry I had to ask you, I'm sorry sweet, I'm sorry, the mouths, the other fire, the caresses with pink edges, the bubble that trembles between the lips, phases of the knowledge, silences in which everything is skin or the slow running along of hair, a wave of eyelids, denial and demand, a bottle of mineral water drunk from the neck which is passed from one mouth to another to quench a single thirst, ending in the fingers that feel on the night table, that light, there's that gesture of covering the lampshade with a slip, with anything, of gilding the air in order to start looking at Lina from behind, at the teddy bear beside him, the cub face down, Lina's tender skin that asks him for a cigarette, that sits against the pillows, you're so bony and hairy, Shepp, wait till I cover you a little if I can find the bedspread, look at it there by your feet, I think the edges have been singed, Shepp.

Then the slow, low fire in the fireplace, in them, grow-

ing smaller and golden, the water drunk now, the cigarettes,
university courses were a pain, it was so boring, I learned the
best things in cafés, reading before going to the movies, talking to Cecilia and Perucho, and he hearing her, the Rubí, so
likely like the Rubí twenty years earlier, Arlt and Rilke and
Eliot and Borges, except that Lina yes, she yes in her hitch-
hiking windjammer, in her day's sail in Renault or Volks-
wagen, the teddy bear among dry leaves and rain on the
bangs, but why so much windjammer and so much Rubí
again, she doesn't know any of it, hadn't even been born, snot-
nosed little Chilean girl vagabond Copenhagen, why from
the beginning, from the soup and white wine going along
dragging so many things past and lost out of his face, so many
buried dogs, so many windjammers for six hundred pesos,
Lina looking at him from half-sleep, slipping down on the
pillows with the sigh of a satisfied animal, searching his face
with her hands, I like you, bones, you've read every book
there is, Shepp, I mean it's nice with you, you're up on everything, you've got those big strong hands, you've got life behind you, you're not old. So the teddy bear felt he was alive
in spite of, more alive than people her age, the corpses from
the Romero movie and who could that be under the bangs
where the little theater damp now slid into sleep, eyes rolling
and looking at him, taking her softly one more time, feeling
her and letting her go at the same time, listening to her purr
of half-protest, I'm sleepy, Marcelo, not like that, yes, my
love, yes, her light hard body, the tense thighs, the attack
returned duplicated without pause, no longer Marlene in
Brussels, the women like him, paused and assured, with all
books read, she the teddy bear, her way of receiving his
strength and answering it but afterward still on the edge of
that wind full of rain and shouts, slipping in turn into half-
sleep, realizing that this too was windjammer and Copen-

hagen, his face sunk between Lina's breasts was the face of
the Rubí, the first adolescent nights with Mabel or with
Nélida in the apartment borrowed from Monk, the furious
and elastic waves and almost immediately why don't we go
out and walk around downtown, give me the candy, if Mama
ever found out.

Then not even like that, not even in love could he get
rid of that rearview mirror, the old portrait of his young self
that Lina put in front of him by stroking him and Shepp and
let's go to sleep now and a little more water please; like having been her, from her in every thing, unbearably absurd
irreversible and finally sleep amidst the last murmured caresses and all the teddy bear's fur brushing his face as if something in her knew, as if she were trying to erase him so that he
would wake up Marcelo again, as he woke up at nine o'clock
and Lina on the sofa was combing her hair humming, already
dressed for another highway and another rainstorm. They
didn't talk too much, it was a brief breakfast and the sun was
out, several miles from Kindberg they stopped to have some
more coffee, Lina four lumps and her face as if washed, absent, a kind of abstract happiness, and then you know, don't
get angry, tell me that you're not going to get angry, but of
course not, tell me anything, if you need anything, stopping
just short of the cliché because the word had been there like
the bills in his wallet, waiting to be used and already on the
verge of being spoken when Lina's timid hand in his, the
bangs covering her eyes and finally asking him if she could
go on a little farther with him even if it wasn't the same
route, what difference did it make, going on a little more
with him because it felt so good, letting it go on a little longer
with this sun, we'll sleep in the woods, I'll show you the
record and the sketches, only until nighttime if you want,
and feeling that yes, that he wanted to, that there was no

reason for him not to want to, and slowly pushing her hand
away and telling her no, best not to, you know, you'll find it
easy here, it's an important crossroads, and the teddy bear
accepting as if suddenly beaten and distant, eating the sugar
lumps head down, watching him paying and getting up and
bringing her the knapsack and kissing her on the hair and
turning his back on her and getting lost in a furious shifting
of gears, thirty, fifty, sixty, a route wide open for a salesman
of prefabricated materials, a route without Copenhagen and
full only of rotting windjammers along the curb, of jobs that
paid better and better, of the Buenos Aires gossip about the
Rubí, of the shadow of the solitary plane tree at the curve,
the trunk against which he was squashed at eighty miles an
hour with his head bent over the steering wheel the way Lina
had lowered her head a few minutes ago because a bear cub
always lowers its head like that to eat sugar.

SECOND

TIME

AROUND

We just waited for them, each one had his date and his time, but there was no rush about it, smoking slowly, every so often Nigger López would come by with coffee and then we'd stop working and talk about what was new, almost always the same things, the boss's visit, the changes higher up, the races at San Isidro. They, of course, had no way of knowing that we were waiting for them, what's called waiting, things like that had to happen without making waves, you people go ahead without worrying, the boss's word, he would repeat it every so often just in case, you people just go ahead nice and easy, when you come down to it, it was easy, if there was a slip they wouldn't take it out on us, the ones responsible were higher up and the boss was okay, just rest easy, boys, if there's any trouble here I'll take the responsibility, the only thing I ask is that you don't get your subjects mixed up on me, an investigation first so you don't get involved where you shouldn't, and then you can go right ahead.

Frankly, they weren't any trouble, the boss had picked out functional offices so that there wouldn't be any crowding, and we received them one at a time, as it should be, with all the time necessary. Nobody with better manners than us, eh, the boss would say from time to time, and it was true, everything was synchronized in a way that would put I.B.M. to shame, things worked Vaseline-smooth here, no getting your piss hot or getting ahead of yourself. We had time for coffee and picking Sunday's races, and the boss was the first to come by to get the sure things because in that business Slats Bianchetti was a regular oracle. So the same thing every day, we'd arrive with the newspapers, Nigger López would bring the first round of coffee, and in a little while they would begin to come by for the procedure. The summons said that, a procedure which concerns you, and us, just there waiting. Now this is important, even if it is written on yellow paper, a summons always has a serious look about it; that's why María Elena had looked at it several times at home, the green stamp around the illegible signature and the date and the place. She took it out of her purse again on the bus and wound her watch just to be safe. They were summoning her to an office on the Calle Maza, it was strange that there should be a ministry there but her sister had told her that they were setting up offices all over because the ministries didn't have enough room anymore, and as soon as she got off the bus she saw that it must have been true, the neighborhood was like any other, with three- or four-story houses and most of all a lot of retail stores, even some of the few trees left in the district.

At least it most likely will have a flag, María Elena thought as she approached the seven-hundred block; it was probably like the embassies, which were in residential districts but could be spotted from a distance by the colored piece of cloth over one of the balconies. Although the number stood out quite clearly on the summons, she was surprised not to see the national flag and for a moment she stood on the corner (she was early, there was plenty of time) and for no particular reason she asked the man in the newsstand if the government office was on that block.

"Yes, indeed," the man said, "down there in the middle of the block, but first why don't you keep me company for a little while; see how all alone I am."

"On the way back." María Elena smiled at him, going away in no hurry and consulting the yellow paper once more. There was almost no traffic and not many people, a cat in front of a grocery store and a fat lady with a little girl coming out of a doorway. The few cars were parked by the government office, almost all of them with someone behind the wheel reading the newspaper or smoking. The entrance was narrow, like all those on the block, with a majolica-tile passageway and a stairway in the rear; the plaque on the door looked like one for a doctor or a dentist, that was all, dirty, and with a piece of paper pasted over the bottom part to cover that line of the inscription. It was strange that there was no elevator, a third-floor walkup after that paper which was so serious with its green stamp and signature and everything.

The door on the third floor was closed and she didn't see any bell or plaque. María Elena tried the knob and the door opened noiselessly; the tobacco smoke reached her before she saw the greenish tiles of the hallway and the benches on both sides with people sitting on them. There weren't many, but with that smoke and such a narrow hallway their knees seemed to be touching, the two old ladies, the bald man, and the boy with the green necktie. They obviously had been chatting in order to kill time, for just as she opened the door María Elena caught the tail end of a phrase from one of the ladies, but, as always, they fell silent almost immediately as they looked at the latest arrival, and also as always and feeling so foolish, María Elena blushed and was barely able to raise enough voice for a good-morning as she stood there by the door until the boy signaled to her, pointing to the empty space on the bench next to him. Precisely as she sat down, thanking him, the door at the other end of the corridor opened to let out a redheaded man who made his way between the knees of the others without taking the trouble to excuse himself. The clerk held the door open with his foot, waiting until one of the two ladies got up with difficulty and, begging their pardon, passed between María Elena and the bald man; the exit door and the office door closed at almost the same time, and those left began to chat again, stretching a little and making the benches creak.

Each one had his or her theme as always: the bald man about the slowness of the procedures, since this is my first time, what can I expect, tell me, over half an hour wasted for what in the end will probably be four or five questions and so long, at least that's what I imagine.

"Don't you believe it," said the boy with the green tie, "it's my second time and I can assure you that it's not so short, with everything that has to be typed up and some guy who can't remember a date, things like that, it ends up lasting quite a while."

The bald man and the old lady listened with interest because it was obviously the first time for them, the same as for María Elena, although she didn't feel she had the right to join in the conversation. The bald man wanted to know how

much time there was between the first and the second summons, and the boy explained that in his case it had been three
days. But why two summonses, María Elena wanted to ask,
and once more she felt the color rising to her cheeks and
she waited for someone to talk to her and give her confidence,
let her form part of the group, not be the last one anymore.
The old lady had taken out a small vial with salts or something in it and took a whiff, breathing in deeply. It might
have been all the smoke that was upsetting her, and the boy
offered to put his cigarette out and the bald man said of
course, this hallway was a disgrace, they'd better put out their
cigarettes if she wasn't feeling well, but the woman said no,
just a touch of fatigue that will go away immediately, her
husband and sons smoked all the time at home, I practically
don't notice it anymore. María Elena, who had also had the
urge to take out a cigarette, saw that the men were putting
theirs out, that the boy was crushing his against the sole of his
shoe: people always smoke too much when they have to wait,
the last time it had been worse because there were seven or
eight people then and in the end you couldn't see a thing in
the hallway with so much smoke.

"Life is a waiting room," said the bald man, carefully
stepping on his cigarette and looking at his hands as if he
didn't know what to do with them, and the old lady sighed an
agreement of many years' standing and put away the vial precisely as the door opened and the other lady came out with
that air they all envied, the almost compassionate good-bye as
she reached the exit door. It doesn't take so long after all,
María Elena thought, three people ahead of her, let's say
three-quarters of an hour; of course, in any one of the cases
the procedure might take longer than in the others, the boy
had already been there a first time and had said so. But when
the bald man went into the office, María Elena got up the

courage to ask in order to feel more secure, and the boy thought for a while and then said that the first time some had taken a long time and others less, you never could tell. The old lady called attention to the fact that the other lady had come out almost at once, but that the redheaded gentleman had been in there for an eternity.

"It's good there are only a few of us left," María Elena said. "These places are depressing."

"You have to be philosophical about it," the boy said. "Don't forget that you're going to have to come back, so you might as well relax. When I came the first time there was no one to talk to, there was a whole bunch of us but, I don't know, no one hit it off, and today, on the other hand, the time has passed nicely from the moment I got here because ideas have been exchanged."

María Elena enjoyed chatting with the boy and the lady; she almost didn't feel the time passing until the bald man came out and the lady got up with a rapidity that one wouldn't have expected at her age. The poor thing probably wanted to get the procedure over with quickly.

"Well, just us now," the boy said. "Would it bother you if I smoked a cigarette? I can't take it anymore, but the lady there seemed so upset . . ."

"I feel like a smoke too."

She accepted the cigarette he offered her and they exchanged names, where they worked; it did them good to swap impressions and forget about the hallway, the silence that seemed too heavy at times, as if the streets and people had been left far behind. María Elena had also lived in Floresta, but when she was a child; now she lived in Constitución. Carlos didn't like that section, he preferred the west side; the air is cleaner, there are trees. His ideal would be to live in Villa del Parque; when he got married he'd probably rent an

apartment over there, his future father-in-law had promised
to help him, he was a man with a lot of connections and he
could get something through one of them.

"I don't know why, but something tells me I'm going to
spend the rest of my life in Constitución," María Elena said.
"It's not so bad, after all. And if sometime . . ."

She saw the door in the rear open and she was almost
surprised as she looked at the boy, who smiled at her as he got
up, see how time flies when you talk, the lady gave them a
friendly nod, she seemed so happy to be leaving, everyone
had a younger, more agile look when they left, as if a weight
had been lifted from them, the procedure over, one thing less
to do and outside the street, the cafés, where they would
probably go to have a drink or a cup of tea in order to feel
that they were really on the other side of the waiting room
and the forms. Now time would drag for María Elena, all
alone; although if it kept on like that Carlos would come out
fairly soon, but some took longer than others because it was
the second time around and who could say what complications there might be.

She almost didn't understand at first when she saw the
door open and the clerk looked at her and nodded for her
to come in. She thought that's how it is, then, that Carlos
would have to stay a while longer filling out forms and in the
meantime they would take care of her. She nodded to the
clerk and went into the office; scarcely had she gone through
the door when another clerk pointed to a chair in front of a
black desk. There were several people in the office, only men,
but she didn't see Carlos. From the other side of the desk a
clerk with a sickly face was looking at a form; without raising
his eyes he held out his hand and it took María Elena an
instant to realize he was asking for the summons; she suddenly understood and looked for it, a little flustered, mur-

muring excuses. She took two or three things out of her purse until she found the piece of yellow paper.

"Start filling this out," the clerk said, handing her a form. "Print it in capital letters, nice and clear."

It was the usual nonsense, first and last name, sex, address. In between two words María Elena got the feeling that something was bothering her, something that wasn't completely clear. Not on the form, where it was easy to go along filling in the blanks; something outside it, something that was missing or wasn't in its place. She stopped writing and took a look around, the other desks with the clerks working or talking among themselves, the dirty walls with posters and photographs, the two windows, the door she had come through, the only door in the office. *Profession*, and next to it the dotted line; she automatically filled in the blank. The only door in the office, but Carlos wasn't there. *Length of time in job*. Capital letters, nice and clear.

When she signed at the bottom, the clerk was looking at her as if she had taken too long in filling out the form. He studied the paper for a moment, found no errors, and put it into a folder. The rest consisted of questions, some of them unnecessary because she had answered them on the form, but about her family too, moves over the past years, insurance, whether she took many trips and where to, whether she had taken out a passport or was planning to. No one seemed very interested in the answers; in any case, the clerk didn't write them down. Suddenly he told María Elena that she could leave but to come back in three days at eleven o'clock; there was no need for a written summons, but she wasn't to forget.

"Yes, sir," María Elena said, getting up. "Thursday at eleven, then."

There was no one in the hallway, and going along it was just as it had been for all the others, a haste, a lightness in her breathing, the urge to get out onto the street and leave the other thing behind. María Elena opened the exit door and as she started down the stairs she thought of Carlos again; it was strange that Carlos hadn't come out like the others. It was strange because the office had only one door, of course at some moment she may not have taken a good look because it couldn't be, the clerk had opened the door for her to come in and Carlos hadn't passed her, he hadn't come out first like all the others, the redheaded man, the ladies, everybody except Carlos.

The sun broke against the sidewalk, it was the noise and the smell of the street; María Elena walked a few steps and stopped, standing by a tree at a spot where no cars were parked. She looked back at the door of the building, told herself that she was going to wait for a moment to see Carlos come out. It was impossible for Carlos not to come out, they'd all left after the procedure was over. She thought that he was probably taking longer because he was the only one who had come for a second time; who knows, that must have been it. It seemed so strange not seeing him in the office, although there probably was a door hidden behind the posters, something she'd missed, but just the same it was strange because everybody had gone out through the hallway like her, all those who had come for the first time had left through the hallway.

Before leaving (she had waited a while, but she couldn't stay there any longer), she thought about the fact that she had to come back on Thursday. Maybe things would be different then and they would have her go out through the other side, although she didn't know where or why. Not her, no, of course, but us, yes, we knew, and we'd be waiting for her and the others, smoking slowly and chatting while Nigger López brewed another of the many rounds of morning coffee.

SEVERO'S PHASES

IN MEMORIAM
REMEDIOS VARO

Everything was sort of quiet, sort of frozen in some way into its own movement, odor, and form, which went on and varied along with the smoke and the soft talk between cigarettes and drinks. Bebe Pessoa had already given out three sure things for the track at San Isidro; Severo's sister was sewing the four coins into the corners of the handkerchief for when sleep overcame Severo. There weren't so many of us but suddenly a house becomes small, between two phrases the transparent cube of two or three seconds of suspension appears, and at moments like that some must have felt like me that all of that, necessary as it might have been, was hurting us because of Severo, Severo's wife, and the friends of so many years.

We'd arrived about eleven at night with Ignacio, Bebe Pessoa, and my brother Carlos. We were kind of family, especially Ignacio, who worked in the same office as Severo, and we came in without anyone's paying too much attention to us. Severo's elder son asked us to go into the bedroom, but Ignacio said that we'd stay in the dining room a while; there were people everywhere in the house, friends or relatives who didn't want to be a bother either and were sitting in corners or gathering beside a table or sideboard to talk or look at each other. Every so often Severo's children or sister would bring coffee and glasses of cane liquor, and at those moments everything would almost always quiet down as if it were freezing into its own movement and in one's memory the idiotic phrase "an angel passing over" began to flutter. But even though afterward I'd comment about a double win by Nigger Acosta at Palermo track or Ignacio would stroke the hair of Severo's younger son, we all felt that underneath everything the immobility persisted, that we were sort of waiting for things that had already happened or that all that could happen was something else perhaps or nothing, as in dreams, even though we were awake and from time to time, without wanting to listen, we heard Severo's wife weeping, almost timidly, in a corner of the room where the closest relatives must have been with her.

You go along forgetting what time it is in cases like that, or as Bebe Pessoa said laughing, it's just the opposite and time forgets you, but in a little while Severo's brother came over to say that the sweating was going to start and we stubbed out our butts and began going into the bedroom one by one, where almost all of us fit because the family had taken out the furniture and there was nothing left but the bed and a night table. Severo was sitting up in bed, supported by the pillows, and a blue serge coverlet and a pale blue towel could be seen at his feet. There was no need to be silent and Severo's brothers with cordial gestures (they're all such nice people) invited us to come closer to the bed, to surround Severo, who had his hands crossed on his knees. Even the younger son, so tiny, was now beside the bed looking at his father with a dream face.

The sweat phase was disagreeable because at the end it was necessary to change the sheets and his pajamas; even the pillows were becoming soaked and were heavy, like enormous tears. Unlike others, who tended to become impatient, Severo remained motionless, not even looking at us, and almost at once the sweat covered his face and hands. His knees stood out like two dark splotches; even though his sister kept drying the sweat on his cheeks, the perspiration would break out again and fall onto the sheet.

"Actually, that's very good," insisted Ignacio, who'd stayed near the door. "It would be worse if he moved, the sheets stick something fierce."

"Papa is a calm man," Severo's elder son said. "He's not the kind to cause people trouble."

"It's ending now," said Severo's wife, who'd come in at the end and was carrying clean pajamas and a set of sheets. I think all of us without exception admired her more than ever at that moment because we knew that she'd been weeping a short time before and now she was capable of attending to her husband with a calm and peaceful, even energetic, face. I suppose that some of the relatives said words of encouragement to Severo; I was in the entranceway once more and the younger daughter was offering me a cup of coffee. I would have liked to have engaged her in conversation to take her mind off things, but other people came in and Manuelita is a little timid: she'd probably think I'm interested in her and I prefer to remain neutral. On the other hand, Bebe Pessoa is

the kind who comes and goes through the house and among
people like nothing, and he, Ignacio, and Severo's brother
had already formed a group with some girl cousins and their
friends, talking about brewing up some bitter maté, which at
that hour would be more than welcome because it would
settle the roast. As it turned out they couldn't, because at one
of those moments when we suddenly remained motionless (I
insist that nothing was changing, we were still talking and
gesticulating, but that's how it was and somehow it's necessary to say it and give it a reason or a name) Severo's brother
came with an acetylene lantern and from the door advised us
that the phase of leaps was going to begin. Ignacio drank
down his coffee in one gulp and said that everything that
night seemed to be moving faster; he was one of those who
placed himself near the bed, with Severo's wife and the small-
est child, who was laughing because Severo's right hand was
oscillating like a metronome. His wife had dressed him in
white pajamas and the bed was impeccable again; we smelled
the cologne and Bebe gave an admiring look to Manuelita,
who must have thought of it. Severo took the first leap and
remained sitting on the edge of the bed, looking at his sister,
who was encouraging him with a somewhat stupid and circumstantial smile. What need was there for that, I thought, as
one who prefers things neat; and what difference could it
make to Severo whether his sister encouraged him or not.
The leaps followed each other rhythmically: sitting on the
edge of the bed, sitting against the headboard, sitting on the
opposite side, standing in the middle of the bed, standing on
the floor between Ignacio and Bebe, squatting on the floor
between his wife and his brother, sitting in the corner of the
doorway, standing in the center of the room, always between
two friends or relatives, falling precisely into the empty
spaces as nobody moved and only eyes followed him, sitting

on the edge of the bed, standing against the headboard, squatting in the middle of the bed, kneeling between his younger son and me, sitting at the foot of the bed. When Severo's wife announced the end of the phase, everyone began to talk at the same time and congratulate Severo, who seemed as though he hadn't been there; I can no longer remember who accompanied him back to the bed because we all went out at the same time, commenting on the phase and looking for something to calm our thirst, and I went out into the courtyard with Bebe to breathe the night air and drink two beers from the bottle.

There was a change in the next phase, I remember, because according to Ignacio it was to be the watch one but we heard Severo's wife weeping again in the living room and almost at once the elder son came to tell us that the moths were already starting to come in. We exchanged slightly puzzled looks with Bebe and Ignacio, but it wasn't impossible for there to be changes and Bebe said the usual thing about the order of factors and things like that; I don't think anybody liked the change but we hid it as we went in again and formed a circle around Severo's bed, which the family had placed in the center of the bedroom.

Severo's brother came last with the acetylene lantern, turned off the spider-legged chandelier on the ceiling and brought the night table over to the foot of the bed; when he put the lantern on the night table we fell silent and motionless, looking at Severo, who had half sat up between the pillows and didn't seem too tired out from the previous phases. The moths began to come in through the door, and the ones that were already on the walls or the ceiling joined the others and began to fly around the acetylene lantern. With his eyes very wide Severo followed the ash-colored whirlwind that kept growing and he seemed to be concentrating all his strength in that unblinking contemplation. One of the moths (it was quite large, I think that it really was a great moth, but in that phase only miller moths were mentioned and no one would have argued over the name) broke away from the others and flew to Severo's face; we saw that it was clinging to his right cheek and that Severo closed his eyes for an instant. One after another the moths abandoned the lantern and flew around Severo, clinging to his hair, his mouth, and his forehead until they had transformed him into an enormous trembling mask in which only the eyes were his and these stared at the acetylene lantern, which one moth insisted on whirling around looking for an entry. I felt Ignacio's fingers digging into my forearm, and only then did I realize that I too was trembling and had a hand sunk into Bebe's shoulder. Someone moaned, a woman, probably Manuelita, who couldn't control herself as well as the others, and at that same instant the last moth flew to Severo's face and was lost in the gray mass. We all shouted at once, embracing and clapping each other on the back while Severo's brother ran to turn on the chandelier; a cloud of moths sluggishly sought the way out and Severo, Severo's face once more, continued looking at the now useless lantern and cautiously moved his lips as if he were afraid of poisoning himself with the silver powder that covered them.

I didn't stay there because they had to wash Severo and somebody was already talking about a bottle of grappa in the kitchen, apart from the fact that in cases like that it's surprising how a sudden falling back into normality, to put it that way, can distract and even deceive a person. I followed Ignacio, who knew all the nooks and crannies, and we latched on to the grappa with Bebe and Severo's elder son. My brother Carlos had lain down on a bench and was smoking with his head tilted to one side, breathing heavily; I brought him a glass and he swallowed it in one gulp. Bebe Pessoa was insisting that Manuelita have a drink, and he was even talking to her about movies and racing; I was putting away one grappa after another, not wanting to think about anything, until I couldn't take it anymore and looked for Ignacio, who seemed to be waiting for me with his arms folded.

"If the last moth had chosen . . ." I began.

Ignacio shook his head negatively. Of course, there was no reason to ask; at least at that moment there was no reason to ask; I don't know if I understood completely, but I had the feeling of a great hollow, something like an empty crypt that was slowly throbbing in some part of my memory with the drip-drip of filtration. In Ignacio's negation (from a distance it had looked to me as if Bebe Pessoa was also shaking his head, and that Manuelita was looking at us anxiously, too timid to say no in turn) there was a kind of suspension of judgment, a not wanting to go further; things were therefore in their absolute present, as they were happening. Then we could go on and when Severo's wife came into the kitchen to tell us that Severo was going to say the numbers, we left our glasses half-finished and made haste, Manuelita between Bebe and me, Ignacio behind, with my brother Carlos, who's always late wherever he goes.

The relatives had already crowded into the bedroom and there wasn't much space to be found. I was just coming in (the acetylene lantern was burning on the floor beside the bed now, but the chandelier was still lighted) when Severo rose up, put his hands in his pajama pockets, and, looking at his elder son, said: "6," looking at his wife, said: "20," looking at Ignacio, said: "23," with a voice that was tranquil and from beneath, without hurrying. To his sister he said 16, to his younger son 28, to other relatives he went along saying numbers that were almost always high, until he told me 2 and

I felt Bebe looking at me out of the corner of his eye and tightening his lips, waiting his turn. But Severo went on to say numbers to other relatives and friends, almost always higher than 5 and without ever repeating them. Almost at the end he said 14 to Bebe, and Bebe opened his mouth and shuddered, as if a great wind had passed between his eyebrows, rubbed his hands, and then was ashamed and hid them in the pockets of his pants precisely as Severo said 1 to a woman with a very ruddy face, probably a distant relative who had come alone and who had spoken to practically no one that night, and suddenly Ignacio and Bebe were looking at each other and Manuelita leaned against the doorframe and it looked to me as if she were trembling, holding back a scream. The rest were no longer paying attention to their numbers, Severo was saying them just the same, but they were beginning to talk, even Manuelita when she recovered and took two steps forward and got 9; no one was interested anymore and the numbers ended with a hollow 24 and a 12 that were for a relative and my brother Carlos; Severo himself seemed less concentrated and with the last one he flung himself backward and let himself be covered by his wife, closing his eyes like a person who is losing interest or forgetting.

"It's a question of time, of course," Ignacio told me as we were leaving the bedroom. "The numbers by themselves have no meaning, you know."

"Do you think so?" I asked him, swallowing the drink that Bebe had brought me.

"But of course," Ignacio said. "Just remember that years can pass between 1 and 2, make it ten or twenty, even more, perhaps, it's a matter of chance."

"Of course," Bebe backed him up. "I wouldn't let it bother me if I were you."

I thought how he had brought me the glass without anyone's asking him, taking the trouble to go to the kitchen with all those people. And he had got 14 and Ignacio 23.

"Not to mention that there's the watch business," my brother Carlos said, having come up beside me and resting his hand on my shoulder. "That's not too easily understood, but it probably has its importance. If it's your turn to fall behind . . ."

"An added advantage," Bebe said, taking the empty glass from my hand as if fearing I would drop it.

We were in the entranceway next to the bedroom and that's how we were among the first to go in when Severo's elder son came to tell us just then that the watch phase was beginning. It seemed to me that Severo's face had suddenly become thin, but his wife had just combed his hair and he smelled of cologne again, which always imparts confidence. I was surrounded by my brother, Ignacio, and Bebe, as if watching over my spirits, and, on the other hand, no one was concerned about the woman relative who had drawn 1 and was at the foot of the bed, her face redder than ever, her mouth and eyelids trembling. Without even looking at her, Severo told his elder son to advance and the kid didn't understand and began to laugh until his mother grabbed him by the arm and took off his wristwatch. We knew that it was a symbolic gesture, all that was necessary was to advance or retard the hands without looking at the hours or minutes, since on leaving the room we would reset our watches to the correct time. Several had already been set ahead or back, Severo was distributing the indications almost mechanically, without taking any interest; when it was my turn to retard, my brother sank his fingers into my shoulder again; this time I thanked him, thinking like Bebe that it might be an added advantage, although nobody could be sure; and also the relative with the red face drew retarding, and the poor woman was drying tears of gratitude, perhaps completely useless after all's said and done, and she was going into the courtyard to have a good nervous attack among the potted plants; something we heard later from the kitchen in the midst of some fresh drinks of grappa and the congratulations of Ignacio and my brother.

"The dream will be soon," Manuelita told us. "Mama says to get ready."

There wasn't much to getting ready: we went slowly back to the bedroom, dragging along the fatigue of the night; soon it would be dawn and it was a working day, our jobs were waiting for most of us at nine or nine thirty; suddenly it was growing colder, the icy breeze in the courtyard coming in through the entranceway, but in the bedroom the lights and the people warmed up the air, there was almost no talking and all we had to do was find room, place ourselves around the bed after putting out our cigarettes. Severo's wife was sitting on the bed, straightening the pillows, but she got up and stood by the head; Severo was looking up, ignoring us, he was looking at the lighted chandelier without blinking, his hands resting on his belly, motionless and indifferent he was looking without blinking at the lighted chandelier and then Manuelita came over to the edge of the bed and we all saw the handkerchief with the coins sewn into the four corners in her hand. There was nothing to do but wait, almost sweating in that close, hot air, thankful for the cologne and thinking about the moment when we would finally be able to leave the house and smoke and talk in the street, discussing or not what happened that night, probably not, but smoking until we were lost at the corner. When Severo's eyelids began to lower slowly, slowly erasing the image of the lighted chandelier, I heard Bebe Pessoa's deep breathing near my ear. There was a sudden change, a loosening, it could be felt as if we were nothing but a single body with countless arms and legs and heads suddenly becoming loose, understanding that it was the end, Severo's dream was beginning, and Manuelita's gesture as she leaned over her father and covered his face with the handkerchief, using the four corners to hold it naturally, without wrinkles or small uncovered spaces, was the same as that contained sigh which enveloped all of us, covered us with the same handkerchief.

"And now he's going to sleep," Severo's wife said. "He's already sleeping, look."

Severo's sister had put a finger to her lips but there was no need, no one would have said anything, we were beginning to move on tiptoe, leaning on one another so as to leave without any noise. Some were still looking back at the handkerchief on Severo's face as if wanting to be sure that Severo was asleep. Against my right hand, I felt stiff and curly hair; it was Severo's younger son, whom a relative had held close to him so that he wouldn't talk or move, and who had come to cling to me now, trying to walk on tiptoe and looking at me from below with questioning and sleepy eyes. I stroked his chin, his cheeks, bringing him along beside me into the entranceway and the courtyard, between Ignacio and Bebe, who were already taking out their packs of cigarettes; the gray of dawn with a rooster out there in the depths was bringing each one of us back to his life, to the future already set up in that grayness and that cold, horribly beautiful. I thought of Severo's wife and Manuelita (maybe the brothers and the elder son), who stayed inside keeping watch over Severo's dream, but we were on our way to the street already, leaving the kitchen and the courtyard behind.

"Aren't you going to play anymore?" Severo's son asked me, dropping with sleepiness but with the obstinacy all kids have.

"No, it's time to get some sleep now," I told him. "Your mother'll put you to bed, get back inside, it's cold."

"It was a game, wasn't it, Julio?"

"Yes, old fellow, it was a game. Go get some sleep now."

With Ignacio, Bebe, and my brother, we reached the first corner, we lighted another cigarette without saying much. Others were already walking far off, some were still standing by the door of the house, talking about trolley cars or taxis; we knew the neighborhood well, we could go on together for the first few blocks, then Bebe and my brother would turn to the left, Ignacio would continue on for a few blocks more, and I would go up to my place and put the kettle on for some maté; after all, it wasn't worth going to bed for such a short time, it would be better to put on my slippers and smoke and drink some maté, things like that, which help.

BUTTERBALL'S
NIGHT

It was typical of Peralta, that idea. Generally he would barely give any explanation to anybody, but this time he opened up a little more and said it was like the tale of the purloined letter. Estévez didn't understand at first and stood looking at him waiting for more; Peralta shrugged his shoulders like someone giving up something and handed him the ticket to the fight. Estévez saw a big number 3 in red on a yellow background and underneath it 235; but then, from the beginning, how could he miss those letters that leaped before his eyes, MONZÓN vs. NÁPOLES. They'll get the other ticket to Walter, Peralta said. You'll be there before the fights start (he never repeated instructions, and Estévez listened so he

could retain each phrase) and Walter will arrive in the middle of the first preliminary, he's got the seat to your right.
Watch out for people who get sharp at the last minute and
start looking for a better seat, say something in Spanish to
him to be sure. He'll come with one of those bags hippies
carry, he'll put it down between the two of you if it's a bench
or on the floor if they're chairs. Don't talk to him about anything except the fights and take a good look around you,
there are sure to be Mexicans or Argentines, have them
spotted when you put the package in the bag. Does Walter
know that his bag has to be open, Estévez asked. Yes, Peralta
said as if brushing a fly from his lapel, only wait till the main
bout when nobody will be looking around. It's hard to look
around with Monzón, Estévez said. Or with Butterball either,
said Peralta. No chatting, remember. Walter will leave first,
let the people start leaving, and you go out a different door.

He thought about all that as in a final review while the
Métro took him to Défense among passengers who, from
their looks, were also going to the fight, men in threes and
fours, Frenchmen bearing the scars of the double beating
Monzón had given Bouttier, seeking a vicarious revenge or
maybe now secretly won over. What a stroke of genius of
Peralta's, giving him that mission, which must be critical,
coming from him, and at the same time letting him watch a
fight that seemed to have been put together for millionaires.
Now he understood the allusion to the purloined letter, who
would ever have thought that Walter and he could meet at
the fights, it really wasn't a question of a meeting because
that could have happened in a thousand crannies in Paris,
but of the responsibility of Peralta, who weighed everything
very slowly. For those who might be following Walter or following him, a movie theater or a café or an apartment was a
possible meeting place, but that fight was like an obligation

for anyone who had the money, and if they followed him there they'd be fucking well disappointed in the circus tent set up by Alain Delon; no one could get in there without the little yellow piece of paper, and tickets had been sold out a week ahead of time, all the papers said so. Even more in Peralta's favor, if they got there by following him or following Walter, it would be impossible to see them together either going in or coming out, two fans among thousands and thousands pouring like mouthfuls of smoke out of subways and buses, clogging up, bit by bit, as the paths merged and the hour approached.

No fool, Alain Delon: a circus tent set up on a vacant lot that was reached by going over a footbridge and following some walkways improvised out of boards. It had rained the night before and the people didn't leave the boards, guiding themselves from the subway exit by the huge arrows that showed the right direction and MONZÓN-NÁPOLES in bright colors. No fool, Alain Delon, capable of putting up his own arrows in the sacred territory of the Métro even if it cost him money. Estévez didn't like the guy, that overbearing way of organizing the world championship on his own, setting up a tent and paying who knows what and how much dough in advance, but you had to hand it to him, he gave you something in exchange, let's not talk about Monzón and Butterball but also the colored arrows in the subway, that way of receiving people like a lord, pointing the way for the fans who would have been confused at the exits and in those vacant lots all full of puddles.

Estévez arrived as he was supposed to, with the tent half-full, and before showing his ticket he stood for a moment looking at the police vans and the large trailers lighted up outside but with dark curtains on the windows, connected to the tent by covered passages, like the ones used to get onto an airplane. The fighters were there, Estévez thought, the newest white trailer most certainly belongs to Carlitos, you don't mix him in with the others. Nápoles would have his trailer on the other side of the tent, it was all scientific and, in passing, pure improvisation, lots of canvas and trailers on a vacant lot. That's how you make dough, Estévez thought, you've got to have big ideas and balls, by God.

His row, the fifth after the ringside section, was a plank with large numbers on it, Alain Delon's courtesy seemed to have ended there, because outside of the chairs at ringside the rest were circus accommodations and a bad circus, plain boards although there were usherettes in miniskirts who made you forget any complaints as soon as you came in. Estévez found 235 on his ticket, although the girl smiled, showing him the number as if he couldn't read, and he sat down to thumb through the newspaper that he would use later as a cushion. Walter would be on his right, and that's why Estévez had the package with the money and papers in the left pocket of his jacket; when the moment came he would take it out with his right hand, bringing it immediately toward his knees, and he would slip it into the open bag beside him.

The wait was getting long; there was time to think about Marisa and the kid, who were probably finishing dinner, the kid already half-asleep and Marisa watching television. They were probably televising the fight and she would see it, but he wasn't going to tell her where he'd been, at least he couldn't now, maybe someday when things had calmed down. He opened the paper listlessly (Marisa watching the fight, it was comical thinking that he wouldn't be able to tell her anything, with the great urge he had to tell her, especially if she said something to him about Monzón and Nápoles); in the midst of reports from Vietnam and the crime news the tent was filling up, a group of Frenchmen behind him were

discussing Nápoles' chances, on his left a snob type was about
to settle himself after having studied for a long time and with
a kind of horror the bench on which he would have to rest his
immaculate blue pants. Farther down there were couples and
groups of friends and among them three who were talking in
an accent that could have been Mexican; although Estévez
wasn't much of an expert on accents, there must have been a
lot of Butterball rooters there that night with the challenger
aspiring to nothing less than taking Monzón's crown. Besides
Walter's there were still a few empty places, but people were
piling up at the entrances to the tent and the girls had to
work extra hard to get everybody seated. Estévez found that
the ring lights were too strong and the music too pop, but
now that the first preliminary was starting the crowd didn't
waste any time on criticisms and eagerly followed a bad
match that was all butting and clinching; at the moment
Walter sat down beside him Estévez was reaching the conclusion that this wasn't a real boxing crowd, at least those
around him; they'd swallow anything out of snobbism just to
see Monzón or Nápoles.

"Excuse me," Walter said, sitting down between Estévez
and a fat woman who was following the fight half hugging
her husband, who was also fat and had the look of someone
who knew what was going on.

"Settle in," Estévez said. "It's not easy, these Frenchmen
always calculate on places for skinny people."

Walter laughed as Estévez pushed gently to the left so as
not to upset the man in blue pants; finally there was room for
Walter to move the blue canvas bag from his knees to the
plank. They were already into the second preliminary, which
was also bad; the people were mostly amusing themselves
with what was going on outside the ring, the arrival of a tight
group of Mexicans with sombreros but dressed as what they

must have been: big shots able to charter a plane to come from Mexico to root for Butterball, broad and chubby types with prominent asses and Pancho Villa faces, almost too typical when they threw their hats into the air as if Nápoles were already in the ring, shouting and arguing before they encrusted themselves into ringside seats. Alain Delon must have foreseen it all because the loudspeakers immediately blatted out a kind of corrido that the Mexicans didn't seem to recognize too well. Estévez and Walter looked at each other ironically, and at that moment in poured through the farther entrance a swarm of people headed by five or six women broader than they were tall, in white sweaters, with shouts of "Argentina, Argentina!" and brandishing an enormous blue and white flag. The group opened its way through usherettes and chairs, determined to advance to the edge of the ring, where their tickets were most certainly not valid. In the midst of delirious shouts they finally formed a line that the usherettes with the help of some smiling gorillas and many explanations led toward two half-empty planks, and Estévez saw that the women displayed a black MONZÓN on the back of each of their sweaters. It was all enjoyed considerably by an audience that cared little about the nationality of the pugilists since they weren't French, and the third prelim was going hard and fast although Alain Delon didn't seem to have spent much dough on the little fish when the two sharks were probably ready in their trailers and were the only thing the public cared about.

There was a kind of instantaneous charge in the air, something climbed up Estévez's throat; from the loudspeakers came a tango played by an orchestra that could well have been Pugliese's. Only then did Walter look at him face on and in a friendly way, and Estévez wondered if he might be a compatriot. They exchanged barely a word except for some

comment having to do with the action in the ring, probably
Uruguayan or Chilean, but no questions, Peralta had been
quite clear about it, people meeting at the boxing match and
chance has it that they both speak Spanish, enough said.

"Well, now's the time," Estévez said. Everybody was
standing up in spite of the protests and the whistling, on the
left a wild uproar and a flight of Mexican hats in the midst of
applause, Butterball climbed into the ring, which suddenly
seemed even brighter, people were looking to the right now,
where nothing was going on, the applause gave way to a
murmur of expectation and from their seats Walter and Estévez couldn't see the entrance to the other side of the ring,
the near silence and suddenly clamor as the only signal, the
white robe outlined suddenly against the ropes, Monzón
showing his back, talking to his people, Nápoles going over to
him, a quick greeting in the midst of flashbulbs and the ref-
eree waiting for the microphone to be lowered, people sitting
back down little by little, one last sombrero flying far off,
returned in the opposite direction out of pure fucking
around, a tardy boomerang amidst the indifference because
now introductions and greetings, Georges Carpentier, Nino
Benvenuti, a French champion, Jean-Claude Bouttier, photographs and applause and the ring slowly emptying, the
Mexican national anthem with more hats and finally the Argentine flag being unfurled to await its anthem, Estévez and
Walter not standing up although it hurt Estévez, but this was
no time to bungle anything, in any case it let him find out
that he didn't have any compatriots too close by, the group
with the flag was singing at the end of the anthem and the
blue and white banner was waving in such a way that it made
the gorillas run to that side just in case, the voice announcing
names and weights, seconds out of the ring.

"Who do you like?" Estévez asked. He was nervous,

childishly worked up now that the gloves were touching in the initial greeting and Monzón, facing him, was using that guard that didn't look like a defense, his arms long and thin, an almost fragile silhouette opposite Butterball, shorter and more muscular, already letting go with two opening punches.

"I've always liked challengers," Walter said, and in back a Frenchman explaining that the difference in height was going to favor Monzón, probing punches, Monzón going in and coming out effortlessly, the round almost had to be even. So he liked challengers, then he wasn't Argentine because otherwise; but the accent, he had to be Uruguayan, he'd ask Peralta, who certainly wouldn't answer him. In any case, he couldn't have been in France for long because the fat man embracing his wife had made some comment to him and Walter answered in such an incomprehensible way that the fat man made a gesture of discouragement and started talking to someone below. Nápoles hits hard, Estévez thought restlessly, twice he'd seen Monzón draw back and the response came a little late, he'd probably felt the blows. It was as if Butterball understood that his only chance was close in, sparring with Monzón wouldn't serve him the way it had always served him, his marvelous speed found a kind of emptiness, a torso that dodged and got away while the champion landed once, twice on the face and the Frenchman behind repeated anxiously, you see, you see how his arms are helping him, maybe the second round went to Nápoles, the people were quiet, every shout came out in isolation and was poorly received, in the third round Butterball gave everything he had and then the expected, Estévez thought, now they're going to see what's coming, Monzón against the ropes, a swaying willow, a one-two like a whiplash, the furious clinch to get off the ropes, a close-in hand-to-hand until the end of the round, the Mexicans up on their seats and the people behind hollering-protestsorstandingupinturntosee.

"Some fight, eh," Estévez said. "This is what makes it all worthwhile."

"Aha."

They took out cigarettes at the same time, exchanged them smiling, Walter's lighter was out first, Estévez looked at his profile for a minute, then he looked at him from the front, it wasn't a question of looking for long, Walter had graying hair but he looked rather young, with his blue jeans and brown polo shirt. Student, engineer? Pulling himself out from down there like so many others, getting into the struggle, with dead friends in Montevideo or Buenos Aires, who knows maybe Santiago, he'd have to ask Peralta, although after everything was over he certainly wouldn't see Walter again, each in his own way would remember some time that they'd met on Butterball's night, as he was going strong in the fifth round, with the crowd on its feet and delirious now, the Argentines and the Mexicans swept away by an enormous French wave that saw the fight more than the fighters, that spotted the reactions, the play of legs; finally Estévez realized that almost all of them really understood the thing, only from time to time some idiot applauding a showy punch that had no effect and he lost what was really happening in that ring, where Monzón was going in and coming out, taking advantage of his speed which more and more left Butterball standing, tired, hurt, fighting with everything he had against the long-armed willow who was once more rocking on the ropes to come in and attack again high and low, dry and precise. When the gong sounded Estévez looked at Walter, who took his cigarettes out again.

"Oh, well, that's the way it goes," Walter said, holding out the pack to him. "If it can't be done, it can't."

It was difficult to talk with all the shouting, the public knew that the next round might be the deciding one, Nápoles'

fans were urging him on almost as if saying good-bye, Estévez thought with a sympathy that no longer went against his
desire now that Monzón was looking for the fight and finding
it and for twenty interminable seconds going for the face and
the body while Butterball tried to clinch like someone diving
into the water, closing his eyes. He can't take any more, Estévez thought, and with effort he took his eyes off the ring to
look at the canvas bag on the plank, he would have to do it
exactly between rounds when everyone was sitting down, exactly at that moment because afterward they would stand up
again and once more the bag would be alone on the board,
two lefts in a row to Nápoles' face as he tried to clinch again,
Monzón out of range, hardly waiting to come back with an
ultra-precise hook to the middle of the face, now the legs, you
had to look especially at the legs, Estévez, an expert at that,
was watching tired Butterball, throwing himself forward
without that precision of his while Monzón's feet slid to the
side or backward, the cadence perfect so that his last right
would land with all it had full in the stomach. A lot of people
didn't hear the bell in the hysterical clamor but Walter and
Estévez did, Walter sat down first, straightening up the bag
without looking at it and Estévez followed him more slowly,
slipped in the package in a fraction of a second and raised his
empty hand again to gesticulate his enthusiasm at the guy in
the blue pants, who didn't seem to be very aware of what was
going on.

"That's a champion," Estévez told him without forcing
his voice, because in any case the other one wouldn't have
heard him in all that noise. "Carlitos, God damn it."

He looked at Walter, who was peacefully smoking, the
man was beginning to give up, what can you do, if it can't be
done it can't. Everybody standing, waiting for the bell for the
seventh round, a quick, incredulous silence and then the

unanimous howl when they saw the towel on the canvas,
Nápoles still in his corner and Monzón coming forward with
his gloves held up, more champion than ever, waving before
he got lost in the whirlwind of congratulations and flashbulbs. It was an ending without beauty but it was incontest-
able, Butterball quitting so he wouldn't be Monzón's punch-
ing bag, all hope lost now that he was getting up to go over to
the winner and lift his gloves to his face, almost a caress,
while Monzón put his on his shoulders and they separated
once more, now yes forever, Estévez thought, now never to
meet again in a ring.

"It was a beautiful fight," he told Walter, who was sling-
ing the bag over his shoulder and working his feet as if he had
a cramp.

"It could have gone on longer," Walter said. "I'm sure
that Nápoles' seconds wouldn't let him go out."

"What for? You could see he'd had it, eh, too much of a
boxer not to realize it."

"Yes, but when you're like him you've got to go on to
the end, finally you never know."

"With Monzón you do," Estévez said, and remembering
Peralta's orders, he held out his hand cordially. "Well, it's
been a pleasure."

"The same here. So long."

"Ciao."

He watched him go out on his side, following the fat
man, who was arguing with his wife in shouts, and he stayed
behind the guy in the blue pants, who wasn't in a hurry; little
by little they headed toward the left to go out between the
boards. The Frenchmen behind were arguing about tech-
niques, but Estévez was amused to see one of the women
embrace her boyfriend or her husband and kiss him on the
mouth and on the neck. Unless the guy is an idiot, Estévez

thought, he has to realize that she's kissing Monzón. The package no longer weighed in his jacket pocket, it was as if he could breathe better, be interested in what was going on, the girl hugging the guy, the Mexicans leaving with their sombreros, which suddenly seemed smaller, the Argentine flag half furled but still waving, the two fat Italians looking at each other with the air of people who understood, and one of them saying almost solemnly *gliel' a messo in culo*, and the other one approving such a perfect synthesis, the way out jammed, a slow tired exit and the board paths up to the gangplank in the cold and drizzly night, finally the gangplank creaking under a critical load, Peralta and Chaves smoking, leaning on the railing, without making a motion because they knew that Estévez would see them and that he would hide his surprise, would come over the way he came over, taking out a cigarette in turn.

"He clobbered him," Estévez informed them.

"I know," Peralta said. "I was there."

Estévez looked at him with surprise, but they turned around at the same time and went down the gangplank among the people, who were already beginning to thin out. He knew he had to follow them and he saw them leave the avenue that led to the subway and go down a darker street, Chaves turned only once to make sure he hadn't lost sight of them, then they went directly to Chaves' car and got in without haste but without losing any time. Estévez got in back with Peralta, the car started up heading south.

"So you were there," Estévez said. "I didn't know you liked boxing."

"I don't give a shit about it," Peralta said, "although Monzón is worth every penny. I went to watch you from a distance just in case, it wasn't a time to leave you alone if at some moment . . ."

"Well, you saw. You know, poor Walter was rooting for Nápoles."

"It wasn't Walter," Peralta said.

The car continued south, Estévez sensed confusedly that by this route they would never get to the Bastille district, he felt it as if from way behind because the rest was an explosion full in his face, Monzón hitting him and not Butterball. He couldn't even open his mouth, he sat looking at Peralta and waiting.

"It was too late to warn you," Peralta said. "Too bad you left your house so early, when we phoned Marisa told us that you'd already left and weren't coming back."

"I felt like walking a bit before taking the subway," Estévez said. "But, then, tell me."

"Everything went to hell," Peralta said. "Walter telephoned when he got to Orly this morning, we told him what he had to do, he confirmed to us that he'd gotten the ticket for the fight, everything was just right. We agreed that he'd call me from Lucho's hideout before leaving, a matter of being sure. At seven thirty he hadn't called, we telephoned Geneviève and she called back to say Walter hadn't gotten to Lucho's."

"They were waiting for him at the exit from Orly," Chaves' voice said.

"But then who was it who . . ." Estévez began, and left the phrase hanging; suddenly he understood and it was cold sweat running off his neck, slipping down inside his shirt, the knot tightening in his stomach.

"They had seven hours to get the information out of him," Peralta said. "For proof, the guy knew every detail of what he was supposed to do with you. You know how they work, not even Walter could take it."

"Tomorrow or the day after they'll find him in some vacant lot," Chaves' voice said, almost bored.

"What difference does it make to you now," Peralta said. "Before coming to the fight I fixed it so they'd scram out of the hideouts. You know, I still had some hope when I went into that shitty tent, but he'd already arrived and there was nothing to do."

"But then," Estévez said, "when he left with the money . . ."

"I followed him, of course."

"But before, if you already knew . . ."

"Nothing to do," Peralta repeated. "It was all lost, the guy would have put up a fight right there and they would have busted us all, you already know how in they are."

"So what happened?"

"Three more of them were waiting outside, one had a pass or something like that and quicker than I can tell you they were in a car in the parking space for Delon's pals and people with dough, and they took off. Then I went back to the gangplank, where Chaves was waiting for us, and there you have it. I took down the number of the car, of course, but that isn't worth shit."

"We're leaving Paris," Estévez said.

"Yes, we're going to a quiet spot. The problem now is you, you must have realized that."

"Why me?"

"Because now the guy knows you and is going to end up finding you. There aren't any more hideouts after the Walter business."

"I've got to get away then," Estévez said. He thought about Marisa and the kid, how could he take them, how could he leave them alone, everything was getting mixed up with the trees at the beginning of some woods, the buzzing in his ears as if the crowd were still there shouting Monzón's name, the instant in which there'd been a pause of disbelief

and the towel fell into the center of the ring, Butterball's
night, poor guy. And the fellow had been rooting for Butterball, now that he thought about it, it was strange that he
should have been on the side of the loser, he should have
been with Monzón, carrying off the money like Monzón, like
someone who turns his back and leaves with everything, making it worse by making fun of the loser, of the poor guy with
the broken face or with his hand held out saying well, it's
been a pleasure. The car put on its brakes among the trees
and Chaves turned off the motor. In the darkness the match
of another cigarette was lighted, Peralta.

"I've got to get away, then," Estévez repeated. "To Belgium, if you think so, the one you know is there."

"You'd be safe if you got there," Peralta said, "but you
already saw with Walter that they've got people everywhere
and a lot of pull."

"They won't grab me."

"Like Walter, who was going to grab Walter and make
him sing. You know different things from Walter, that's the
bad part."

"They won't grab me," Estévez repeated. "Look, it's just
that I've got to think of Marisa and the kid, now that everything's turned to shit I can't leave them here, they'll take it
out on her. I'll make all the arrangements in one day and
take them with me to Belgium, I'll see the one you know and
go on alone to somewhere else."

"One day is too much," Chaves said, turning in his seat.
His eyes were getting used to the darkness, Estévez saw his
profile and Peralta's face when he raised the cigarette to his
mouth and dragged on it.

"All right, I'll leave as soon as possible," Estévez said.

"Right now," said Peralta, taking out the pistol.

TRADE WINDS

Who can say who got the idea, Vera maybe on the night of her birthday, when Mauricio insisted that they open another bottle of champagne and between glasses they danced in the living room, sticky with cigarette smoke and midnight, or maybe Mauricio at the moment when *Blues in Thirds* was bringing back the memory of the earliest times to them from so far back, from the first records, when birthdays were more than a rhythmic and recurring ceremony. Like a game, talking while they danced, smiling accomplices in the gradual lethargy of alcohol and smoke, asking themselves why not, since after all, since they could do it and it would be summer there, together and indifferent they'd looked over the travel

agency folder, suddenly the idea, Mauricio or Vera, just a
phone call, going to the airport, to see if the game was worthwhile, things like that are done right away or not at all, besides what was it, at worst returning with the same friendly
sarcasm that had brought them back from so many boring
trips, but proving something in a different way now, playing
the game, balancing things, deciding.

Because this time (and that's what's new about it, the
idea had occurred to Mauricio but it could just as well have
come out of a casual reflection or Vera's pout, twenty years of
life in common, the mental symbiosis, sentences started by
one and finished at the other end of the table or on the other
telephone), this time it might be different, there was nothing
to do but lay down the rules, get some fun out of the absolute
absurdity of leaving on different planes and arriving at the
hotel like strangers, letting chance introduce them in the dining room or on the beach after one or two days, mingling
with the new acquaintances of the summer vacation, treating
each other courteously, talking about profession and family
during the round of cocktails in the midst of so many other
professions and other lives that were probably searching like
them for the brief contact of vacations. No one would think
anything of the coincidence of last names because it was a
common name, it would be so much fun to calibrate the slow
mutual acquaintance, attuning it to the rhythm of the other
guests, each having fun with people individually, leaving
meetings to chance and from time to time finding themselves
alone and looking at each other as now while they danced to
Blues in Thirds and stopped every so often to lift their glasses
of champagne and clink them softly in exact time to the
music, courteous and mannerly and tired and one thirty already in the midst of so much smoke and perfume which
Mauricio had tried to place that night on Vera's skin, won-

dering if she hadn't made a mistake in perfumes, if Vera
would lift her nose a little and approve, Vera's difficult and
rare approval.

They had always made love at the end of their birthday
parties, waiting with amiable coolness for the last friends to
leave, and this time there was no one, because they hadn't
invited anyone since being with people bored them more
than being alone; they danced until the record was over and
remained embracing, looking at each other in a mist of half-
sleep, went out of the living room still keeping an imaginary
rhythm, lost and almost happy and barefoot on the bedroom
rug, they lingered in a slow disrobing beside the bed, helping
each other and getting mixed up and kisses and clasps and
once more the encounter with its inevitable preferences, the
adjustment of each to the light of the lamp that was condemning them to the repetition of tired images, known
murmurs, the slow sinking into the unsated drowsiness after
the repetition of the formulas that returned to words and
bodies like a necessary, almost tender duty.

In the morning it was Sunday and rain, they had breakfast in bed and decided on it seriously; now they had to legis-
late, set up each phase of the trip so that it wouldn't turn into
just another departure and, most of all, just another return.
They figured it out by counting on their fingers: they would
travel separately, one; they would stay in different rooms
with nothing to prevent them from taking advantage of the
summer, two; there would be no censuring or looks like the
ones they knew so well, three; a meeting without witnesses
would let them exchange impressions and find out if it had
been worth the trouble, four; the rest was routine, they
would come back on the same plane since the other people
would no longer matter (or they would, but that was to be
seen in accordance with article four), five. What would hap-

pen afterward wasn't numbered, it was going into a zone determined and uncertain at the same time, an aleatory sum in
which anything could happen and about which nothing
should be said. The flights to Nairobi left on Thursdays and
Saturdays, Mauricio took the first one after a lunch at which
they had salmon just in case, declaiming toasts and exchanging talismans, don't forget the quinine, remember, you always leave your shaving cream and sandals behind.

It was amusing to arrive in Mombasa after an hour in a
taxi that took her to the Trade Winds, to a bungalow on the
beach with monkeys cavorting in the coconut palms and smiling African faces, seeing Mauricio from a distance, already
master of his house, playing on the beach with a couple and
an old man with red sideburns. Cocktail hour caught up with
them on the open veranda by the sea talking about reefs and
seashells, Mauricio came along with a woman and two young
men, at some moment he asked where Vera was from and
explained that he had arrived from France and was a geologist. Vera thought it was nice that Mauricio was a geologist
and answered the other tourists' questions, the pediatrics that
every so often demanded a few days' rest so as not to sink
you into depression, the old man with red sideburns was a
retired diplomat, his wife dressed as if she were twenty years
old but it didn't look so bad on her in a place where almost
everything looked like a Technicolor movie, waiters and
monkeys included, and even the name Trade Winds, which
reminded one of Conrad and Somerset Maugham, cocktails
served in coconut shells, shirttails, the beach, where one
could stroll after dinner under a moon so pitiless that the
clouds projected their moving shadows on the sand to the
surprise of the people who had been squashed down by dirty,
misty skies.

The last shall be first, Vera thought when Mauricio said

that they had given him a room in the more modern part of
the hotel, comfortable but without the charm of the bunga-
lows on the beach. They played cards at night, day was an
endless dialogue of sun and shade, sea and refuge under the
palm trees, rediscovering the pale and tired body with each
lash of the waves, going to the reefs in a dugout to dive with
masks and see the blue and red coral, the fish so innocently
close by. There was a lot of talk on the second day about the
encounter with two starfish, one with red spots and the other
violet and covered with triangles, unless it was the third day
already, time slipped away like the warm sea on the skin,
Vera was swimming with Sandro, who had surfaced between
two cocktails and said he was sick of Verona and automobiles,
the Englishman with red sideburns had had too much sun
and the doctor was coming from Mombasa to have a look at
him, the lobsters were incredibly huge in their last dwelling
of mayonnaise and lemon slices, vacations. All that had been
seen of Anna was a distant and kind of distancing smile, the
fourth night she came to get a drink at the bar and took her
glass out onto the veranda, where the three-day veterans received her with information and advice, there were dangerous sea urchins in the northern part, she should by no means
go out in a dugout without a hat and something to cover her
shoulders, the poor Englishman was paying dearly for it and
the blacks forget to warn tourists because for them, of course,
and Anna thanking them quietly, drinking her martini
slowly, almost demonstrating that she had come to be alone
from some Copenhagen or Stockholm that needed to be forgotten. Without even thinking about it, Vera decided that
Mauricio and Anna, of course, Mauricio and Anna before
twenty-four hours were up, she was playing Ping-Pong with
Sandro when she saw them go to the beach and lie down on
the sand. Sandro was joking about Anna, who didn't seem

very communicative to him, Nordic mists, he was easily win-
ning the games but the Italian gentleman ceded a few points
from time to time and Vera realized it and thanked him in
silence, twenty-one to eighteen, she hadn't been bad, she was
making progress, a matter of applying herself.

At some moment before sleep Mauricio thought that,
after all, they were doing quite well, it was almost comical to
think that Vera was sleeping a hundred yards away from his
room in the enviable bungalow caressed by the palms, you
were lucky, baby. They'd coincided on a trip to the nearby
islands and had had a lot of fun swimming and playing with
the others; Anna's shoulders had been burned and Vera gave
her a cream that never failed, you know that a baby doctor
ends up knowing everything about creams, the hesitant return of the Englishman protected by a pale blue robe, the
radio at night talking about Jomo Kenyatta and tribal problems, somebody knew a lot about the Masai and over many
drinks entertained them with legends and lions, Karen
Blixen and the authenticity of elephant skin amulets, pure
nylon and that's the way everything was going in those coun-
tries. Vera didn't know whether it was Wednesday or Thursday when Sandro accompanied her to the bungalow after a
long walk on the beach where they'd kissed as that beach and
that moon had demanded, she let him come in as soon as he
put a hand on her shoulder, let herself be loved all night,
heard strange things, learned some differences, slept slowly,
savoring every minute of the long silence under an almost
inconceivable mosquito netting. For Mauricio it was the siesta, after a lunch during which his knees had found Anna's
thighs, accompanying her to her rooms, murmuring a so-long
by the door, seeing how Anna kept her hand on the latch,
going in with her, losing himself in a pleasure that only re-
leased them at nightfall, when some people were already

wondering if they were ill and Vera smiled uncertainly between two drinks, burning her tongue on a mixture of
Campari and Kenyan rum that Sandro had mixed at the bar
to the astonishment of Moto and Nikuku, those Europeans
would all end up crazy.

The rules had set Saturday at seven in the evening, Vera
took advantage of a meeting without witnesses on the beach
and pointed out a propitious palm grove in the distance.
They embraced with an old love, laughing like kids, obeying
article four, good people. There was a soft solitude of sand
and dry branches, cigarettes and those bronzed people on the
fifth or sixth day whose eyes began to glow like new, to whom
talk is a festival. It's going very well for us, Mauricio said
almost at once, and Vera, yes, of course it's going very well for
us, I can see it in your face and in your hair, why in my hair,
because it shines differently, it's the salt, silly, maybe but salt
mats hair together instead, laughter wouldn't let them talk, it
was good not talking while they laughed and looked at each
other, a last sun going down quickly, the Tropics, take a good
look and you'll see the legendary green ray, I already tried
from my balcony and didn't see anything, ah, of course, the
gentleman has a balcony, yes ma'am, a balcony, but you've
got a bungalow for enjoying ukuleles and orgies. Slipping
along the slope without effort, with another cigarette, really,
he's marvelous, he's got a way of. It must be, if you say so.
What about yours, speak. I don't like your saying yours, it's
like a distribution of prizes. It is. All right, but not like that,
not Anna. Oh, my, what a voice, all full of glucose, you say
Anna as if you were sucking on every letter. Not every letter,
but. Pig. What about you, then. In general it's not me who does
the sucking, although. I imagined so, all those Italians are
right out of *The Decameron*. Just a minute, we're not in group
therapy, Mauricio. I'm sorry, it's not jealousy, what right do I

have. Oh, good boy. Yes, then? Yes, then, perfect, slowly, interminably perfect. I congratulate you, I wouldn't have liked
for it to be any less good for you than for me. I don't know
how it's going with you, but article four demands. Agreed,
although it isn't easy to put it into words, Anna is a wave, a
starfish. The red one or the violet one? All of them together, a
golden river, pink coral. This man is a Scandinavian poet.
And you're a Venetian libertine. He isn't from Venice, he's
from Verona. It's the same thing, it always makes you think
of Shakespeare. You're right, I hadn't thought of that. So
that's how we're doing, right? That's how we're doing,
Mauricio, and we've still got five days left. Five nights,
above all, make good use of them. I think I shall, he's
promised me some new things that he calls tricks to reach
reality. You can explain them to me, I'll wait. In detail, you
can be sure, and you'll tell me about your river of gold and
the blue coral. Pink coral, little girl. Well, you can see that
we haven't been wasting our time. That remains to be seen,
in any case, we're not wasting the present and talking about
it, it's no good for us to spend too much time on article four.
Another dip before whisky? Whisky, how common, I get
served Carpano mixed with gin and bitters. Oh, I beg your
pardon. That's all right, refinement takes time, let's go look
for the green ray, one of these times, who can say.

Friday, Robinson Crusoe day, someone remembered between drinks and there was talk for a while about islands and
shipwrecks, there was a brief and violent hot downpour that
silvered the palm trees and brought a new sound of birds
afterward, migrations, the Ancient Mariner and his albatross,
they were people who knew how to live, every whisky came
with its ration of folklore, of old songs from the Hebrides or
Guadeloupe, at the end of the day Vera and Mauricio were
thinking the same thing, the hotel deserved its name, it was

the hour of trade winds for them, Anna the giver of forgotten vertigos, Sandro the maker of subtle machines, trade winds bringing them back to other times without customs, when they too had had a time like that, inventions and enlightenments on the bed-sheet sea, except that now, except that no longer and therefore, therefore the trade winds that would blow till Tuesday, precisely until the end of the interregnum that was the remote past once more, an instantaneous trip to fountains in flower again, bathing them in a present delight but one already known, known sometime before there were rules, before *Blues in Thirds*.

They didn't talk about that when they met on the Boeing in Nairobi, while they lighted the first cigarette of their return together. Looking at each other as before filled them with something for which there were no words and about which they both kept silent in the midst of drinks and anecdotes about the Trade Winds, in some way they had to preserve the Trade Winds, the winds had to keep driving them, that wonderful old sailing before the wind coming back to destroy propellers, to do away with the slow dirty petroleum of every day that contaminated glasses by birthday champagne, the hope of every night. The trade winds of Anna and Sandro, keeping on drinking while they looked at each other between puffs of smoke, why Mauricio now if Sandro was still there, his skin and his hair and his voice sharpening Mauricio's face as Anna's hoarse laugh in full love dissolved that smile that in Vera was an amiable absence. There was no article six, but they could invent one without words, it was so natural that at some moment he would invite Anna to have another whisky, that she, accepting it with a stroke on the cheek, would say yes, would say yes, Sandro, it would be so nice if we had another whisky in order to get rid of the fear of height, playing like that during the whole flight, there was no longer any need for rules to decide that at the airport Sandro would offer to see Anna home, that Anna would accept with a simple respect for gentlemanly duties, that once at the house she would be the one to look for her keys in her purse and invite Sandro to have another drink, have him leave his bag in the foyer and show him the way to the living room, making excuses for the traces of dust and the closed-in air, opening the drapes and getting ice while Sandro with an appreciative air examined the stacks of records and the Friedlander print. It was after eleven o'clock at night, they drank their glasses of friendship and Anna brought a tray with pâté and crackers, Sandro helped her make canapés and they didn't get to taste them, hands and mouths sought each other, rolling around on the bed and getting undressed, clinging already, looking for each other in the midst of belts and clothing, pulling off the last pieces and turning down the bed, lowering the lights and taking each other slowly, searching and murmuring, above all hoping and murmuring the hope.

Who can say when the drinks and cigarettes came back, the pillows to sit up in bed with and smoke by the light of the lamp on the floor. They almost didn't look at each other, the words went to the wall and came back in a slow game of catch for blind people, and she first, wondering as if to herself what could have become of Vera and Mauricio after the Trade Winds, what could have become of them after their return.

"They've probably realized by now," he said. "They've probably understood and after that they won't be able to do anything more."

"Something can always be done," she said. "Vera's not going to stay that way, you only had to look at her."

"Mauricio either," he said. "I barely knew him but it

was so obvious. Neither one is going to stay like that and it's almost easy to imagine what they're going to do."

"Yes, it's easy, it's like seeing it from here."

"They probably haven't gone to sleep, just like us, and now they're probably talking slowly, without looking at each other. They won't have anything more to say to each other, I think it'll be Mauricio who opens the drawer and takes out the blue vial. Like this, see, a blue vial like this."

"Vera will count them and divide them up," she said. "Practical things are always left to her, she'll do it well. Sixteen apiece, not even the problem of an odd number."

"They'll swallow them by twos, with whisky and at the same time, without getting ahead of each other."

"They'll taste a little bitter," she said.

"Mauricio will say no, more acidy."

"Yes, they could be more acidy. And then they'll turn out the light, no one knows why."

"No one ever knows why, but it's true, they'll turn out the light and embrace. That's for sure, I know they'll embrace."

"In the dark," she said, looking for the switch. "Like this, right?"

"Like this," he said.

MANUSCRIPT
FOUND
IN
A
POCKET

Now that I'm writing this, it might seem like roulette or the racetrack to others, but it wasn't money I was looking for; at some moment I'd begun to feel, to decide that a Métro window might give me the answer, the finding of a happiness, here precisely where everything happens under the sign of the most implacable break, in a below-ground time that traveling between stations sketches out and limits in that way, unappealingly under ground. I say break in order to get a better understanding (I've had to understand so many things since I've begun to play the game) of that hope of a convergence that I might receive from the reflection on a window-pane. Going beyond the break that people don't seem to

understand even though who knows what those people
crammed together getting on and off the Métro cars are thinking, what, besides transportation, are those people getting on
sooner or later to get off later or sooner looking for, only
coming together in the zone of a car where everything
has been decided beforehand, without anyone's knowing
whether we'll get off together, whether I'll get off first or
that skinny man with a roll of papers, whether the old woman
in green will go to the end of the line, whether those children
will get off now, it's clear that they'll be getting off because
they're picking up their notebooks and rulers and playing by
the door while in the corner there's a girl who's settled down
to endure, to stay for many stations to come in the seat that's
free at last, and that other girl is unpredictable, Ana was unpredictable, she sat very stiffly against the back of the window
seat, she was already there when I got on at the Étienne
Marcel station and a black man left the seat opposite and it
didn't seem to interest anyone and I was able to slip in between the knees of the two passengers sitting on the outside
seats with a vague apology and remained opposite Ana and
almost immediately, because I'd gone down into the Métro to
play the game once more, I looked for Margrit's profile in the
reflection on the windowpane and I thought she was pretty,
that I liked her black hair cut in a kind of short bob that she
combed diagonally across her forehead.

It isn't true that the names Margrit or Ana came later or
that it's a way now of differentiating between them in writing, things like that are decided instantaneously by the game,
I mean that the reflection in the window could in no way be
named Ana, just as the girl sitting opposite me without looking at me couldn't be named Margrit, her eyes lost in the
boredom of that interregnum where everybody seems to consult a zone of vision not in his immediate vicinity, except

children, who stare fully at things until the day when they too
are taught to place themselves at the interstices, to look without seeing with that civil ignorance of neighboring appear-
ances, of all sensible contact, each one installed in his bubble,
lined up between parentheses, watching out for the viable
space of the minimal free air between others' knees and elbows, taking refuge in *France-Soir* or paperback books even
though always, like Ana, a pair of eyes fills the gap between
what is really seeable in that neutral and stupid distance that
goes from my face to that of the man concentrating on *Le
Figaro*. But then Margrit, if there was something I could
have foreseen it was that at some time Ana would turn distractedly toward the window and then Margrit would see my
reflection, the crossing of looks in the images of that glass
where the darkness of the tunnel has spread its thin quicksilver, its purple, moving felt which gives faces a life on other
planes, takes away from them that horrible chalk mask of the
municipal car lights and above all, oh yes, you couldn't have
denied it, Margrit, makes them really look at the other face in
the glass, because during the instantaneous time of the double look there's no censure, my reflection on the glass was not
the man sitting opposite Ana, whom Ana couldn't look at
fully in a subway car, and, besides, the one who was looking
at my reflection was no longer Ana but Margrit at the moment in which Ana had quickly averted her eyes from the
man sitting opposite her because it wasn't right to look at him
and on turning toward the window she'd seen my reflection,
which was waiting for that instant to smile slightly, without
insolence or expectation, when Margrit's look landed on his
look like a bird. It must have lasted a second, maybe a little
more, because I felt that Margrit had noticed the smile that
Ana reproved even though it was only by the gesture of lowering her face, of vaguely examining the clasp of her red leather

purse; and it was almost proper to keep on smiling even though Margrit was no longer looking at me because in some way Ana's expression acknowledged my smile, she continued knowing that and it wasn't necessary any longer for her or Margrit to look at me, concentrating with application on the trivial task of testing the clasp on the red purse.

As with Paula (with Ofelia) already and with so many others who had concentrated on the task of checking a clasp, a button, the fold of a magazine, once more it was the pit where hope becomes enmeshed with fear in a deadly cramp of spiders fighting in his stomach, where time begins to throb like a second heart in the pulse of the game; from that moment on every station of the subway was a different plotting of the future because the game had so decided; Margrit's look and my smile, Ana's instantaneous withdrawal to the contemplation of the clasp on her purse were the opening of a ceremony that had begun to be celebrated contrary to everything reasonable, preferring the worst missed meetings to the stupid chains of everyday causality. It isn't hard to explain it but playing it had a lot of blind combat about it, a quivering colloidal suspension in which every path raised a tree of unforeseeable courses. A map of the Paris subway encompasses in its Mondrianesque skeleton, its red, yellow, blue, and black branches, a vast but limited surface of subtended pseudopodia; and that tree is alive twenty out of twenty-four hours, a tormented sap runs through it with precise finalities, the one that gets off at Châtelet or gets on at Vaugirard, the one that changes at Odéon to continue on to La Motte-Picquet, the two hundred, three hundred, who knows how many possible combinations, for each codified and programmed cell enters one sector of the tree and comes to the surface in another, comes out at Galeries Lafayette to deliver a package of towels or a lamp to a third floor on the Rue Gay-Lussac.

My rules for the game were maniacally simple, they were beautiful, stupid, and tyrannical: if I liked a woman, if I liked a woman sitting opposite me, if I liked a woman sitting opposite me beside the window, if her reflection in the window crossed glances with my reflection in the window, if my smile in the reflection in the window disturbed or pleased or repelled the reflection of the woman in the window, if Margrit saw me smile and then Ana lowered her head and began to examine the clasp on her red purse with concentration, then there was a game, it was exactly the same if the smile was respected or answered or ignored, the first time the ceremony didn't go beyond that, a smile registered by one who'd deserved it. Then the combat in the pit began, the spiders in the stomach, the wait, with its pendulum, from station to station. I remember how I awoke that day: now they were Margrit and Ana, but a week before they'd been Paula and Ofelia; the blond girl had gotten off at one of the worst stations, Montparnasse-Bienvenüe, which opens its foul-smelling hydra to the maximum possibilities of failure. My connection was with the Porte de Vanves line and almost at once, in the first passageway, I understood that Paula (that Ofelia) would take the passageway leading to the connection with the Mairie d'Issy line. Impossible to do anything, just look at her for the last time where the passageways cross, see her move away, go down some stairs. Those were the rules of the game, a smile in the window glass and the right to follow a woman and hope desperately that her connection would coincide with the one decided on by me before each trip; and then—always until now—seeing her take another passageway and being unable to follow her, being obliged to return to the upper world and go into a café and continue to live until little by little, hours or days or weeks, the thirst again demanded the possibility that everything would coincide someday, woman and window glass, accepted or rejected smile, train connection, and then finally yes, then the right to go over and say the first word, thick with stagnant time, with endless ravaging at the bottom of the pit among the cramp of spiders.

Now we were coming into the Saint-Sulpice station, someone beside me was getting up; Ana, too, was left alone opposite me, had stopped looking at her purse, and once or twice her eyes swept me distractedly before losing themselves in the ad for the thermal baths that was repeated in the four corners of the car. Margrit hadn't looked at me again in the window but that proved the contact, her stealthy throb; Ana was timid perhaps or it simply seemed absurd to her to accept the reflection of that face which would smile again at Margrit; and, besides, reaching Saint-Sulpice was important because if there were still eight stations left to the end of the line at Porte d'Orléans, only three had connections with other lines, and only if Ana got off at one of those three would the possibility of coinciding be left to me; when the train began to brake at Saint-Placide I looked and I looked at Margrit, looking in her for the eyes that Ana still had resting softly on the things in the car as if admitting that Margrit wouldn't look at me anymore, that it was useless to hope that she'd look at the reflection which was waiting to smile at her again.

She didn't get off at Saint-Placide, I discovered that before the train began to slow down, there's that haste of a passenger, especially the women, who nervously check their packages, button their coats, or look to the side as they get up, avoiding knees at that instant in which the loss of speed make bodies clumsy and confused. Ana vaguely reviewed the ads in the station, Margrit's face was being erased under the platform lights and I couldn't find out if she'd looked at me again; or if my reflection had been visible in that morass of neon and photographic ads, of bodies getting on and off. If Ana got off at Montparnasse-Bienvenüe my possibilities were minimal; how could I forget Paula (Ofelia) there where a possible quadruple combination made all predictions tenuous; and yet on Paula's (Ofelia's) day I had been absurdly certain that we would coincide, until the last minute I'd walked nine feet behind that slow blond woman dressed as if in dry leaves and her turn to the right had caught my face like the lash of a whip. That's why now Margrit no, that's why the fear, it could happen again abominably at Montparnasse-Bienvenüe; the memory of Paula (of Ofelia), the spiders in the pit against the tiny confidence that Ana (that Margrit). But who can do anything against the innocence which goes on letting us live, almost immediately I told myself that maybe Ana (maybe Margrit) wouldn't get off at Montparnasse-Bienvenüe but at one of the other possible stations, that maybe she wouldn't get off at one of the intermediate ones where I wasn't allowed to follow her; that Ana (that Margrit) wouldn't get off at a Montparnesse-Bienvenüe (she didn't), that she wouldn't get off at Vavin, and she didn't, that maybe she'd get off at Raspail, which was the first of the last two possible ones; and when she didn't get off and I knew that only one station was left where I could follow her as against the last three where everything would already be the same, I looked for Margrit's eyes once more in the window glass, I called her from a silence and an immobility that must have reached her like a demand, like a breaking wave, I smiled at her with a smile that Ana could no longer ignore, that Margrit had to admit even though she wasn't looking at my reflection lashed by the half-lights of the tunnel as it came out into Denfert-Rochereau. Maybe the first touch of the brakes had made the smooth purse on Ana's thighs quiver, maybe only boredom moved her hand to the lock of black hair that crossed

her forehead; in those three, four seconds in which the train
came to a halt at the platform, the spiders sank their claws
into the skin of the pit to conquer me once more from inside;
when Ana stood up with a single and clean bend of her body,
when I saw her from behind between two passengers, I think
I still absurdly looked for Margrit's face in the passive
shadow of that body that went out onto the platform, until
I awoke to what was about to come, the irrevocable fulfillment of the final double choice.

I think it's clear, Ana (Margrit) would take a daily or
circumstantial route while I, before getting on that train, had
decided that if anyone got into the game and got off at Denfert-Rochereau, my connection would be the Nation-Étoile
line, in the same way that if Ana (if Margrit) had got off at
Châtelet I could only have followed her if she took the Vin-
cennes-Neuilly connection. In the last moment of the ceremony the game was lost if Ana (if Margrit) took the connection with the Ligne de Sceaux or went directly out onto the
street; immediately, right then, because there weren't the
endless passageways of other times in that station and the
stairs led rapidly to destiny, to what methods of transportation also called destination. I was watching her move among
the people, her red purse like a toy pendulum, lifting her
head in search of the directional signs, hesitating an instant
before going toward the left; but the left was the exit that
led to the street.

I don't know how to put it, the spiders were biting too
much, I wasn't being dishonest during the first minute, I simply followed her perhaps in order to accept it later, to let her
go off in one of her directions up there; halfway up the stairs
I understood that it wasn't that, that maybe the only way to
get rid of them was to deny, one time, the law, the code. The
cramp that had gripped me during the second in which Ana

(in which Margrit) had begun to climb the forbidden stairs gave way suddenly to a dreamy lassitude, to a slow-moving golem; I refused to think, it was enough knowing that I could still see her, that the red purse was going up onto the street, that the black hair trembled on her shoulders with every step. It was already night and the air was icy, with a few snowflakes among the gusts of wind and the drizzle; I know that Ana (that Margrit) wasn't afraid when I moved alongside her and said: "We just can't separate like this before we meet."

In the café later on, now only Ana as the reflection of Margrit gave way to a reality of Cinzano and words, she told me that she didn't understand anything, that her name was Marie-Claude, my smile in the reflection had annoyed her, that for a moment she'd thought of getting up and changing her seat, that she hadn't seen me follow her and that on the street she hadn't been afraid, contradictorily, looking into my eyes, drinking her Cinzano, smiling without being ashamed to smile, of having accepted my harassment right on the street almost immediately. At that moment of happiness, like the one when you let yourself go in the waves, or the one you get in a timber-drift between poplar trees, I couldn't tell her what she would have taken for madness or a mania, which it was, but in another way, as seen from other shores of life; I spoke to her about her lock of hair, her red purse, her way of looking at the ad for the thermal baths, said that I hadn't smiled at her as a Don Juan or out of boredom but to give her a flower I didn't have, a sign that I liked her, that she did me good, that riding across from her, that another cigarette and another Cinzano. At no moment were we emphatic, we spoke as if from a known and accepted already, looking at each other without doing harm; I think that Marie-Claude was letting me come and be in her present as perhaps Margrit would have answered my smile in the glass if so much previous molding hadn't intervened, so much you don't have to answer if you're spoken to on the street or offered candy and invited to the movies, until Marie-Claude, freed now from my smile to Margrit, Marie-Claude on the street and in the café had thought that it was a good smile, that the stranger down there hadn't smiled at Margrit in order to test new terrain, and my absurd way of coming up to her had been the only comprehensible thing, the only reason to say yes, we could have a drink and a chat in a café.

I don't remember what I was able to tell her about me, maybe everything except the game but so little then, at some moment we laughed, someone cracked the first joke, we discovered that we liked the same cigarettes and Catherine Deneuve, she let me see her to the door of her building, shook hands simply, and consented to the same café at the same time on Tuesday. I took a taxi back to my neighborhood, in myself for the first time as if in an incredible foreign country, repeating to myself yes, Marie-Claude, Denfert-Rochereau, closing my eyes tightly to hold on better to her black hair, to that way of tilting her head before speaking, of smiling. We were punctual and we told each other about movies, work, we verified partial ideological differences, she continued accepting me as if miraculously that present without reasons, without interrogation was enough; she didn't even seem to realize that any imbecile would have thought her easy or foolish; observing that I didn't so much as try to share the same bench in the café, that going along the Rue Froidevaux I didn't put my arm around her shoulder in the first gesture of intimacy, that knowing she was practically alone—a younger sister, often absent from the apartment on the fourth floor—I didn't ask her to let me come up. If there was something she couldn't suspect it was the spiders, we'd met three or four times without their biting, motionless in the pit and waiting until the day when I found out, as if I hadn't known it all the time, but Tuesdays, arriving at the café, imagining that Marie-Claude was probably there already or watching her come in with her agile steps, the dark revival that had foolishly fought against the spiders who were awake again, against the betrayal of the game that only she had been able to defend with nothing more than giving me a brief, warm handclasp, with nothing but that lock of hair that strolled across her forehead. At some moment she must have realized, she sat looking at me, silent, waiting; it was impossible now for me not to be given away by the effort of making the truce last, not to admit that they were coming back little by little in spite of Marie-Claude, against Marie-Claude, who couldn't understand, who sat looking at me, silent, waiting; drinking and smoking and talking to her, defending the sweet interregnum without spiders until the last, learning about her simple life and schedule and student sister and allergies, desiring so much that black lock which was combed across her forehead, desiring her as something terminal, as really the last station on the last subway of life, and then the pit, the distance from my chair to that bench where we could have kissed, where my mouth could have drunk in Marie-Claude's first whiff of perfume before taking her home in an embrace, going up the stairs, freeing ourselves finally from so much clothing and so much waiting.

Then I told her, I remember the cemetery wall and that Marie-Claude leaned on it and let me talk with her face hidden in the warm moss of her overcoat, who knows if my voice reached her with all of its words, if it was possible for her to understand; I told her everything, every detail of the game, the confirmed improbabilities after so many Paulas (so many Ofelias) lost at the end of a passageway, the spiders in every ending. She was weeping, I felt her tremble against me although she continued sheltering me, sustaining me with all of her body leaning against the wall of the dead; she didn't ask me anything, she didn't want to know why or how long, it didn't occur to her to fight against a machine put together by a whole life against its own grain, against the city and its countersigns, just that weeping there like a wounded little animal, resisting without effort the triumph of the game, the exasperated dance of the spiders in the pit.

At the door of her building I told her that everything wasn't lost, that an attempt at a legitimate meeting depended on both of us; she knew the rules of the game now, maybe they'd be favorable to us since all we had to do was look for each other. She told me that she could ask for two weeks off, ride carrying a book so that time would be less damp and hostile in the world below, going from one connection to another, waiting for me, reading, looking at the ads. We refused to think about the improbability, the fact that maybe we would meet on a train but that it wouldn't be enough, that this time the pre-established would have to be followed; I asked her not to think, to let the subway run, never to cry during those two weeks while I searched for her; it was understood without words that if the time limit ended without our seeing each other again or only seeing each other until two passageways separated us, it wouldn't make any more sense to go back to the café, to the door of her building. At the foot of that neighborhood stairway where an orange light stretched softly upward, toward the image of Marie-Claude in her apartment, among her furniture, naked and asleep, I kissed her on the hair, stroked her hands; she didn't seek my mouth, she drifted off and I saw her from behind, going up one more of the innumerable stairs that took them away without my being able to follow them; I walked back to my place, without spiders, empty and washed by the new

wait; now they couldn't do anything to me, the game was going
to begin again like so many other times but only with Marie-
Claude, Monday going into the Couronnes station in the
morning, coming out at Marx Dormoy at night, Tuesday
going in at Crimée, Wednesday at Philippe Auguste, the precise rules of the game, fifteen stations in which four had
connections, and then at the first of the four knowing that it
was up to me to follow the Sèvres-Montreuil line as at the
second she would have to make the Clichy-Porte Dauphine
connection, each itinerary chosen without any special reason
because there could be no reason, maybe Marie-Claude
would come out near her place, at Denfert-Rochereau or at
Corvisart, she would be changing at Pasteur to continue on to
Falguière, the Mondrianesque tree with all of its dry
branches, the chance of the red, blue, white, dotted tempta-
tions; Thursday, Friday, Saturday. Watching the trains come
in on some platform or other, the seven or eight cars, letting
myself look while they passed slower and slower, running to
the last one and getting on a car without Marie-Claude, getting off at the next station and waiting for another train,
going on to the first station to get another line, watching the
cars arrive without Marie-Claude, letting a train or two pass,
getting on the third, going to the end of the line, returning to
a station from where I could get another line, deciding that
I'd only take the fourth train, abandoning the search and
going up to eat, returning almost immediately with a bitter
cigarette and sitting on a bench until the second, until the
fifth train. Monday, Tuesday, Wednesday, Thursday, without spiders because I was still hoping, because I still am hoping on this bench in the Chemin Vert station, with this notebook where a hand writes in order to invent a time that won't
just be that interminable gust of wind that flings me toward
the Saturday when everything will perhaps have ended, when

I'll return alone and feel them wake up and bite, their raven-
ous pincers demanding a new game from me, other Marie-
Claudes, other Paulas, the repetition after each defeat, the
cancerous beginning all over again. But it's Thursday, the
station is Chemin Vert, night is falling outside, it's still possible to imagine something, it doesn't even seem too incredible that in the second train, that in the fourth car, that Marie-
Claude in a window seat, that she's seen and stands up with a
shout that nobody but me can hear full in the face like that,
at a full run to jump into the loaded car, pushing indignant
passengers, muttering excuses that no one expects or accepts,
standing against the double seat occupied by legs and umbrellas and packages, by Marie-Claude with her gray coat by
the window, the black lock, which the sudden lurch of the
train barely agitates as her hands tremble on her thighs in a
call that has no name, that's all that's going to happen now.
There's no need to talk, nothing could be said about that
impassable and mistrusting wall of faces and umbrellas between Marie-Claude and me; there are three stations left that
connect with other lines, Marie-Claude will have to choose
one of them, cross the platform, follow one of the passageways
or look for the exit stairs, alien to my choice, which I can't
betray this time. The train enters the Bastille station and
Marie-Claude sits there, the people get off and get on, someone leaves the seat next to her empty but I don't go over, I
can't sit there, I can't tremble next to her as she is probably trembling. Now come Ledru-Rollin and Faidherbe-
Chaligny, Marie-Claude knows I can't follow her at those stations with no connections and she doesn't move, the game has
to be played out at Reuilly-Diderot or Daumesnil; while the
train is entering Reuilly-Diderot I turn my eyes away, I don't
want her to know, I don't want her to be able to understand
that it's not there. When the train starts up I see that she

hasn't moved, that we have one last hope left, at Daumesnil there's only one connection and the exit to the street, red or black, yes or no. Then we look at each other, Marie-Claude has lifted her face to look at me directly, clinging to the handle of the seat, I'm the thing she's looking at, something as pale as what I'm looking at, the bloodless face of Marie-Claude who squeezes her red purse, who's going to make the first gesture toward getting up as the train enters the Daumesnil station.

APOCALYPSE

AT

SOLENTINAME

Ticos, Costa Ricans, are always like that, rather quiet but full of surprises; you land in San José and waiting for you there are Carmen Naranjo and Samuel Rovinski and Sergio Ramírez (who's from Nicaragua and not a Tico, but what difference does that make since it's all the same after all, what difference does it make that I'm Argentine although out of niceness I should say Tino, and the rest of them Nicas or Ticos). It was one of those hot spells and to make things even worse it all got started right away, a press conference with the usual business, why don't you live in your own country, why was *Blow Up* so different from your short story, do you think a writer must be involved? With things going like that I can

see that my final interview will be at the gates of hell and
there're sure to be the same questions, and if by chance it's
chez St. Peter it won't be any different: don't you think that
you're writing over the heads of the people down there?

Afterward the Hotel Europa and that shower which caps
trips with a long monologue of soap and silence. Except that
at seven o'clock it was already time to take a stroll through
San José and see if it was as simple and smooth as they had
told me, a hand tugged at my jacket and there was Ernesto
Cardenal behind me and such an embrace, poet, how wonderful for you to be there after our meeting in Rome, after so
many meetings on paper over the years. It always surprises
me, always moves me that someone like Ernesto should come
to see me and seek me out, you're probably saying what a
crock of false modesty, but you just go right on saying it, old
man, the jackal howls, but the bus passes, I'll always be an
amateur, someone who from way down loves some people so
much that one day it turns out that they love him too, those
are things that are beyond me, we'd better get on to the next
line.

The next line was that Ernesto found out I was coming
to Costa Rica and zip, he'd come by plane from his island
because the little bird that brings him news had told him that
the Ticos were planning a trip to Solentiname for me and the
idea of coming to pick me up seemed irresistible to him, so
two days later Sergio and Oscar and Ernesto and I were filling up the all too fillable capacity of a little Piper Aztec, the
name of which will always be a mystery to me, but which flew
with hiccoughs and bowel rumblings while the blond pilot
hummed some countervailing calypso songs and seemed
completely unconcerned by my notion that the Aztec was taking us straight to the sacrificial pyramid. It didn't turn out
that way, as can be seen, we came down at Los Chiles and

from there an equally bouncy Jeep brought us to the farm of the poet José Coronel Urteche, whom more people would do well to read and at whose house we rested, talking about so many other poet friends, Roque Dalton and Gertrude Stein and Carlos Martínez Rivas, until Luis Coronel arrived and we left for Nicaragua in his Jeep and his outboard of frightening speed. But first there were souvenir photographs with one of those cameras that let the little piece of sky-blue paper pop out right there and little by little and miraculously and Polaroid it fills up little by little with images, first disturbing ectoplasms and little by little a nose, some curly hair, Ernesto's smile and his Nazarene headband, Doña María and Don José outlined against the porch. That seemed quite normal to all because, of course, they were accustomed to using that camera, but not to me, I was filled with amazement as I saw those faces and those good-bye smiles coming out of nothing and I told them so, I remember asking Oscar what would happen if sometime after a family snapshot the sky-blue paper started to fill up with Napoleon on horseback, and Don José Coronel's laugh, listening to everything as always, the Jeep, let's go to the lake now.

We got to Solentiname late at night, waiting there were Teresa and William and a gringo poet and the other young people from the community; we went to bed almost immediately but first I looked at the paintings in a corner, Ernesto was talking to his people and was taking the provisions and gifts he was bringing from San José out of a bag, someone was asleep in a hammock and I saw the paintings in a corner, I began to look at them. I don't remember who explained to me that they were the work of peasants from the region, this one was painted by Vicente, this is by Ramona, some signed and others not, but all so beautiful, once more the first vision of the world, the clean look of a person who describes what's around him like a song of praise: midget cows in poppy fields, the sugar-making shed with people coming out like ants, the horse with green eyes against a background of cane fields, a baptism in a church that doesn't believe in perspective and climbs up or falls down on top of itself, the lake with little boats like shoes and in the background an enormous fish laughing with turquoise teeth. Then Ernesto came over to explain to me that the sale of the paintings helped things along, in the morning he would show me some work in wood and stone done by the peasants and also some of their own sculptures; we were falling asleep but I kept on looking at the little pictures piled up in a corner, taking out the great piles of canvases with little cows and flowers and that mother with two children on her knees, one in white, the other in red, under a sky so full of stars that the single cloud hung in a corner as if in humiliation, squeezing up against the frame of the picture, already pushing out of the canvas from pure fear.

The next day was Sunday and eleven o'clock mass, the Solentiname mass in which the peasants and Ernesto and the visiting friends comment together on a chapter of Scripture which that day was Jesus' arrest in the garden, a theme that the people of Solentiname treated as if they were talking about themselves, about the threat of being pounced on at night or in broad daylight, that life of permanent uncertainty on the islands and on the mainland and in all of Nicaragua and, yes, almost all of Latin America, a life surrounded by fear and death, life in Guatemala and life in El Salvador, life in Argentina and Bolivia, life in Chile and Santo Domingo, life in Paraguay, life in Brazil and Colombia.

A while later we had to think about going back and it was then that I thought about the paintings again; I went to the community hall and began to look at them in the dazzling light of noon, the bright colors, the acrylics or oils facing each other out of their ponies and sunflowers and fiestas in the symmetrical fields and palm groves. I remembered that I had a roll of color film in my camera and I went out onto the porch with an armful of paintings; Sergio, who was coming up, helped me stand them up in a good light, and I went along photographing them carefully one by one, centering them so that each painting filled the viewer completely. Chance is like that: I had just the number of exposures as there were paintings, not one was left out and when Ernesto came to tell us that the outboard was ready, I told him what I'd done and he laughed, art thief, image smuggler. Yes, I told him, I'm taking all of them, I'll show them on my screen back there and they'll be bigger and brighter than these, screw yourself.

I returned to San José, I was in Havana and I did some things there, back in Paris with a weariness that was full of nostalgia, Claudine silently waiting for me at Orly, once more the life of wristwatch and *merci, monsieur, bonjour, madame*, committees, movies, red wine and Claudine, Mozart quartets and Claudine. In among so many things the toad suitcases had spat out onto the bed and rug, magazines, clippings, handkerchiefs and books by Central American poets, the gray plastic tubes with the rolls of film, so many things over two months, the sequence of the Lenin School in Havana, the streets of Trinidad, the outline of the Irazú volcano and its vat of boiling green water, where Samuel and I and Sarita had imagined ourselves already roasted and floating in the midst of sulfur smoke gases. Claudine took the rolls to be developed; one afternoon while walking through the Latin Quarter I remembered and since I had the stub in my pocket I picked them up and there were eight of them. I immediately thought about the little paintings from Solentiname and when I got home I opened the boxes and looked at the first slides in each series, I remembered that before I had photographed the paintings I'd been shooting Ernesto's mass, some children playing among the palm trees, just as in the paintings, children and palms and cows against a brilliantly blue sky and a lake that was just a touch greener, or maybe just the opposite, I wasn't sure about it anymore. I put the slides of the children and the mass into the projector; I was aware that the paintings began afterward and I went on to them.

It was growing dark and I was alone, Claudine would come by after work to listen to some music and stay with me; I fixed the screen and some rum with lots of ice, the projector and its carrousel and its remote-control button all ready; there was no need to draw the curtains, the cooperative night was there already, lighting up the lamps and the aroma of the rum; it was pleasant thinking that everything would be revealed to me again little by little, after the paintings from Solentiname I would go through the boxes with the Cuban photographs, but why the paintings first, why the professional deformation, art before life, and why not, the one said to the other in their eternal unresolvable fraternal and rancorous dialogue, why not look at the Solentiname paintings first since they're life too, since it's all the same.

The photographs of the mass went by first, rather poor because of errors of exposure, the children, on the other hand, playing in full light and with such white teeth. I was unwillingly pushing the change button, I would have lingered a while longer looking at each photograph that was sticky with memory, the small fragile world of Solentiname, surrounded by water and police, the same way the boy I was looking at was surrounded and didn't understand, I'd pushed the button and the boy was there very clearly in the background, a broad, smooth face, as if full of incredulous surprise as his body pitched forward, the neat hole in the middle of his forehead, the officer's pistol still marking the trajectory of the bullet, the others on the side with their submachine guns, a confused background of houses and trees.

You think what you think, it always gets ahead of you and leaves you so far behind; I stupidly told myself that they must have made a mistake at the camera place and given me some other customer's pictures, but the mass then, the children playing on the grass, how then. Nor did my hand obey when I pushed the button and it was an endless sand flat at noon with two or three rusty-roofed sheds, people gathered on the left looking at the bodies laid out face up, their arms open to a naked gray sky; you had to look closely to make out a uniformed group in the background with their backs turned and going away, the Jeep waiting at the top of a rise.

I know that I continued on, in the face of what resisted all sanity the only thing I could do was keep on pressing the button, seeing the corner of Corrientes and San Martín in Buenos Aires and the black car with the four guys taking aim at someone on the sidewalk in a white shirt and loafers who was running, two women trying to take cover behind a parked truck, someone looking straight out, a face of horrified disbelief, raising a hand to his chin as if to touch himself and feel that he's still alive, and suddenly the room that's almost in darkness, a dirty light falling from the barred little window up high, the table with the naked girl on her back, her hair hanging down to the floor, the shadow of shoulders putting a wire between her open legs, the two guys in front talking to each other, a blue necktie and a green sweater. I never knew if I kept on pushing the button or not, I saw a clearing in the jungle, a cabin with a thatched roof and trees in the foreground, against the trunk of the nearest one a thin fellow looking to the left where a confused group, five or six of them close together, were aiming rifles and pistols at him; the fellow with a long face and a lock of hair falling down over his dark forehead was looking at them, one hand half-raised, the other probably in his pants pocket, it was as if he were saying something to them unhurriedly, almost listlessly, and even though the photograph was hazy I sensed and I knew that the fellow was Roque Dalton, and then I did press the button as if with that I could save him from the infamy of that death and I managed to see an automobile flying into pieces right in the heart of a city that could have been Buenos Aires or São Paulo, I kept on pressing and pressing through the waves of bloody faces and parts of bodies and women running and children on a Bolivian or Guatemalan hillside, suddenly the screen filled with mercury and with nothing and with Claudine, who was coming in silently, casting her shadow on the screen before she bent over and kissed me on the hair and asked me if they came out well, if I was pleased with the pictures, if I felt like showing them.

I clicked the carrousel and put it back to zero, you don't know how or why you do things when you've gone beyond a limit that you don't understand either. Without looking at her, because she might have understood or would simply be afraid of what my face must have looked like, without ex-plaining anything because everything was one single knot from my throat down to my toenails, I got up and slowly sat her down in my chair and I must have said something to her about going to get her a drink. In the bathroom I think I threw up or I didn't do anything and just sat on the edge of the bathtub letting time pass until I could go to the kitchen and fix Claudine her favorite drink, fill it with ice, and then feel the silence, realize that Claudine wasn't shouting or run-ning to ask me, silence, nothing else and for a moment the sugary bolero that filtered in from the apartment next door. I don't know how long it took me to cover the distance between the kitchen and the living room, to see the back part of the screen precisely as she was coming to the end and the room filled up with the instantaneous mercury reflection and then the shadows, Claudine turning off the projector and settling back in the chair to take the glass and smile at me slowly, happy and cat and so content.

"They came out so well, that one with the smiling fish and the mother with the two children and the cows in the field; wait, and that other one with the baptism in the church, tell me who painted them, you couldn't see the signatures."

Sitting on the floor, not looking at her, I reached for my glass and drank it down in one swallow. I wasn't going to tell her anything, what could I tell her now, but I do remember that I vaguely thought about asking her something idiotic, asking her if at some moment she'd seen a photograph of Napoleon on horseback. But I didn't, of course.

San José, Havana,
April 1976

FOOTSTEPS
IN
THE
FOOTPRINTS

*A rather tedious chronicle, more in
the style of an exercise than in the
exercise of a style, say that of a
Henry James who might have sipped
maté in some Buenos Aires or Mar
del Plata courtyard in the twenties*

Jorge Fraga had just turned forty when he decided to study
the life and works of the poet Claudio Romero.

The whole thing was born out of a café conversation in
which Fraga and his friends were forced to admit once more
the uncertainty that surrounded Romero's person. The author of three books passionately read and envied and which
had brought him an ephemeral fame during the years following the Centenary, Romero had an image that was confused
with his creations. He suffered from the lack of a systematic
criticism and even a satisfactory iconography. Aside from par-
simoniously laudatory articles in the magazines of the period
and a book committed by an enthusiastic professor from

Santa Fe, for whom lyricism replaced ideas, not even the
slightest investigation into the life or work of the poet had
been attempted. A few anecdotes, some hazy photographs;
the rest was legends for café talk and panegyrics in antholo-
gies put out by obscure publishers. But Fraga's attention had
been called to the fact that a lot of people were still reading
Romero's poetry with the same fervor as that of Carriego
or Alfonsina Storni. He had discovered it himself during his
high school years and in spite of the lower-class tone and the
images that had been worn out by his followers, the poems by
the Bard of the River Plate had been one of the decisive
experiences of his youth, like Almafuerte or Carlos de la Púa.
Only later on, when he had become known as a critic and
essayist, did it occur to him to think seriously about Romero's
work and he didn't take long to realize that almost nothing
was known of its more personal and perhaps deeper meaning.
Compared to the poetry of other good turn-of-the-century
poets, that of Claudio Romero was distinguished by a special
quality, a less emphatic resonance that immediately earned
him the trust of the young, tired of high-sounding tropes and
padded evocations. When he spoke to students or friends
about the poems, Fraga came to wonder whether or not
underneath it all the mystery might be what lent prestige to
that poetry of obscure keys, evasive intent. He ended up
being irritated by the facility with which ignorance favors
admiration; after all, Claudio Romero's poetry stood too high
to have a better knowledge of its origins bring it down. On
leaving one of those café get-togethers where Romero had
been discussed with the usual admiring vagueness, he felt a
kind of obligation to get down to serious work on the poet.
He felt, too, that it shouldn't be a mere essay with philological or stylistic intent, as were almost all of those that had been
written. The notion of a biography in the highest sense of the

word imposed itself upon him from the beginning: man, land, and work must rise up out of a single act of living, even though the undertaking seemed impossible in all that mist of time. When the period of note taking was over, he would have to arrive at the synthesis, to provoke, unthinkably, the encounter of the poet with his pursuer; only that contact would reinvest Romero's work with its deepest reason.

When he decided to undertake the study, Fraga was entering a critical segment of his life. A certain academic prestige had earned him an adjunct professorship at the university and the respect of a small group of readers and students. At the same time, a recent attempt to attain the official backing that would have allowed him to work in certain libraries in Europe had failed for reasons of bureaucratic politics. His publications were not those that open the doors of ministries without knocking. The novelist in vogue, the literary columnist received more than he. Fraga was not unaware that if his book on Romero was a success, the basest problems would be solved all by themselves. He wasn't ambitious, but it irritated him to see himself left behind by the scribes of the moment. Also, Claudio Romero, in his day, had complained haughtily that the poetaster of elegant salons had gotten the diplomatic post denied him.

For two and a half years he gathered material for the book. The task wasn't difficult, but it was lengthy and, in some respects, boring. It included trips to Pergamino, Santa Cruz, and Mendoza, correspondence with librarians and archivists, the examination of collections of newspapers and magazines, the collation of texts, parallel studies of the literary currents

of the period. Toward the end of 1954, the central elements
of the book were collected and evaluated, although Fraga had
still not written a word of text.

While he was inserting a new card into his black cardboard file one September night, he wondered if he was in
shape to undertake the task. He wasn't worried about obstacles, but, quite the contrary, rather about how easy it would
be to run across a field so well known. The information was
there and nothing important would come out of the files or
memories of Argentines of the time anymore. He'd collected
news items and events, apparently unknown, that would perfect the image of Claudio Romero and his poetry. The only
problem was that of making a mistake in the central focus,
the lines of flight, and the composition of the whole.

"But is that image clear enough for me?" Fraga would
wonder, looking at the glow of his cigarette. "The affinities
between Romero and me, our common preference for certain
aesthetic and poetic values, the thing that makes the choice of
theme inevitable for the biographer, won't that make me fall
into a disguised autobiography more than once?"

He could answer that with the fact that he hadn't been
endowed with any creative capacity, that he wasn't a poet but
one who enjoyed poetry, and that his faculties had been
affirmed in criticism, in the pleasure that accompanies
knowledge. An alert attitude would be sufficient, a watchful-
ness as he faced submersion in the work of the poet so as to
avoid any unwarranted transfusion. He had no reason not to
trust his sympathy for Claudio Romero and his fascination
with his poems. As with good photographic equipment, the
necessary adjustment would have to be made so that the subject would remain precisely framed without the shadow of
the photographer treading on his toes.

Now that the first blank page was awaiting him like a
door that it would be necessary to start opening from one

moment to the next, he went back to wondering whether or not he would be capable of writing the book as he had imagined it. The biography and criticism could verge dangerously on the facile, being oriented only toward that type of reader who expects a book that is the equivalent of a movie or of André Maurois. The problem consisted in not sacrificing that anonymous and multitudinous consumer whom his socialist friends called the people to the erudite satisfaction of a handful of colleagues. To find the angle that would permit him to write a book of impassioned reading without falling into the recipes of a best seller; to earn simultaneously the respect of the academic world and the enthusiasm of the man on the street who wants to be entertained in his easy chair on Saturday night.

It had a touch of Faust's moment, the time of the pact. Almost at dawn, the cigarette consumed, the glass of wine in his indecisive hand. *Wine, like a glove of time,* Claudio Romero had written somewhere.

"Why not?" Fraga said to himself, lighting another cigarette. "With everything I know about him now, it would be stupid for me to stick with a mere essay, in an edition of three hundred copies. Juárez or Ricardi could do that just as well. But nobody knows anything about Susana Márquez."

An allusion by the justice of the peace in Bragado, the younger brother of a deceased friend of Claudio Romero's, had put him on the track. Someone who worked in the civil registry in La Plata had gotten an address in Pilar for him after much searching. Susana Márquez's daughter was a woman of some thirty years, small and sweet. She had refused to talk at first, under the pretext that she had to take care of the business (a vegetable store); then she allowed Fraga to come into the parlor, sit in a dusty chair, and ask her questions. In the beginning she looked at him without answering; then she wept a little, put her handkerchief to her eyes, and spoke about her poor mother. It was hard for Fraga to make her understand that he already knew something about the relationship between Claudio Romero and Susana, but he ended up telling himself that the love of a poet was just as good as a marriage license, and he hinted at it with the necessary delicacy. After a few minutes of strewing flowers along the way, he saw her come toward him, totally convinced and even moved. A moment later he had in his hands an extraordinary photograph of Romero, never published, and another one, smaller and yellowed, where next to the poet was seen a woman as small as her daughter and with just as sweet a look.

"I have some letters too," Raquel Márquez said. "If they can be of any help to you, since you say you're going to write about him . . ."

She searched for a long time, selecting from a pile of papers that she had taken out of a music cabinet, and finally she handed him three letters that Fraga put away without reading, after ascertaining that they were in Romero's handwriting. At this point in the conversation he was already sure that Raquel wasn't the poet's daughter, because with the first insinuation he saw her lower her head and fall silent for a moment, as if thinking. Then she explained that her mother later on had married a military man from Balcarce ("Fangio's town," she said, almost as if it were proof), and that they had both died when she was only eight years old. She remembered her mother very well, but didn't remember much about her father. He was a strict man, that he was.

When Fraga returned to Buenos Aires and read Claudio Romero's three letters to Susana, the final fragments of the mosaic seemed to fall into place quickly, revealing a completely unexpected composition, a drama that the ignorance and prudery of the poet's generation hadn't even suspected. In 1917 Romero had published the series of poems dedicated to Irene Paz, among which the famous "Ode to Your Double Name" figured, the one that critics had proclaimed the most beautiful love poem ever written in Argentina. And, nevertheless, a year before the appearance of the book, another woman had received those three letters where the tone that defined the best poetry of Romero reigned, a mixture of exaltation and disengagement, like that of a person who was simultaneously the motive and the subject of the action, protagonist and chorus. Before reading the letters, Fraga had suspected the usual amorous correspondence, the mirrors face to face, isolating and petrifying their reflection, important only to them. In every paragraph, on the contrary, he discovered the reiteration of Romero's world, the richness of a totalizing vision of love. Not only had his passion for Susana Márquez not cut him off from the world, but with every line one could feel throbbing a reality that amplified the beloved, the justification and demand of a poetry that was doing life-size battle.

The story itself was simple. Romero had met Susana at a dull literary salon in La Plata and the beginning of their relationship coincided with an almost total eclipse of the poet, one which his few biographers had not explained or attributed to the first attacks of the tuberculosis that was to kill him two years later. The story of Susana Márquez had escaped everybody, as befitted her hazy image, the great frightened eyes that stared fixedly from the old photograph. She was an unemployed schoolteacher, the only daughter of old and poor parents, lacking friends who might take an interest in her, and their simultaneous disappearance from literary gatherings in La Plata had coincided with the most dramatic

period of the European war, other public interests, new literary voices. Fraga could consider himself fortunate in having
heard the casual allusion by a country justice of the peace;
with that thread between his fingers he managed to locate the
gloomy house in Burzaco where Romero and Susana had
lived for almost two years; the letters that Raquel Márquez
had entrusted to him corresponded with the end of that
period. The first, postmarked La Plata, referred to a previous
piece of correspondence in which he had dealt with his marriage to Susana. The poet confessed his anguish at feeling ill,
and his scruples about marrying someone who would have to
be a nurse rather than a wife. The second letter was admirable, the passion gave ground to a feeling of almost unbearable purity, as if Romero were struggling to awaken in his
beloved an analagous lucidity that would make the necessary
break less painful. One sentence summed it all up: "No one
has any reason to know about our life and I offer you freedom with silence. Free, you will be even more for eternity. If
we were to marry, I would feel like your executioner every
time you came into my room with a flower in your hand."
And he added harshly: "I don't want to cough in your face, I
don't want you to dry my sweat. You've known a different
body, I've given you different roses. I need the night for myself alone, I won't let you see me weep." The third letter was
more serene, as if Susana had begun to accept the poet's sacrifice. Somewhere it said: "You insist I magnetize you, oblige
you to do my will. . . . But my will is your future, let me sow
these seeds that will be the consolation of a stupid death."

In the chronology established by Fraga, the life of
Claudio Romero from that moment entered a monotonous
stage, one of almost continuous reclusiveness in his parents'
home. No other testimony led one to suppose that the poet
and Susana Márquez had ever met again, although it was also

impossible to state the contrary; nevertheless, the best proof that Romero's renunciation had been consummated and that Susana must finally have preferred freedom to condemning herself to the side of the sick man was the ascendancy of the new and resplendent planet in the heavens of Romero's poetry. One year after that correspondence and that renunciation, a magazine in Buenos Aires published "Ode to Your Double Name," dedicated to Irene Paz. Romero's health seemed to have improved and the poem, which he himself had read in some salons, suddenly brought him the glory that his previous work had paved the way for almost secretly. Like Byron, he could say that one morning he had awakened to discover that he was famous, and, like Byron, he never stopped saying so. But, contrary to what one might have hoped for, the poet's passion for Irene Paz was not returned, and, judging from a series of mundane episodes related by the wits of the period in a contradictory way, the personal prestige of the poet plunged suddenly, obliging him to retreat once more into his parents' home, removed from friends and admirers. His last book of poems was from that period. A brutal hemoptysis caught Romero in the street a few months after, and three weeks later he was dead. His funeral brought together a group of writers, but from the tone of the funeral orations and the chronicles it was obvious that the world to which Irene Paz belonged had not been present, nor had it rendered the homage that might have been expected under those circumstances.

It wasn't difficult for Fraga to understand that Romero's passion for Irene Paz must have flattered and scandalized the aristocratic world of La Plata and Buenos Aires in equal measure. He hadn't been able to get a clear idea of Irene; the photos of her at twenty attested to her beauty, but the rest was nothing but society news. The true heiress to the traditions of the Pazes, she had an attitude toward Romero that was easy to imagine; she must have met him at some gathering that her people gave from time to time to listen to those they called, stressing the quotation marks with their inflection, the "artists" and "poets" of the moment. If the ode flattered her, if the admirable initial invocation revealed to her like a flash of lightning the truth of a passion that demanded her in the face of all obstacles, only Romero, perhaps, could have known it, and even that wasn't certain. But at that point Fraga understood that the problem ceased being such and that it had lost all importance. Claudio Romero had been too lucid to have imagined for a single instant that his passion was returned. The distance, the barriers of all kinds, Irene's complete inaccessibility, sequestered within the double prison of her family and herself, faithful mirror of her caste, had made her unattainable from the beginning. The tone of the ode was unmistakable and went well beyond the current images of love poetry. Romero called himself "the Icarus of your honeyed feet"—an image that earned him the mockery of an Aristarchus from *Caras y Caretas*—and the poem was nothing more than a supreme leap in quest of the impossible and therefore most beautiful ideal, the ascent through verse of a desperate flight toward the sun that would burn him and fling him to his death. Even the poet's final withdrawal and silence poignantly resembled the phases of a fall, of a lamentable return to the earth he had dared abandon for a dream beyond his forces.

Yes, Fraga thought, pouring himself another glass of wine, everything coincides, everything falls into place; now all I have to do is write it.

The success of *Life of an Argentine Poet* went beyond anything the author and publishers could have imagined.

Though the book was barely commented on during the first weeks, an unexpected article in *La Razón* awoke the people of Buenos Aires from their cautious drowsiness and incited them to taking a position that few refused to assume. *Sur, La Nación*, the best provincial newspapers took over the theme of the moment, which immediately invaded café conversations and after-dinner talk. Two violent polemics (about the influence of Darío on Romero and a chronological question) converged to interest the public. The first edition of the *Life* was sold out in two months—the second in a month and a half. Obliged by the circumstances and the advantages offered him, Fraga consented to do a dramatic adaptation and another for radio. The time had arrived when the interest and the novelty of a work reach the fearful apex behind which the unknown successor is already lurking; inevitably, and as if it were meant to redress an injustice, the National Prize cleared a way for itself to Fraga through the intervention of two friends who had preceded the telephone calls and the shrill chorus of the first congratulations. Laughing, Fraga recalled that being awarded the Nobel Prize hadn't stopped Gide from going to see a Fernandel movie the same night; maybe that's why he enjoyed seeking refuge at a friend's place and avoiding the first avalanche of collective enthusiasm with a tranquillity which even his accomplice in that friendly kidnapping found excessive and almost hypocritical. But, during those days, Fraga had his doubts, without any explanation, as to why a kind of desire for solitude was taking root in him, a wish to be on the margin of his public figure, which by means of photography and radio was breaching walls, reaching provincial circles, and appearing in the foreign media. The National Prize wasn't a surprise, merely a reparation. Now the rest would come, what underneath it all had driven him to write the *Life*. He wasn't

wrong: a week later the Minister of Foreign Relations received him at home ("we diplomats know that good writers
aren't interested in the official apparatus") and offered him
the post of cultural attaché in Europe. Everything had an
almost oneiric air about it: it all went so much against the
current that Fraga had to make an effort to accept fully the
ascent up the stairway of honors; step by step, starting with
the first reviews, the smiles and embraces of his publishers,
invitations from literary societies, he had reached the landing
from which, by just leaning over, he would be able to take in
the whole of the fashionable salon world, dominate it alle-
gorically, and scrutinize it to its last corner, to the last white
tie and last chinchilla of the protectors of literature, between
mouthfuls of foie gras and Dylan Thomas. Further off—or
closer by, it depended on the angle of vision, the momentary
state of mind—he also saw the humble and sheeplike multi-
tude of magazine devourers, of televiewers and radio listen-
ers, the many who on a certain day, without knowing how or
why, submit to the imperative of buying a washing machine
or a novel, an object of thirty cubic feet or three hundred
eighteen pages, and they buy it, buy it immediately, making
some kind of sacrifice, and take it home where madam and
the children are waiting anxiously because the neighbor
woman already has one, because the commentator in vogue
on Radio El Mundo has praised it again on his eleven fifty-five
broadcast. The startling thing had been that his book had entered the catalogue of things that must be bought and read,
after so many years during which the life and works of
Claudio Romero had been nothing more than a mania of intel-
lectuals—which is to say, of almost no one. But when, time
and again, he felt the necessity of remaining alone once more
and thinking about what was happening (it was the week of
contacts with movie producers now), the initial surprise gave

way to a nervous expectation of he didn't know what. Nothing could come that wasn't another step on the stairway of honor, except the inevitable day when, as on garden bridges, the last rising step is followed by the first descending one, the respectable path toward public satiety and a turn in search of new emotions. When he had to isolate himself in order to prepare his acceptance speech for the National Prize, the synthesis of the dizzying experiences of those weeks was summed up in an ironic satisfaction with what his triumph had of retaliation about it, softened by that inexplicable restlessness which at moments rose to the surface and tried to project itself toward a territory to which his sense of balance and humor were resolutely denied. He thought that the preparation of the lecture would bring the pleasure of work back to him, and he went to Ofelia Fernández's country place to write it, a place where he would have peace and quiet. It was the end of summer, the woods were already taking on the colors of autumn, which he liked to look at from the porch while he chatted with Ofelia and petted the dogs. In a room on the second floor his working materials were waiting; when he lifted the cover of his main file box, running through it distractedly like a pianist warming up, Fraga told himself that all was well, that in spite of the inevitable vulgarity of all literary triumphs on a grand scale, the *Life* was an act of justice, an homage to the race and to the nation. He could sit down and write his speech, receive the prize, get ready for his trip to Europe. Dates and notes were mingled in his mind with the clauses of contracts and dinner invitations. Soon Ofelia would come in with a decanter of sherry, she would come over, silent and attentive, would watch him work. Yes, everything was fine. There was nothing to do but take a sheet of paper, adjust the lamp, light up a Havana cigar listening to the distant call of a tero bird.

He never knew exactly whether the revelation had come at that moment or later, after making love to Ofelia, while they were smoking, lying in bed and looking at a small green star high up on the window. The invasion, if one were to call it that (but its true name or nature didn't matter), might have coincided with the first sentence of his speech, drawn up swiftly to a point at which it had been interrupted suddenly, replaced, swept by something like a wind that took all meaning from it. The rest had been a long silence, but perhaps everything was already known when he came down out of the hall, known and formulated, weighing like a headache or the beginning of the flu. Ungraspable, at some indefinable moment, the confused weight, the black wind had been resolved in certainty: the *Life* was false, the story of Claudio Romero had nothing to do with what he had written. No reasons, no proofs: everything false. After years of work, of gathering facts, of following tracks, of avoiding personal excesses: everything false. Claudio Romero had not sacrificed himself for Susana Márquez, nor had he given her back her freedom at the cost of his renunciation, he had not been the Icarus at the honeyed feet of Irene Paz. As if he were swimming underwater, unable to return to the surface, lashed by the roar of the current in his ears, he knew the truth. And it was not sufficient torture; behind it, still lower in the water that was mud and filth now, dragging him along was the certainty that he'd known it from the first moment. It was useless to light another cigarette, plead neurosis, kiss the thin lips that Ofelia offered him in the shadows. Useless to argue that the excessive dedication to his hero might have provoked that momentary hallucination, that rejection, because of an excess of energy. He felt Ofelia's hand stroking his chest, the intermittent warmth of her breathing. Inexplicably, he fell asleep.

In the morning he looked at the open file, the papers, and they were more alien than the feelings of the night before. Downstairs Ofelia was busy telephoning the station to get the train connections. He got Pilar around eleven thirty and went directly to the vegetable store. Susana's daughter received him with a curious air of simultaneous resentment and adulation, like a dog after a kick. Fraga asked her to give him five minutes and once more went into the dusty parlor and sat down in the same white-bottomed chair. He didn't have to talk much because Susana's daughter, after drying a few tears, began to approve, with her head tilted, leaning more and more forward.

"Yes, sir, that's how it was. Yes, sir."

"Why didn't you tell me the first time?"

It was difficult to explain why she hadn't said so the first time. Her mother had made her swear that she would never mention certain things and she'd married the non-commissioned officer from Balcarce later on, so . . . She'd almost thought of writing him when they'd begun to talk so much about the book on Romero because . . .

She looked at him perplexed, and from time to time a tear fell down to her mouth.

"How did you find out?" she asked him then.

"Don't worry about that," Fraga said. "Everything comes out in the end."

"But you wrote it so differently in the book. I read it, you know. I have it and everything."

"The blame for its being so different is on you. There are other letters from Romero to your mother. You gave me the ones that fitted, the ones that flattered Romero and, by ricochet, your mother. I need the others right now. Give them to me."

"There's only one," Raquel Márquez said. "But Mama made me swear, sir."

"If she kept it without burning it, it's because it wasn't so important. Let me have it. I'll buy it from you."

"Mr. Fraga, that's not why I won't give it to you . . ."

"Here," Fraga said brutally. "You won't get money like this selling pumpkins."

While he watched her bending over the music case, going through papers, he thought that what he knew now he'd already known (in a different way, perhaps, but he'd known it) the day of his first visit with Raquel Márquez. The truth didn't take him completely by surprise, and now he could judge himself in retrospect and wonder, for example, why he'd abbreviated his first interview with Susana's daughter in such a way, why he'd accepted Romero's letters as if they were the only ones, without insisting, without offering something in exchange, without getting to the bottom of what Raquel knew and was keeping quiet. It's absurd, he thought. At that moment I had no way of knowing that Susana had prostituted herself and the fault was Romero's. But why, then, had he deliberately abbreviated his conversation with Raquel, appearing satisfied with the photographs and the three letters. Oh, yes, I knew it, who knows how, but I knew it, and I wrote the book knowing it, and maybe the readers know it too, and the critics, and it's all an immense lie in which we're all caught up . . . But it was easy to get out of it by way of generalizations, accepting only a small part of the blame. Also a lie: there was only one guilty party, he.

The reading of the letter was a mere superimposition of words on something that Fraga already knew from a different angle and which the epistolary proof could only reinforce in case of a polemic. The mask fallen, an almost ferocious Claudio Romero appeared in those phrases, so cutting and having an unanswerable logic. Condemning Susana to the filthy profession in which she was to drag herself along during her last years and which was alluded to in two passages, he imposed silence, distance, and hate on her forever. He pushed her with sarcasm and threats toward a downhill course that he himself must have prepared in two years of slow and minute corruption. The man who weeks before had taken pleasure in writing: "I need the night for myself alone, I won't let you see me weep" now finished off a paragraph with a filthy allusion whose effect he must have malignantly foreseen, and he piled up sarcastic recommendations and advice, light farewells interrupted by explicit threats in case Susana tried to see him again. Nothing of that surprised Fraga anymore, but he remained for a long time with his shoulder leaning against the window of the train, the letter in his hand, as if something in him were struggling to awaken from a slow, unbearable nightmare. And that explains the rest, he heard himself think. The rest was Irene Paz, "Ode to Your Double Name," Claudio Romero's final failure. Without proof or reasons, but with a certainty much deeper than could emanate from just any letter or testimony, the last two years of Romero's life were ordered day by day in the memory—if there was some name you could give it—of a person who, in the eyes of the passengers on the train from Pilar, must have been a gentleman who had drunk one vermouth too many. When he got off at the station it was four o'clock in the afternoon and starting to rain. The gig that took him to the farm was cold and smelled of rancid leather. How much good sense had dwelt under the haughty brow of Irene Paz, from how much long aristocratic experience had the negative of her world been born. Romero had been capable of magnetizing a poor woman, but he didn't have the wings of Icarus that his poem claimed. Irene, or not even she, her mother or her brothers, had immediately guessed the attempt of the arriviste, the grotesque leap of the social climber who begins by denying his origins, killing them if that failed (and the crime was called Susana Márquez, schoolteacher). All they had needed was a smile, the refusal of an invitation, a retreat to their ranch, the sharp weapons of money and butlers with instructions. They hadn't even bothered to attend the poet's funeral.

Ofelia was waiting on the porch. Fraga told her that he had to get to work right away. When with a cigarette between his lips and an enormous fatigue that sank his shoulders he faced the page begun the night before, he told himself that nobody knew anything. It was like the time before he'd written the *Life* and he was still the master of the keys. He just smiled and began to write his speech. Much later he realized that at some point on the trip he'd lost Romero's letter.

Anyone can read in the files of Buenos Aires newspapers the comments aroused by the National Prize award ceremony in which Jorge Fraga had deliberately provoked the upset and wrath of sound minds when from the platform he presented an absolutely wild version of the life of the poet Claudio Romero. One reporter pointed out that Fraga had given the impression of being indisposed (but the euphemism was clear), among other things because several times he had spoken as if he were Romero himself, correcting himself immediately only to fall back into the absurd aberration a moment later. Another reporter called attention to the fact that Fraga had a few scribbled pages that he scarcely looked at during the course of the speech, giving the feeling of his being his own audience, approving or disapproving certain phrases that were scarcely spoken, until he produced a grow-

ing and an ultimately unbearable irritation in the vast audience that had gathered together with the express intention of
applauding him. Another writer reported the violent alterca-
tion between Fraga and Dr. Jovellanos after the lecture,
when a large part of the audience had abandoned the hall
with exclamations of chagrin, and reported with grief that in
reply to Dr. Jovellanos' intimation that he present convinc-
ing proof of the fearful affirmations of calumny to the sacred
memory of Claudio Romero, the lecturer had shrugged his
shoulders and ended by raising a hand to his forehead as if
the required proof had not gone beyond his imagination;
and, lastly, he had remained motionless, looking into the air,
as aloof from the tumultuous departure of the audience as to
the provocative applause and congratulations of a small
group of youths and humorists who seemed to find that particular manner of accepting a National Prize admirable.

When Fraga reached the farm two hours later, Ofelia
silently handed him a long list of telephone calls, one from
the Foreign Ministry to another from a brother with whom
he had broken. He looked distractedly at the series of names,
some underlined, others poorly written. The piece of paper
fell from his hand and onto the rug. Without picking it up, he
began to climb the stairs that led to his workroom.

Much later Ofelia heard him walking about the room.
She went to bed and tried not to think. Fraga's steps came
and went, halting at times as if he had stopped by the desk for
a moment, to look something up. An hour later she heard
him come downstairs, come into the bedroom. Without opening her eyes she felt the weight of his body as he slipped in
beside her and lay on his back. A cold hand squeezed hers.
In the darkness Ofelia kissed him on the cheek.

"The only thing I don't understand," Fraga said as if he
weren't talking to her, "is why it took me so long to know

that I'd always known it all. It's idiotic to suppose that I'm a medium, I've had absolutely nothing to do with him. Even up to a week ago I had nothing to do with him."

"If you could only get a bit of sleep," Ofelia said.

"No, I've got to find it. There are two things: what I don't understand and what's going to start tomorrow, what's already started this afternoon. I'm finished, you understand, they'll never forgive me for having put the idol into their arms and then making it fly into pieces. Just look how absolutely imbecilic it all is, Romero will go on being the author of the best poems of the twenties. But idols can't have feet of clay and, using the same banality, my dear colleagues are going to tell me that tomorrow."

"But if you thought that your duty was to proclaim the truth . . ."

"I didn't think it, Ofelia, I did it. That's all. Or someone did it for me. Suddenly there wasn't any other way after that night. It was the only thing that could have been done."

"It probably would have been better if you'd waited a bit," Ofelia said timidly. "All of a sudden, just like that, in front of . . ."

She was going to say "of the Minister," and Fraga heard the words as clearly as if she'd said them. He smiled, stroked her hand. Little by little the waters began to recede; something still obscure was trying to bring itself into view, define itself. Ofelia's long, anguished silence helped him grasp things better, looking into the darkness with his eyes wide open. He would never understand why he hadn't known before that everything was known, why he kept denying that he, too, was a swine, as much a swine as Romero himself. The idea of writing the book had already taken on the aim of a social revenge, of a facile triumph, of the vindication of everything he deserved and which other opportunists were

taking away from him. Apparently rigorous, the *Life* had
been born armed with all the resourses to open a way into the
show windows of bookstores. Every step of the triumph was
waiting, minutely prepared in every chapter, in every phrase.
His ironical, almost disenchanted progressive acceptance of
those stages didn't go beyond one of the many masks of infamy. Behind the anodyne cover of the *Life*, radio, TV, movies, the National Prize, the diplomatic post in Europe, the
money, and the lionizing had been lurking. Except that
something unforeseen had been waiting until the last moment to land on the painstakingly constructed machine and
blow it up. It was useless to want to think about that, useless
to be afraid, to feel possessed by the succubus.

"I've had nothing to do with him," Fraga repeated, closing his eyes. "I don't know how it happened, Ofelia, but I've
had nothing to do with him."

He could hear her weeping in silence.

"But then it's even worse. Like an infection under the
skin, hidden for so long and suddenly bursting and spattering
you with rotten blood. Every time it was my turn to choose,
to decide on the conduct of that man, I chose the reverse,
what he tried to make people believe while he was alive. My
choices were his, when anyone could have been able to de-
cipher a different truth in his life, in his letters, in that last
year when death was hemming him in and stripping him. I
didn't want to see it, I refused to show the truth because,
then, Ofelia, then, Romero wouldn't have been the famous
person who needed me as I needed him to put together the
legend, in order to . . ."

He fell silent, but everything kept on taking shape and
falling into place. Now, from out of the depths, he was arriving at his identity with Claudio Romero, and it had nothing
to do with the supernatural. Brothers in the farce, in the lie

and the hope of a blazing ascent, brothers in the brutal fall that struck them down and destroyed them. Clearly and simply, Fraga felt that anyone like him would always be Claudio Romero, that the Romeros of yesterday and tomorrow would always be Jorge Fraga. Just as he had been afraid one distant September night, he had hypocritically written his autobiography. It gave him an urge to laugh and at the same time he thought of the pistol he kept in the desk.

He never knew whether it had been at that moment or later that Ofelia had said: "The only thing that counts is that today you showed them the truth." She hadn't meant to make him think about that, to bring back the almost incredible hour in which he had spoken, facing looks that passed progressively from the admiring or courteous smile to the wrinkled brow, the disdainful grimace, the arm rising in a sign of protest. But that was the only thing that counted, the only certain and solid thing in the whole story; no one could take that hour when he had really triumphed away from him, beyond the simulacra and his avid supporters. When he leaned over Ofelia to stroke her hair it seemed to him that she was a little like Susana Márquez and that his caress was saving her and keeping her close to him. And at the same time the National Prize, the post in Europe, and the honors were Irene Paz, something that had to be rejected and abolished if he didn't want to sink completely into Romero, miserably identified until the end with a false hero of the printed word and soap operas.

Later on—the night spun slowly in its heaven boiling with stars—other decks of cards became mingled in the interminable insomnia solitaire. Morning would bring the telephone calls, the newspapers, the scandal well tailored to fit into two columns. It seemed mad to him to have thought for a moment that everything was lost when a minute of assurance and skill was all that was needed to win the game, point by point. Everything depended on a few hours, a few interviews. If he felt like it, the cancellation of the prize, the refusal of the Foreign Ministry to confirm its proposal could be converted into news that would throw him into the international world of vast printings and translations. But he could also stay on his back in bed, refusing to see anyone, shutting himself up for months on the farm, picking up and continuing with his old philological studies, his best and now hazy friendships. In six months he would be forgotten, admirably replaced by the most stolid newspaperman of the moment in the listings of success. Both paths were equally simple, equally secure. It was all a matter of choosing. And even though he'd already decided, he still thought, just for something to think about, choosing and giving reasons for his choice until dawn began to brush against the window, against the hair of Ofelia asleep and the silk-cotton tree in the garden, imprecisely outlined like a future that takes shape as present, hardens little by little, enters into its everyday form, accepts it and defends it and condemns it in the morning light.

ENCOUNTER

WITHIN

A

RED

CIRCLE

FOR BORGES

It seems to me, Jacobo, that you must have been very cold that night and that the persistent Wiesbaden rain was closing in to make you decide to go into the Zagreb. Maybe your appetite was the dominant reason, you'd worked all day and now it was time to have dinner in some quiet, peaceful spot; if the Zagreb lacked other qualities, it did combine those two and you, shrugging your shoulders, I think, as if teasing yourself a little, decided to dine there. In any case, there were plenty of tables in the shadows of the vaguely Balkan dining room and it was nice to be able to hang your soaked raincoat

This tale was included in the catalogue of an exhibit by the Venezuelan painter Jacobo Borges.

on the old rack and search out that corner where the green
candle on the table softly moved the shadows and let ancient
silverware and a very tall glass show through where the light
took refuge like a bird.

First there was the usual feeling in an empty restaurant,
something between annoyance and relief; from its looks it
shouldn't be bad, but the absence of customers at that hour
gave cause for thought. In a foreign city meditations like that
don't last long: what does a person know about customs and
schedules, what counts is the warmth, the menu where surprises or reappearances are proposed, the tiny woman with
large eyes and black hair who arrived as if out of nowhere,
suddenly outlined against the white tablecloth, a slight fixed
smile as she waited. You thought that perhaps it was already
too late in the routine of the city, but you almost didn't have
time to raise a look of touristic interrogation; a small, pale
hand deposited a napkin and lined up the saltshaker that had
been out of rhythm. As was logical, you chose shish kebab
with onions and red peppers, and a thick and fragrant wine
that had nothing Western about it; like me on other occa-
sions, you liked to escape from hotel meals where the fear of
the too typical or exotic is resolved with insipidness, and you
even ordered black bread, which might not have been the
thing to go with shish kebab, but which the woman brought
immediately. Only then, smoking a first cigarette, did you
look somewhat intently at the Transylvanian enclave that was
protecting you from the rain and a not excessively interesting
German city. The silence, the absences, and the vague light
from the wicks were already almost your friends; in any case,
they put you at a distance from the rest and left you beautifully alone with your cigarette and your weariness.

The hand that poured the wine into the tall glass was
covered with hair, and it took you a startled second to break

the absurd logical chain and understand that the pale woman
was no longer by your side and in her place a swarthy and
silent waiter was inviting you to taste the wine with a gesture
that seemed to be only an automatic expectation. It's rare for
anyone to find the wine bad, and the waiter finally filled the
glass as if the interruption had been but a minor part of the
ceremony. Almost at the same time another waiter, curiously
resembling the first (but the native costumes, the black sideburns made them uniform), put the steaming platter on the
table and with a rapid movement pushed the meat off the
skewers. The few necessary words had been exchanged in the
bad German foreseen in the guest and those serving him; he
was surrounded once more by the calm of the shadows in the
room and the weariness, but now you heard the rain beating
more strongly on the street. That too ceased almost immediately and you, barely turning, saw that the entrance door had
been opened to let in another customer, a woman who must
have been myopic, not only because of the thickness of her
glasses, but also because of the senseless assuredness with
which she advanced among the tables to sit down in the opposite corner of the room, lighted only by one or two candles
that flickered as she passed and mingled her uncertain figure
with the furnishings and the walls and the thick-curtained
red of the background, there where the restaurant seemed to
lean against the rest of an unpredictable house.

While you ate you were vaguely amused that the English
tourist (she couldn't have been anything else with that raincoat and a peep of blouse that was between mauve and to-
mato) was concentrating her myopia on a menu that must
have been totally beyond her, and that the woman with the
large black eyes had remained in the third corner of the
room, where there was a counter with mirrors and wreaths
of dry flowers, letting the tourist finish not understanding

before she went over. The waiters had placed themselves behind the counter, on both sides of the woman, and were also
waiting with their arms folded, so similar to each other that
the reflection of their backs in the aged quicksilver had something false about it, like a difficult or tricky quadruplication.
They were all looking at the English tourist, who didn't seem
to realize the passage of time and still had her face glued to
the menu. There was still a wait while you took out another
cigarette, and the woman finally came over to your table and
asked if you wanted some soup, perhaps some Greek goat
cheese, continued the questions with each polite negative, the
cheeses were quite good, well, then, perhaps some regional
pastries. You wanted only some Turkish coffee because the
dinner had been abundant and you were starting to feel
sleepy. The woman seemed indecisive, as if giving you an
opportunity to change your mind and order a platter of
cheeses, and when you didn't, she repeated mechanically,
Turkish coffee, and you said yes, Turkish coffee, and the
woman took a kind of short, quick breath, raised her hand to
the waiters, and went on to the English tourist's table.

The coffee was a long time coming, in contrast to the
quick start of the dinner, and you had time to smoke another
cigarette and slowly finish the bottle of wine while you
amused yourself watching the English tourist let a thick-
lensed look stroll all about the room without stopping on
anything particular. There was something stupid or timid in
her, she went through a rather long set of vague movements
until she decided to take off the raincoat that was glistening
with rain and hang it on the nearest rack; when she sat down
again she naturally must have wet her behind, but that didn't
seem to worry her as she finished her uncertain observation of
the room and remained quite still looking at the tablecloth.
The waiters had gone back to their positions behind the

counter, and the woman was waiting beside the small window
to the kitchen; the three were looking at the English tourist,
looking at her as if expecting something, for her to call to
complete an order or maybe change it or leave, they were
looking at her in a way that seemed to you too intense, un-
justified in any case. They had stopped paying attention to
you, the two waiters had their arms folded again, and the
woman had her head a bit tilted and her long hair covered
her eyes, but it was she, perhaps, who was staring hardest at
the tourist and that seemed disagreeable and discourteous to
you, even though the poor myopic mole couldn't have been
aware of anything now that she was digging in her purse and
pulling out something that couldn't be seen in the shadows
but which could be identified by the noise the mole made as
she blew her nose. One of the waiters brought her meal (it
looked like goulash) and returned immediately to his post as
sentinel; the double mania of folding their arms as soon as
they finished their work should have been amusing but in
some way it wasn't, nor was the woman's placing herself in
the most distant angle of the counter and from there continuing to concentrate her attention on the operation of drinking
coffee that you were bringing to a conclusion with all the
slowness that its good quality and aroma demanded. Suddenly the center of attention seemed to have changed, because the two waiters were also watching you drink your
coffee, and before you finished the woman came over to ask if
you wanted another, and you accepted, almost perplexed because in all that, which wasn't anything, there was something
that was escaping you and which you would have liked to
have understood better. The English tourist, for example,
why was it that the waiters suddenly seemed to be in such a
hurry for the tourist to finish eating and leave and they took
away her plate right after her last mouthful and gave her

the menu opened up in her face as one of them went off with the empty plate while the other waited as if urging her to decide.

You, as happens so many times, couldn't have been able to identify the precise moment in which you thought you understood; in chess and in love, too, there are those moments when the mist breaks and it is then that plays or acts are performed which would have been inconceivable one second before. Without even an idea you could articulate you smelled the danger and said to yourself that no matter how long the English tourist dragged out her dinner it was necessary for you to remain there smoking and drinking until the defenseless mole decided to encase herself in her plastic bubble and go out onto the street once more. Since you had always enjoyed sport and absurdity, you found it amusing to consider as such something that at gut level was far from being so; you made a signal and ordered another coffee and a glass of barack, which was advisable in the enclave. You had three cigarettes left and you thought they would last until the English tourist decided on some Balkan dessert; naturally, she wouldn't have any coffee, it was something that could be seen in her eyeglasses and blouse; nor would she ask for tea because there are things one doesn't do outside the mother country. With a little luck she would pay the bill and leave after some fifteen more minutes.

They served you the coffee but not the barack, the woman took her eyes out of her mat of hair to put on the expression that fitted the delay; they were looking for a new bottle in the wine cellar, if the gentleman would be so kind as to wait a few minutes. The voice articulated the words clearly even if they were mispronounced, but you noticed that the woman remained intent on the other table, where one of the waiters was presenting the bill with the gesture of a robot, stretching out his arm and remaining motionless within a perfectly respectful discourtesy. As if she finally understood, the tourist set about digging into her purse; everything about her was clumsy, she was probably running into a comb or a mirror instead of the money that finally must have come to the surface because the waiter brusquely left the table at the moment the woman arrived with the glass of barack. Nor did you know too well why you simultaneously asked her for the check, now that you were sure the tourist would leave first and you could dedicate yourself to savoring the barack and smoking the last cigarette. Maybe the idea of remaining alone once more in the place that had been so agreeable on arriving and was different now, things like the double image of the waiters behind the counter and the woman who seemed to hesitate at the request, as if it were indolence to be in such a hurry, and then turned her back and returned to the counter to close the trio and the wait again. After all, it must have been depressing to work in such an empty restaurant, so far from light and fresh air; those people had begun to wither, their paleness and their mechanical gestures were the only possible response to so many interminable nights. And the tourist gesticulated around her raincoat, went back to the table as if she thought she had forgotten something, looked under the chair, and then you got up slowly, incapable of staying a second longer, and halfway there you ran into one of the waiters, who held out the silver tray on which you put a bill without looking at the check. The gust of wind coincided with the gesture of the waiter as he looked in the pockets of his red vest for the change, but you knew that the tourist had just opened the door and you didn't wait any longer, you raised your hand in a good-bye that took in the waiter and those who continued looking from the counter, and calculating the distance exactly, you picked up your

raincoat as you went by and went out into the street, where it
was no longer raining. Only there did you really breathe, as if
until then and without realizing it you had been holding
your breath; only there did you really feel fear and relief at
the same time.

The tourist was a few steps ahead, walking slowly in the
direction of your hotel, and you followed her with the vague
suspicion that suddenly she would remember that she had
forgotten something and it would occur to her to return to
the restaurant. It was no longer a question of understanding
anything, everything was a simple block, evidence with no
reason: you had saved her and you had to be sure that she
wouldn't return, that the clumsy mole stuck in her damp
bubble would arrive with a total, happy unawareness at the
shelter of her hotel, at a room where no one would look at
her the way they had been looking at her.

When she turned the corner, and even though there was
no longer any reason to hurry, you wondered whether or not
it wouldn't be better to follow her closely in order to be sure
that she wouldn't go around the block in her erratic myopic
clumsiness; you hastened to reach the corner and saw the
poorly lighted and empty alleyway. The two long stone walls
showed in the distance nothing but a doorway, which the
tourist could not have reached; only a toad, enlivened by the
rain, was hopping across from one sidewalk to the other.

For a moment it was rage, how could that stupid . . .
Then you leaned against one of the walls and waited, but it
was almost as if you were waiting for yourself, for something
that had to open and function in the deepest part so that all
of it would come to some meaning. The toad had found a
hole at the base of the wall and was also waiting, perhaps for
some insect that had nested in the hole or for a passageway to
get into a garden. You never knew how long you had stayed

there or why you went back to the street where the restaurant was. The windows were dark but the narrow door was still ajar; it almost didn't startle you that the woman was there as if waiting for you without surprise.

"We thought you'd come back," she said. "You see now that there was no reason for you to have left so soon."

She opened the door a little more and stood aside; now it would have been so easy to turn your back and go away without even answering, but the street with the walls and the toad was like a denial of everything you had imagined, of everything you had believed to be an inexplicable obligation. In some way it was all the same to you to go in as to go away, even though you felt the twitching that was pushing you back; you went in before deciding to on that level where nothing had been decided that night, and you heard the sound of the door and the lock behind you. The two waiters were very near, and there were only a few lighted wicks in the room.

"Come," said the voice of the woman from some corner, "everything is prepared."

Her voice sounded as if it were distant, something coming from the other side of the mirror at the counter.

"I don't understand," you managed to say, "she was there and suddenly . . ."

One of the waiters laughed, just the beginning of a dry laugh.

"Oh, that's the way she is," the woman said, coming toward you. "She did what she could for you, she always tries, poor thing. But they haven't got the strength, they can only do certain things and they always do them poorly, it's so different from how people imagine them."

You felt the two waiters by your side, the rub of their vests against your raincoat.

"We almost feel sorry," the woman said, "it's already been twice that she's come and has had to leave because nothing comes out right for her. Nothing ever works out, all you have to do is take a look at her."

"But, she . . ."

"Jenny," the woman said. "That's all we could find out about her when we first met her, she managed to say that her name was Jenny, unless she was calling to someone else, then there was nothing but the screams, it's absurd how they scream so much."

You looked at them without speaking, knowing that even looking at them was useless, and I felt so sorry for you, Jacobo, how could I know that you were going to think what you thought of me and that you were going to try to protect me, I who was there for that reason, to get them to let you go. There were too many distances, too many impossibilities between you and me; we'd played the same game, but you were still alive and there was no way to make you understand. From now on it would be different if you wanted it that way, from now on we would be two coming in on rainy nights, maybe it would turn out better that way, or at least it would be that, we would be two on rainy nights.

THE
FACES
OF
THE
MEDAL

The offices of CERN opened onto a gloomy hallway, and Javier liked to leave his office and smoke a cigarette, walking back and forth, imagining Mireille behind the door on the left. It was the fourth time in three years that he'd gone to work as a temporary in Geneva, and every time he returned Mireille would greet him cordially, invite him to have tea at five o'clock with two other engineers, a female secretary, and a male stenographer, poet and Yugoslavian. We liked the little ritual because it wasn't daily and therefore mechanical; every three or four days, when we would come together in an elevator or in the hall, Mireille would invite him to join his colleagues over tea, which would be improvised on her desk.

Maybe she liked Javier because he didn't disguise his boredom and his desire to get the contract over with and return to
London. It was difficult to know why they hired him; in any
case, Mireille's colleagues were surprised at his disdain for
the work and the soft music from the Japanese transistor with
which he accompanied his calculations and designs. Nothing
seemed to bring us closer in those days, Mireille remained in
her office for hours on end and it was useless for Javier to
invent absurd cabals to see her come out after thirty-three
turns up and down the hall; but if she had come out, they
would only have exchanged a couple of ordinary phrases
without Mireille's imagining that he was strolling with the
hope of seeing her come out, just as he was making a game
out of his stroll, to see if before thirty-three it was Mireille or
defeat once more. We almost didn't know each other, at CERN
almost no one really knows anyone else, the obligation of
coexistence for so many hours a week weaves spiderwebs of
friendship or enmity that any wind of vacation or retirement
can send to the devil. We played at that for those two weeks
which came back every year, but for Javier the return to
London was also Eileen and a slow, irresistible degradation of
something that at one time had had the grace of desire and
pleasure, Eileen a cat up on a barrel, a pole dancer above
boredom and habit. With her he had lived out a safari in the
middle of the city, Eileen had gone with him to hunt ante-
lope in Piccadilly Circus, to light campfires in Hampstead
Heath, everything had speeded up as in silent movies until
one last love race in Denmark, or had it been Romania, suddenly the differences, always known and denied, the cards
that changed position in the deck and modified fortunes, Eileen preferring the movies to concerts or vice versa, Javier
going alone to look for records because Eileen had to wash
her hair, she who had only washed it when there had really

been nothing else to do, protesting against hygiene and please dry my face I've got shampoo in my eyes. The first contract with CERN had arrived when there was already nothing to be said except that the apartment in Earl's Court was still there with the morning routine, love like soup or the *Times*, like Aunt Rosa and her birthday at the country place in Bath, the gas bills. All that was now a muddy emptiness, a past present of contradictory recurrences filled with Javier's back and forth along the hallway by the offices, twenty-five, twenty-six, twenty-seven, perhaps before thirty the door and Mireille and hi, Mireille, who would be going to pee or to check a fact with the English statistician with white sideburns, Mireille dark and silent, blouse up to her neck where something must have been slowly throbbing, a little bird of life without too many ups and downs, a distant mother, some love affair that was unfortunate and had no sequels, Mireille already a little bit old maid, a little bit office worker but sometimes whistling a theme from Mahler on the elevator, dressed without fantasy almost always in gray or a tailored suit, an age too settled, a discretion too withdrawn.

Only one of the two is writing this but it's all the same, it's as if we were writing it together, even though we're never going to be together anymore, Mireille will stay on at her little house on the outskirts of Geneva, Javier will travel about the world and return to his apartment in London with the obstinacy of the fly that alights a hundred times on an arm, on Eileen. We write it in the same way that a medal is obverse and reverse at the same time in the double play of the mirrors of life. We'll never really know which of us two is more sensitive to this way of not being that each had for the other. Both on their own side, Mireille weeps sometimes as she listens to a certain Brahms quintet, alone at dusk in her living room of dark beams and rustic furniture, where at moments the scent from the roses in the garden reaches. Javier doesn't know how to weep, his tears choose to condense into nightmares which awaken him brutally alongside Eileen, which are gotten rid of by drinking cognac and writing texts that inevitably don't contain the nightmares although sometimes they do; sometimes he pours them out in useless words and for a while is the master, the one who decides what will be said or what will slip little by little into the false oblivion of a new day.

In our way we both knew that a mistake had been made, a reparable error, but no one was capable of repairing it. We were certain that we had never judged ourselves, had simply accepted the fact that things were that way and nothing more could be done beyond what we did. I'm not sure if at that time we thought about things like pride, renunciation, deception, whether only Mireille or only Javier thought about them while the other one accepted them as something fateful, submitting to a system that took them in and submitted them; it's too easy now to say to oneself that everything could have depended on some instantaneous rebellion, lighting the lamp by the side of the bed when Mireille refused, keeping Javier by her side all night when he was already looking for his clothes to get dressed again; it's too easy to put the blame on delicacy, on the impossibility of being brutal or obstinate or generous. Between simpler or more ignorant beings it wouldn't have happened like that, maybe a slap or an insult would have contained the charity and the right road that decorum courteously forbade us. Our respect came from a way of life that brought us close together like the two faces of a medal; we accepted it each on his own side, Mireille in a silence of distance and renunciation, Javier murmuring his now ridiculous hope to her, finally falling silent in the middle of a phrase, in the middle of a last letter. And in the end all we had left, have left is the mournful task of still being worthy, still living with the vain hope that forgetfulness will not forget us too much.

One noon we came together at Mireille's house, almost by obligation she had invited him to have lunch with some other colleagues, she couldn't leave him out when Gabriela and Tom mentioned the lunch while they were having tea in her office, and Javier had thought that it was sad that Mireille had invited him because of simple social pressures but he'd bought a bottle of Jack Daniel's and gotten to know the cabin on the outskirts of Geneva, the small rose garden and the barbecue where Tom officiated among cocktails and a Beatles record that didn't belong to Mireille, that certainly wasn't part of Mireille's stern collection, but which Gabriela had put on the turntable because for her and Tom and half of CERN the air was unbreathable without that music. We didn't talk much, at some moment Mireille took him through the rose garden and he asked her if she liked Geneva and she answered him by just looking at him and shrugging her shoulders, he watched her busy herself with plates and glasses, heard her curse because of a spark on her hand, the fragments were coming together and perhaps it was then that he desired her for the first time, the lock of hair falling over her dark forehead, the blue jeans marking her waist, the somewhat grave voice that must have known how to sing lieder, say important things in a simple murmur. He returned to London at the end of the week and Eileen was in Helsinki, a piece of paper on the table told about a well-paying job, three weeks, there was a chicken in the freezer, kisses.

The next time CERN was aglow with a high-level conference, Javier really had to work and Mireille seemed to feel

sorry for him when he mournfully told her between the fifth
floor and the street; she suggested going to a piano concert,
they went, they coincided on Schubert but not on Bartók,
they had some drinks in an almost deserted little café, she had
an old English car and dropped him off at his hotel, he'd
brought her a record of some madrigals and it was good to
know that she didn't know it, that he wouldn't have to exchange it. Sunday and the country, the transparency of an
afternoon that was almost too Swiss, we left the car in a village and walked through the wheat fields, at some moment
Javier told her about Eileen, just for something to tell her,
without any precise necessity, and Mireille listened to him in
silence, she held back the pity and the comments that he
might have wanted in some way because he was expecting
something from her that would begin to resemble what he
felt, his desire to kiss her softly, lean her against the trunk of
a tree and know her lips, her whole mouth. We almost didn't
talk about ourselves on the way back, we let ourselves go
along through the paths that proposed their themes at every
turn, the hedges, the cows, a sky with silvered clouds, the
postcard of a good Sunday. But when we ran down a hill
between fences, Javier felt Mireille's hand near his and he
squeezed it and they kept on running as if they were drawn
along and back in the car Mireille invited him to have tea at
her cabin, she liked to call it cabin because it wasn't a cabin
but it had so much of a cabin about it, and listen to records.
It was a halt in time, a line that suddenly ceases in the rhythm
of the sketch before starting up again on some other part of
the paper, seeking a new direction.

We made a very clear balance that afternoon: Mahler
yes, Brahms yes, the Middle Ages in toto yes, jazz no (Mireille), jazz yes (Javier). We didn't talk about the rest, left to
explore were the Renaissance, baroque, Pierre Boulez, John

Cage (but Mireille Cage certainly not, even if they hadn't mentioned him, and probably Boulez the musician no, although the conductor yes, those important nuances). Three days later we went to a concert, had dinner in the old city, there was a postcard from Eileen and a letter from Mireille's mother but we didn't talk about them, everything was still Brahms and a white wine that Brahms would have liked. Mireille dropped him at the hotel and they kissed on the cheek. That night Javier answered Eileen's card, and Mireille watered her roses in the moonlight, not because of any romanticism because there was nothing romantic about her, but because sleep was slow in coming.

Politics was missing, except for isolated comments that little by little showed our partial differences. Maybe we hadn't wanted to face it, maybe in a cowardly way; tea in the office unleashed it, the poet stenographer came down hard on the Israelis, Gabriela found them wonderful, Mireille only said that they were in the right and what the hell, Javier smiled without sarcasm and observed that the same exact thing might be said of the Palestinians. Tom was for an international arrangement with blue helmets and the rest of the show, otherwise it was tea and forecasts of the week's work. We would talk seriously about all that some time, now we just liked to look at each other and feel good, tell each other that soon we would have a Beethoven night at Victoria Hall; we talked about it at the cabin, Javier had brought cognac and an absurd toy that according to him had to please Mireille but that she found exceedingly silly, which didn't stop her from putting it on a shelf after having wound it up and watching in a pleasant way its contortions. That afternoon was Bach, Rostropovich's cello, and a light that descended slowly like the cognac in the bubbles of the glasses. Nothing could have been more ours than that agreement on silence, we had never needed to raise a finger or hush a comment; only afterward, with the gesture of changing the record, did the first words come. Javier said them, looking at the floor; he asked simply if sometime he would be able to know what she already knew about him, her London and her Eileen.

Yes, of course he could, but no, in any case, not now. Sometime, when young, nothing to tell except that, well, there were days when everything weighed so much. In the shadows Javier felt that the words were reaching him as if wet, an instantaneous giving in but drying her eyes with the back of her sleeve now, without giving him time to ask anything more or beg her pardon. Confused, he put an arm around her, sought the face that she didn't refuse but which was as if somewhere else, in some other time. He tried to kiss her and she slipped away, murmuring a bland excuse, a little more cognac, there was no need to pay any attention to her, no reason to insist.

Everything mixes in little by little, we wouldn't remember in detail the before or after of those weeks, the order of the walks or the concerts, the meetings in museums. Perhaps Mireille might have ordered the sequence of things better, all Javier did was lay his few cards down face up, the return to London was drawing near, Eileen, the concerts, discovering Mireille's religion through a simple phrase, her faith and her precise values, what in him was nothing more than the hope of a present that was almost always repealed. In a café, after a laughing dispute over the question of who was going to pay, we looked at each other like old friends, comrades suddenly, we called ourselves dirty words that were deprived of meaning, the claws of bears at play. When we listened to music in the cabin again there was a different way of talking between

us, a different familiarity of the hand that helped a waist
through the door, Javier's right to get a glass by himself or
request Telemann no, first Lotte Lehmann and lots, lots of
ice in the whisky. Everything was all as if it had been subtly
reversed, Javier felt it and something, he didn't know what,
was disturbing him, a having arrived before arriving, a key to
the city that no one had given him. We never looked at each
other during music time, it was enough being there on the
old leather couch and letting the sun set and Lotte Lehmann.
When he searched for her mouth and his fingers brushed the
curve of her breasts, Mireille remained motionless and let
herself be kissed and answered his kiss and ceded her tongue
and her saliva to him for a second, but still without moving,
without answering his gesture of raising her up from her seat,
silent while he babbled his request to her, he was calling her
to everything that was waiting for them on the first step of the
stairs, in the whole night.

He waited too, thinking that he understood, he begged
her pardon but first, with his mouth still close to her face, he
asked her why, he asked her if she was a virgin, and Mireille
said no, tilting her head, smiling at him a little as if asking, it
was foolish, useless. They listened to another record, eating
crackers and drinking, night had fallen and he would have to
leave. We got up at the same time, Mireille let herself be
hugged as if she'd lost her strength, she didn't say anything
when he murmured his desire again; they went up the narrow staircase and on the landing they separated, there was
that pause in which doors are opened and lights turned on, a
request to wait and a disappearance which was prolonged
while in the bedroom Javier felt beside himself, incapable of
thinking that he shouldn't have let that happen, that it
couldn't be that way, the intervening wait, the probable precautions, the almost debasing routine. He saw her come back

wrapped in a white terrycloth bathrobe, go over to the bed and reach her hand out to the lamp. "Don't put the light out," he asked her; Mireille refused with a nod and turned it off, leaving him to get undressed in total darkness, feel for the edge of the bed, slide up against her motionless body in the shadows.

We didn't make love. We were one step away after Javier knew with hands and lips the silent body that awaited him in the darkness. His desire was different, seeing her in the light of the lamp, her breasts and her stomach, stroking a defined back, seeing Mireille's hands on his own body, detail in a thousand fragments, the pleasure that precedes pleasure. In the total silence and darkness, in the distance and timidity that fell over him from Mireille, invisible and mute, everything gave way to an unreality of half-sleep and at the same time he was incapable of standing up to her, of leaping from the bed and turning on the light and imposing a necessary and beautiful will once more. He thought confusedly that afterward, after she had known him, when true intimacy would begin, but the silence and the shadows and the ticking of that clock on the dresser were more powerful. He babbled an excuse that she muted with a friendly kiss, squeezed himself against her body, felt unbearably tired, perhaps slept for a moment.

Perhaps we slept, yes, perhaps at that moment we were left to ourselves and were lost. Mireille got up first and turned on the light, wrapped in her robe she went back to the bathroom while Javier got dressed mechanically, incapable of thought, his mouth as if dirty and the residue of the cognac biting his stomach. They scarcely spoke, they scarcely looked at each other, Mireille said it was nothing, that there were always taxis on the corner, she'd go down with him. He couldn't break the rigid chain of causes and consequences,

the obligatory routine that from long before them had demanded that he lower his head and leave the cabin in the
middle of the night; his only thought was that the next day
they would talk more calmly, that he would try to make her
understand, but understand what. And it's true that they
talked in the usual café and that Mireille once again said it
was nothing, it wasn't important, maybe it would be better
another time, you mustn't think about it. He would be going
back to London three days later, when he asked her to let him
go to the cabin she said no, better not. We didn't know what
to do or what else to say, we didn't even know how to be
silent, embrace at some corner, find each other in some look.
It was as if Mireille were waiting for something from Javier
that he was waiting for from Mireille, a question of initiatives
or priorities, of the gestures of a man and the compliance of a
woman, the immutability of sequences decided by others, received from without; we had advanced along a road where no
one had wanted to face the march, break the harmonious
parity; not even now, after knowing that we'd taken the
wrong road, were we capable of a shout, a hand reaching for
the lamp, the impulse above useless ceremonies, bathrobes
and it's nothing, don't worry about it, it'll be better another
time. It would have been preferable to accept it then, at once.
It would have been preferable to repeat together: we lose our
life because of niceties; the poet would have pardoned us if
we were also talking for ourselves.

We didn't see each other for months. Javier wrote, of course,
and a few words from Mireille, cordial and distant, reached
him punctually. Then he began to telephone her at night,
almost always on Saturdays when he imagined her alone in
the cabin, begging her pardon if he was interrupting a quar-

tet or a sonata, but Mireille would always answer that she'd been reading or working in the garden, that it was fine to call at that time. When she traveled to London six months later to visit a sick aunt, Javier got her a hotel room, they met at the station and went to visit the museums, King's Road, enjoyed a film by Milos Forman. That time, as in the past, in a small restaurant in Whitechapel, their hands met with a confidence that wiped out memory, and Javier felt better and told her so, he told her that he wanted her more than ever but that he'd never talk to her about that again, that it all depended on her, on the day she decided to return to the first step of the first night and simply held out her arms to him. She nodded without looking at him, without agreement or negation, she just found it absurd that he kept turning down the contracts they offered him in Geneva. Javier went back to the hotel with her and Mireille said good-bye in the lobby, she didn't ask him up but she smiled when she kissed him softly on the cheek, murmuring a see-you-soon.

We know so many things, that arithmetic is false, that one and one aren't always one but two or zero; we have more than enough time to thumb through the album of holes, of closed windows, of letters without voice or scent. The daily office, Eileen convinced and lavishing happiness, weeks and months. Geneva in summer again, the first stroll along the lake shore, a concert by Isaac Stern. Left in London now was the tiny shadow of María Elena, whom Javier had met at a cocktail party and who had given him three weeks of light games, pleasure for its own sake where everything else was an amiable daily emptiness with María Elena becoming tireless at tennis and at the Rolling Stones, a good-bye without melancholy after a last weekend enjoyed like that, like a good-bye without melancholy. He told Mireille, and without need of asking her he knew that she no, that she the office and girl-friends, that she always the cabin and the records. He thanked her without words that Mireille listened to with her grave, attentive, comprehensive silence, leaving his hand in hers while they watched sunset over the lake and decided on a place for dinner.

Afterward it was work, a week of isolated meetings, night in the Romanian restaurant, tenderness. They'd never spoken of what was once again there in the gesture of pouring the wine or looking at each other slowly at the end of a con-versation. True to his word, Javier was waiting for a time he didn't think he had the right to wait for. But the tenderness, then, something present there among so many other things, a gesture of Mireille's as she lowered her head and passed her hand over her eyes, her simple phrase to tell him that she would go with him to his hotel. In the car they kissed again as on the night in the cabin, he held her body and felt her thighs open under the hand that was rising and caressing. When they went into the room Javier couldn't wait and embraced her standing up, losing himself in her mouth and her hair, leading her step by step to the bed. He heard her murmur a muffled no, ask him to wait a moment, felt her break away from him and look for the bathroom door, close it and time, silence and water and time while he pulled down the bed-spread and left only a light in a corner, took off his shoes and shirt, wondering whether to get completely undressed or to wait because his robe was in the bathroom and if the light was on, if Mireille on coming back found him naked and stand-ing, his erection grotesque, or if he turned his back even more grotesquely so that she wouldn't see him like that as she would really have to see him now that she was coming out with a bath towel wrapped around her, going over to the bed with her eyes lowered and he had his pants on, they'd have to be taken off and he'd have to take off his shorts and then yes embrace her, pull away the towel and lay her down on the bed and see her golden and dark and kiss her again to the deepest and caress her with fingers that hurt her perhaps because she moaned, threw herself back, stretching out on the farthest part of the bed and blinking at the light, asking once more for a darkness that he wouldn't give her because he wouldn't give her anything, his suddenly useless sex searching for a passage that she was offering him and that would not be crossed, the exasperated hands trying to excite him and excite himself, the mechanics of gestures and words that Mireille would slowly reject, rigid and distant, understanding that not now either, that tenderness and all of that had become unreconcilable, that her acceptance and her desire had only served to leave her once more beside a body that had ceased to struggle, that was clinging to her without moving, that wasn't even trying to begin again.

It might be that we slept, we were too distant and alone and dirty, the repetition had been fulfilled as in a mirror, except that now it was Mireille who was getting dressed to leave and he went with her to the car, he heard her say goodbye without looking at him and the soft kiss on the cheek, the car that started up in the silence of the late night, the return to the hotel and not even knowing how to cry, not even knowing how to kill himself, only the couch and the alcohol and the ticking of the night and the dawn, the office at nine o'clock, Eileen's card and the telephone waiting, the inside number that he would have to dial at some moment because at some moment he would have to say something. Because yes, don't worry, all right, in the café at seven o'clock. But telling him that, telling him don't worry, in the café at seven o'clock was coming after that interminable trip to the cabin,

getting into a cold bed and taking a useless sleeping pill, seeing every scene of that progression toward nothingness once
more, repeating in the midst of nausea the instant they had
stood up in the restaurant and she had said she would go to
the hotel with him, the rapid operations in the bathroom, the
towel to drape around her loins, the hot strength of the arms
that were leading her and laying her down, the murmuring
shadow stretching out on top of her, the caresses and that
flaming feeling of a hardness against her stomach, between
her thighs, the useless protest about the lighted lamp and
suddenly the absence, the hands slipping away lost, the voice
murmuring delays, the useless waiting, the drowiness, all
again, all why, why tenderness, why acquiescence, why the
hotel, and the innocuous sleeping pill, the office at nine
o'clock, a special meeting of the council, impossible to be
absent, everything impossible except the impossible.

We won't have spoken of this, imagination brings us together
today as uselessly as reality then. Together we'll never seek
blame or responsibility or the maybe not unimaginable new
beginning. There is only a feeling of punishment in Javier,
but what does punishment mean when one loves and desires,
what grotesque atavism is unleashed there where happiness
was waiting, why before and after this present Eileen or
María Elena or Doris in which a past Mireille will plunge her
knife of silence and disdain to the hilt. Of silence only even
though he thinks disdain with every nauseous moment of
memory, because there isn't any disdain in Mireille, silence
yes, and sadness, telling herself that she or he but also she and
he, telling herself that not every man fulfills the moment of
love and not every woman knows how to find a man in him.
The mediations remain, the last recourses, Javier's invitation

to take a trip together, spend two weeks in some distant corner to break the curse, vary the formula, find each other
finally in a different way without towels or waits or summonses. Mireille said yes, later on, he should phone her from
London, maybe she could get two weeks' leave. They were
saying good-bye at the railroad station, she was taking the
train back to the cabin because there was something wrong
with her car. Javier could no longer kiss her on the mouth
but he held her against him, he asked her again to accept the
trip, he looked at her until it hurt her, until she lowered her
eyes and repeated yes, that everything would come out all
right, that he should go to London in peace, that everything
would end up turning out well. We also talk to children like
that before taking them to the doctor or doing something that
hurts them, Mireille from her side of the medal probably no
longer expected anything, she wouldn't come to believe in
anything, she would simply go back to the cabin and the
records, without even imagining another way of running
toward what they hadn't reached. When he phoned her from
London proposing the Dalmatian coast, giving her dates and
directions with a detail that barely hid the fear of a negative
answer, Mireille answered that she'd write him. From his side
of the medal Javier was only able to say yes, that he'd keep on
waiting, as if in some way he already knew that the letter
would be brief and gracious and no, it was useless to begin
something lost again, better to be just friends; in scarcely
eight lines a hug from Mireille. Each on his and her side,
incapable of turning over the medal with a push, Javier
wrote a letter that might have tried to show the only path left
to them by inventing together, the only one that hadn't already been traced by others, by usage and acceptance, that
would not of needs pass through a staircase or an elevator to
arrive at a bedroom or a hotel, that would not demand his

taking off his clothes at the very same moment in which she was taking off hers; but his letter was only a wet handkerchief, he couldn't even finish it and he signed it in the middle of a sentence, he buried it in the envelope without rereading it. From Mireille there was no reply, the offers of work in Geneva were courteously turned down, the medal was there between us, we live at a distance from each other and we will never write each other again, Mireille in her little house in the suburbs, Javier traveling about the world and returning to his apartment with the obstinacy of the fly that alights on an arm a hundred times. One day at dusk Mireille wept while she listened to a certain Brahms quintet, but Javier doesn't know how to cry, he only has nightmares from which he frees himself by writing texts that try to be like nightmares, there where no one has his true name but perhaps his truth, there where there is no medal standing on edge with obverse and reverse, where there are no consecrated steps to climb; but, of course, they're only texts.

SOMEONE WALKING AROUND

TO ESPERANZA MACHADO,
CUBAN PIANIST

Jiménez had been put ashore as soon as night fell, accepting all the risks of the cove's being so close to the docks. They made use of an electric launch, of course, capable of slipping along as silent as a ray and losing itself in the distance again while Jiménez waited in the underbrush for a moment until his eyes got used to the dark, until every sense adjusted to the hot breeze and the sounds from inland. Two days before it had all been a plague of hot asphalt and city sizzle, the barely disguised disinfectant in the lobby of the Atlantic, the almost pathetic camouflage of bourbon with which they all tried to cover the memory of rum; now, although tense and on guard and barely letting himself think, the smell of Oriente was

penetrating him, the single unmistakable call of the night
bird that might have been welcoming him: it was better to
think of it that way, like an incantation.

At first York had thought it mad for Jiménez to go
ashore so close to Santiago, it was against all principles; for
that very reason and because Jiménez knew the terrain like
no one else, York accepted the risk and arranged for the electric launch. The problem was not to get his shoes dirty, to
arrive at the motel with the look of a tourist from the provinces who was traveling around his country; there Alfonso
would take charge of getting him set up, the rest was a matter
of a few hours, the plastic charge in the place agreed upon
and back to the shore where the launch and Alfonso would be
waiting; the remote control was on board and once they were
at sea the reverberation from the explosion and the first
flames from the factory would send them off with full honors.
For the moment it was necessary to go to the motel using the
old road, abandoned since they'd built the new highway farther to the north, resting a bit before the last leg so that no
one would suspect the weight of the suitcase when Jiménez
met Alfonso and the latter would take it with the gesture of a
friend, avoiding the solicitous bellboy and taking Jiménez to
one of the better-located rooms in the motel. It was the dangerous part of the whole thing, but the only possible access
was through the motel garden; with luck, with Alfonso,
everything would turn out well.

Of course there was no one on the road that had been
invaded by underbrush and disuse, only the smell of Oriente
and the complaint of the bird that bothered Jiménez for a
moment, as if his nerves needed some pretext to relax a little,
so that against his will he could accept the fact that he was
defenseless there, without a pistol in his pocket because York
had been firm about that, the mission would be accomplished

or would fail, but a pistol was of no use in either case and, in fact, it could ruin everything. York had his ideas about Cuban character and Jiménez knew it and cursed him from deep inside while he climbed up the road and the lights of the few houses and the motel were opening up like yellow eyes in the last part of the underbrush. But there was no need for cursing, everything was going according to schedule, as that fairy York would have said, and Alfonso in the garden of the motel yelling out—if you can believe it!—and where the hell did you leave the car, fellow, the two bellboys watching and listening, I've been waiting for you a quarter of an hour, yes but we got here late and I left the car with a comrade who needed it to go to her family's, she dropped me off at the bend, hey, you're always the perfect gentleman, cut it out, Alfonso, it's nice walking around here, the suitcase going from one hand to the other with perfect lightness, the muscles tense but the gesture muffled, nothing, let's go get your key and then we can have a drink, how did you leave Choli and the kids, a little sad, old man, they wanted to come but you know school and work, this time we didn't coincide, tough luck.

The quick shower, checking that the door locked well, the suitcase open on the other bed and the green bundle in the dresser drawer among shirts and newspapers. At the bar Alfonso had already asked for some extra-drys with plenty of ice; they smoked and talked about Camagüey and Stevenson's last fight, the piano reached them as if from far away although the piano player was right there at the end of the bar, playing something very softly, a habanera and then something by Chopin, going on to a danzón and an old song from the movies, something that in the good old days must have been sung by Irene Dunne. They had another rum and Alfonso said that he'd come by for him in the morning to take him around and show him the new parts of town, there was so much to see in Santiago, they were working hard to finish the plans and go beyond them, the microbrigades were wild, Almeida would come to open two factories, one of those times out there even Fidel dropped by, the comrades were putting their shoulders to the wheel in a way that was a sheer delight.

"Santiagans don't sleep," the bartender said, and they laughed in approval, there were few people in the dining room and Jiménez had already been assigned a table near a window. Alfonso said good night after repeating that he'd come by the next morning; at the table, stretching out his legs, Jiménez began to study the menu. A fatigue that wasn't just in his body obliged him to be careful about every movement. Everything there was placid and cordial and calm and Chopin, who was returning now with that prelude that the pianist was playing very slowly, but Jiménez felt the threat like an ambush, the slightest slip and those smiling faces would turn into masks of hate. He knew those feelings and he knew how to control them; he ordered a mojito in order to pass the time and let himself by advised on the meal, fish rather than meat that night. The dining room was almost empty, a young couple at the bar and farther on a man who looked foreign and was drinking without looking at his glass, his eyes lost on the piano player who was repeating the Irene Dunne theme, now Jiménez recognized "Smoke Gets in Your Eyes," that Havana of times gone by, the piano went back to Chopin, one of the études Jiménez had also played when before the big panic, as a boy, he had taken piano lessons, a slow and melancholy étude that brought back the living room of his house, his dead grandmother, and almost against his will the image of his brother who'd stayed behind in spite of the paternal curse, Robertico who was killed like an imbecile at the Bay of Pigs instead of helping to reconquer the true freedom.

He was almost surprised to find himself eating with a good appetite, savoring what his memory hadn't forgotten, admitting ironically that it was the only good thing after the soggy food they swallowed on the other side. He wasn't sleepy and he liked the music, the piano player was a woman still young and pretty, she played as if for herself without ever looking at the bar, where the foreign-appearing man continued to fiddle with his hands, and began another rum and another cigarette. After coffee Jiménez thought that it was going to be a long time waiting for the moment in his room and he went over to the bar to have another drink. The bartender wanted to chat but he did so with respect for the pianist, almost a murmur as if he understood that the foreigner and Jiménez liked that music, now it was one of the waltzes, the simple melody into which Chopin had put something like slow rain, like talcum powder or pressed flowers in an album. The bartender didn't pay any attention to the foreigner, maybe he couldn't speak Spanish well or was a man of silence, the dining room was closing now and he would have to go sleep, but the pianist went on playing a Cuban melody that Jiménez was leaving behind as he lighted a cigarette and with a sweeping good-night headed for the door and entered what was waiting for him as soon as four a.m. sharp synchronized on his watch and the one on the launch.

Before going into his room he let his eyes become accustomed to the darkness of the garden to be sure of what Alfonso had explained to him, he follows the path about three hundred feet away, goes off it toward the new highway, crosses the highway carefully and continues on toward the west. From the motel he could only see the shadowy place where the path began, but it was useful to detect the lights in the background, two or three toward the left, in order to have a notion of the distance. The factory area began several hundred yards to the west, next to the third concrete post he would find the hole in the fence. Normally it was rare for the sentries to be on that side, they made a round every fifteen minutes, but they preferred chatting with each other on the other side, where there were light and coffee; in any case, getting his clothes dirty no longer mattered, he would have to crawl through the bushes up to the place that Alfonso had described in detail to him. The return would be easy without the green bundle, without all those faces that had surrounded him until now.

He stretched out on his bed almost at once and turned out the light to smoke peacefully; he would even sleep for a while in order to relax his body, he had the habit of waking up on time. But first he made sure that the door locked tightly from the inside and that his things were as he had left them. He hummed a little waltz that had stuck in his memory, mixing up past and present for him, he made an effort to exchange it for "Smoke Gets in Your Eyes," but the little waltz came back or the prelude; he dozed off without being able to get rid of them, still seeing the very white hands of the piano player, her head leaning over to listen attentively to herself. The night bird sang again in some bush or in the palm grove to the north.

Something darker than the darkness of the room woke him, darker and heavier, vaguely at the foot of the bed. He'd been dreaming about Phyllis and the pop music festival, with such intense lights and sounds that opening his eyes was like falling into pure space without barriers, a pit filled with nothing, and at the same time his stomach told him it wasn't like that, that part of it was different, had a different consistency and blackness. He found the light switch with his hand; the foreigner from the bar was sitting at the foot of his bed and looking at him unhurriedly, as if until that moment he'd been watching over his sleep.

Doing something and thinking something were equally inconceivable. Viscera, pure horror, an interminable and perhaps instantaneous silence, the double bridge of gazes. The pistol, the first useless thought; if at least the pistol. A panting that restaged time, rejection of the last possibility that it was still the dream where Phyllis, where the music and the lights and the drinks.

"Yes, that's the way it is," the foreigner said, and Jiménez felt the thick accent as if on his skin, the proof that he wasn't from there, like something about his head and his shoulders already when he'd seen him for the first time at the bar.

Inching himself up, seeking an equality of height at least, a total disadvantage of position, the only thing possible was surprise, but even in that he would be completely lost, broken ahead of time; his muscles weren't going to respond for him, he wouldn't have the leverage in his legs for the desperate shove, and the other one knew it, he was quiet and almost lax at the foot of the bed. When Jiménez saw him take out a cigarette and lose the other hand, sinking it into his pants pocket to get the matches, he knew that he would be wasting his time if he leaped on him; there was too much disdain in his way of paying no attention to him, of not being on the defensive. And something even worse, his own precautions, the door locked, the bolt thrown.

"Who are you?" he heard being asked absurdly from what couldn't be dream or wakefulness.

"What difference does it make?" the foreigner said.

"But Alfonso . . ."

He saw himself watched by something that had a kind of different time, a hollow distance. The flame of the match was reflected in a pair of hazel eyes. The foreigner blew out the match and looked at his hands for a moment.

"Poor Alfonso," he said. "Poor, poor Alfonso."

There was no pity in his words, only a kind of indifferent verification.

"But who the hell are you?" Jiménez shouted, knowing that it was hysteria, the loss of his last control.

"Oh, someone walking around," the foreigner said. "I always come by when they play my music, especially here, you know. I like to hear it played here, on these pitiful little pianos. In my time it was different, I've always had to listen to it away from my own land. That's why I like to come by, it's a kind of reconciliation, justice."

Clenching his teeth in order to control the trembling that gripped him from head to foot, Jiménez managed to think that the only sane thing to do was to decide that the man was mad. It no longer mattered how he'd gotten in, how he knew, because he did know of course, but he was crazy and that was the only possible advantage. To gain time, then, drift with the current, ask him about the piano, the music.

"She plays well," the foreigner said, "but, of course, only what you heard, the easy things. Tonight I would have liked for her to have played that étude they call the Revolutionary, I really would have liked it very much. But she can't, poor thing, she hasn't got the fingers for it. For that you need fingers like these."

His hands raised to shoulder level, he showed Jiménez his separated fingers, long and tense. Jiménez saw them only a second before he felt them on his throat.

Cuba, 1976

THE
FERRY,
OR
ANOTHER
TRIP
TO
VENICE

*Ever since I was young I've been tempted by the idea of
rewriting literary texts that have moved me but the making of which seemed to me to be inferior to their internal
possibilities; I think some stories by Horacio Quiroga
brought this temptation to a limit that dissolved, as is
preferable, into silence and abandonment. What might
have been attempted through love would only be received
as insolent pedantry; I accepted the fact of having to
deplore in my heart of hearts that certain texts had come
to me at a lower level than what something in them and
in me had demanded in vain.*

Fate and a pile of old papers give me today an

analogous opening into that unrealized desire, but the temptation is legitimate in this case since it deals with a text of my own, a long tale entitled The Ferry. *On the last page of the rough draft I find this notation: "How awful! I wrote this in Venice in 1954; I reread it ten years later and I like it, and it's so bad."*

The text and the marginal note were forgotten; twelve more years have been added to the first ten, and rereading these pages now I agree with my note, except that perhaps I'd like to know better why the tale seemed and still seems bad to me and why I liked it and still like it.

What follows is an attempt to show myself that the text of The Ferry *is poorly written because it's false, because it takes place alongside a truth that I was unable to grasp at the time and that has become obvious to me now. Rewriting it would be wearisome and, in some hazy way, disloyal, almost as if it were some other author's tale and then I would be falling into the pedantry I mentioned earlier. I can, on the other hand, leave it just as it was born, and at the same time show what I can now manage to see in it. That's where Dora comes on the scene.*

If Dora had thought of Pirandello, she would have immediately sought out the author to reproach him for his ignorance and his persistent hypocrisy. But I'm the one who's going in her direction now so that in the end she'll lay down the cards face up. Dora can't know who the author of the tale is and her criticism is directed only at what happens in it as seen from within, there where she exists; but the fact that these events happen to be a text and she a character in the writing of it has no effect at all on her equally textual right to rebel at a chronicle she judges insufficient or insidious.

Therefore, from time to time today, Dora's voice will interrupt the original text, which, apart from corrections that are nothing but details and the elimination of short repetitious passages, is the same that I wrote by hand in the Pensione dei Dogi in 1954. In it the reader will find all that seems bad to me as writing and bad to Dora as content, and which, perhaps once again, is the reciprocal effect of a cause that is one and the same.

Tourism plays games with its adepts: it inserts them into a deceptive temporality, it fixes it so that leftover English coins emerge from a pocket in France, one searches in vain in Holland for a taste that only Poitiers can give. For Valentina, the small Roman bar on the Via Quattro Fontane was reduced to Adriano, to the taste of a lingering martini and Adriano's face, which had begged her pardon for having pushed her against the bar. She almost couldn't remember if Dora had been with her that morning, she most likely had been because they were "doing" Rome together, organizing a camaraderie that, like so many, had begun in a silly way at Cook's and American Express.

Of course I was. Right from the start she pretends not to see me, reducing me to the role of an extra who is sometimes a comfort and sometimes an annoyance.

In any case, that bar near the Piazza Barberini was Adriano, another traveler, another idle person circulating the way all tourists circulate in cities, a phantom among men who come and go to and from work, have families, speak the same language, and know what's happening at that moment and not in the archeology of the Blue Guide.

The parts of Adriano that faded away immediately were

his eyes, his hair, his clothing; all that remained was his large and sensuous mouth, the lips that trembled a little after he spoke, while he listened. He listens with his mouth, Valentina had thought when out of the first dialogue there was born an invitation to have one of the bar's famous cocktails, which Adriano recommended and which Beppo, shaking it in a chrome container, proclaimed the jewel of Rome, the whole Tyrrhenian Sea distilled into a glass along with its tritons and sea horses. That day Dora and Valentina found Adriano nice;

Hm.

he didn't look like a tourist (he considered himself a traveler and emphasized the distinction with a smile) and the noon-time dialogue was one more enchantment of Rome in April. Dora forgot him immediately,

> *Not true. Distinguishing between savoir faire and silli-*
> *ness. No one like me (or Valentina, of course) could for-*
> *get someone like Adriano just like that; but it so happens*
> *that I'm intelligent and from the word go I could feel*
> *that my wavelength wasn't his. I'm talking about friend-*
> *ship, not about something else because you can't even*
> *talk about waves in that. And since nothing was possible,*
> *why waste time?*

so busy visiting the Lateran, St. Clement's, everything in one afternoon because they were leaving two days later, Cook's had ended up selling them a complicated itinerary; for her part, Valentina found the pretext of some shopping in order to return to Beppo's bar the following morning. When she saw Adriano, who was staying at a nearby hotel, neither of the two pretended surprise. Adriano was going to Florence a week later and they discussed itineraries, exchange, hotels, guidebooks. Valentina believed in buses but Adriano was pro-train; they went to argue the problem at a trattoria on the Suburra where one could eat fish in an atmosphere that was picturesque for those who were only going there once.

From guidebooks they went on to personal information; Adriano learned about Valentina's divorce in Montevideo and she about his family life on a country estate near Osorno in Chile. They swapped impressions of London, Paris, Naples. Valentina kept looking at Adriano's mouth, she looked at it nakedly at the moment his fork brought the food to the lips that opened to receive it, when one shouldn't look. And he was aware of it and tightened his mouth on the piece of fried octopus as if it were a woman's tongue, as if he were already kissing Valentina.

Not true because of omission: Valentina didn't look at just Adriano that way, she looked at everybody who attracted her; she'd done it to me the moment we met at the counter of American Express, and I know that I wondered if she wasn't probably like me; the way she had of fixing her always somewhat dilated eyes on me . . . Almost at once I found out she wasn't, it wouldn't have bothered me personally to get close to her as part of the no man's land of the trip, but when we decided to share the hotel room I knew that there was something else, that the look came from something that could have been fear or the need to forget. Exaggerated words in that time of simple laughter, shampoo, and touristic happiness; but afterward . . . In any case, Adriano must have taken as a mark of courtesy what a friendly bartender or a woman selling wallets would have received too. By the by, there's also some before-the-fact plagiarism from a famous scene in the movie Tom Jones.

He kissed her that afternoon in his hotel on the Via Nazionale after Valentina telephoned Dora to tell her that she wouldn't be going with her to the Baths of Caracalla.

Wasting a phone call like that!

Adriano had some chilled wine sent up and in his room there were English magazines and a large window facing the western sky. Only the bed was uncomfortable, too narrow for them, but men like Adriano almost always make love on small beds, and Valentina had too many bad memories of her double bed not to enjoy the change.

If Dora suspected anything, she didn't say so.

Not true: I already knew. True: I didn't say anything.

Valentina told her that night that she'd happened to run into Adriano, and that maybe they'd see him again in Florence; when they met him coming out of Orsanmichele three days later, Dora seemed to be the happiest of the three.

In cases like that you have to play dumb so they don't think you are dumb.

Adriano had found the separation unexpectedly exasperating. Suddenly he realized that he missed Valentina, that the promise of meeting again, the hours they would spend together hadn't been enough for him. He was jealous of Dora, he could barely hide it while she—more ugly, more common —carefully repeated to him what she'd read in the guidebook of the Touring Club Italiano.

I've never used Touring Club Italiano guidebooks because they were incomprehensible to me; the Michelin

in French is more than adequate for me. Passons sur le
reste.

When they met at Adriano's hotel at dusk, Valentina mea-
sured the difference between that date and the first one in
Rome; preparations had been made now, the bed was perfect
and on a curiously inlaid table a little box wrapped in blue
paper awaited her, inside it an admirable Florentine cameo
that she—much later, when they were drinking by the
window—pinned to her breast with the easy, almost familiar
gesture of one turning a key in the everyday lock.

> *I have no way of knowing what Valentina's gestures were
> like at that moment, but, in any case, they could never
> have been easy; everything in her was knot, chain, and
> whip. At night, from my bed, I would look at her walk-
> ing around before going to bed, time and again picking
> up and putting down a vial of perfume, a bottle of pills,
> going to the window as if she heard strange noises; or,
> later on, while she was sleeping, that way of sobbing in
> the middle of a dream, waking me up suddenly, making
> me come over to her bed, get her a glass of water, stroke
> her forehead until, calmed down, she went back to sleep.
> And her challenges that first night in Rome when she
> came to sit down beside me: you don't know me, Dora,
> you haven't the slightest idea of what's going on inside
> me, this emptiness full of mirrors that show me a street
> in Punta del Este, a child who's crying because I'm not
> there. Easy, her gestures? For my part, at least, they'd
> shown me from the beginning that I had nothing to ex-
> pect from her on an affectionate level, apart from cam-
> araderie. It's hard for me to imagine that Adriano, mas-
> culinely blind as he might have been, wouldn't come to
> suspect that Valentina was kissing nothingness on his*

> *mouth, that before and after love Valentina would keep
> on crying in her sleep.*

Until then he hadn't fallen in love with the ones he made love to; something in him made him take them too quickly, as if to create the aura, the necessary zone of mystery and desire, to organize the mental hunt that sometimes might be called love. With Valentina it had been the same, but during the days they were separated, during those last sunsets in Rome and the trip to Florence, something different had burst forth in Adriano. Without surprise, without humility, almost without marvel, he saw her rise up in the golden shadows of Orsanmichele, emerging out of Orcagna's tabernacle as if one of the innumerable small stone figures had broken away from the monument to come to meet him. Only then perhaps did he realize that he was falling in love with her. Or perhaps afterward, in the hotel, when Valentina had wept as she embraced him without giving any reasons, letting herself go like a child who gives in to a long-contained necessity and finds relief mingled with shame, with disapproval.

As for what was immediate and superficial, Valentina was weeping over the precariousness of the meeting. Adriano would go on his way a few days later; they wouldn't meet again because the episode was going into a vulgar calendar of vacations, a framework of hotels and cocktails and ritual phrases. Only their bodies would emerge sated, as always, for a while they would have the filled-up feeling of a dog who finishes his chewing and flops down in the sun with a grunt of contentment. In itself the meeting was perfect, bodies brought to press together, entwine, hold back or provoke delight. But when she looked at Adriano sitting on the edge of the bed (and he looked at her with his thick-lipped mouth) Valentina felt that the rite just fulfilled had no real content, that the instruments of passion were hollow, that there was no spirit in them. All of that had been tolerable and even favorable in other situations during that hour, and yet this time she would have wanted to have held Adriano, delayed the moment of getting dressed and leaving, those gestures that in some way were already announcing a farewell.

Something was meant to be said here without being said, without understanding anything but an uncertain rumor. Valentina had also looked at me while we bathed and got dressed in Rome, before Adriano; I too had felt that those breaks in the continuum were doing her harm, were pulling her toward the future. The first time I made the mistake of implying it, of going over and stroking her hair and suggesting we have some drinks sent up and watch the sunset from the window. Her answer was dry, she hadn't come out of Uruguay to spend her time in a hotel. I thought simply that she still didn't trust me, that she attributed a precise meaning to that hint of a caress, just as I had misunderstood her first look in the travel agency. Valentina looked, without knowing exactly why; it was the rest of us who gave in to that obscure interrogation that had something of a pursuit about it, but a pursuit that didn't concern us.

Dora was waiting for them in one of the cafés on the Signoria, she had just discovered Donatello and explained him much too emphatically, as if her enthusiasm were serving her as a cape to help hide some irritation.

"Of course we're going to see the statues," Valentina said, "but we couldn't go into museums this afternoon, there was too much sun to go to museums."

"You won't be here long enough to afford to sacrifice all that for the sun."

Adriano made a vague gesture, waiting for Valentina's words. It was hard to tell what Dora represented for Valentina, whether the pair's trip was already laid out and wouldn't allow any changes. Dora returned to Donatello, piling up the useless references one makes in the absence of a work. Valentina was looking at the tower of the Signoria, mechanically taking out her cigarettes.

I think it happened exactly like that, and for the first time Adriano really suffered, he was afraid that I represented the sacred trip, culture as a duty, train and hotel reservations. But if someone had asked him about the other possible solution, he would only have been able to think about something like that beside Valentina, with no precise goal.

The next day they went to the Uffizi. As if hiding from the necessity of a decision, Valentina clung obstinately to Dora's presence so as not to leave any opening for Adriano. Only for one fleeting moment, when Dora hung back looking at a portrait, was he able to speak to her intimately.

"Will you come this afternoon?"

"Yes," Valentina said without looking at him, "at four o'clock."

"I love you so much," Adriano murmured, stroking her shoulder with fingers that were almost timid. "Valentina, I love you so much."

A group of American tourists entered, preceded by the nasal voice of their guide. Their faces drew apart, avidly empty, falsely interested in the painting they would forget an hour later with spaghetti and wine at the Castelli Romani.

Dora was also coming along thumbing through her guide-book, lost because the numbers in the catalogue didn't correspond with those on the pictures.

> *On purpose, of course. In order to let them talk, make a date, get fed up. Not him, I already knew that, but her. And not to get fed up, but, rather, to get back to the ever-present impulse to flee, which might bring her back to my way of accompanying her without badgering her, waiting simply by her side, even though it did no good.*

"I love you so much," Adriano repeated that afternoon as he leaned over Valentina, who was resting on her back. "You can feel it, can't you? It's not in the words, it's got nothing to do with saying it, with looking for names for it. Tell me you can feel it, that you can't explain it but that you can feel it now that . . ."

He sank his head between her breasts, kissing her for a long time, as if he were drinking in the fever that throbbed in Valentina's flesh as she stroked his hair with a distant, distracted gesture.

> *D'Annunzio lived in Venice, didn't he? Unless it was Hollywood scriptwriters . . .*

"Yes, you love me," she said. "But it's as if you were also afraid of something, not of loving me, but . . . Not afraid, maybe, anxious, rather. You're worried about what's going to happen now."

"I don't know what's going to happen; I haven't got the slightest idea. How could I be afraid of so much emptiness? My fear is you, it's a concrete fear, here and now. You don't love me as much as I love you, Valentina, or you love me in a different way, limited or held back, who knows for what reason."

Valentina was listening to him, closing her eyes. Slowly, coinciding with what he had just said, she glimpsed something behind, something that at first was only an empty space, a restlessness. She felt too happy at that moment to let the slightest fault mingle with that pure and perfect hour in which both had made love with no thought other than that of not wanting to think. At the same time, however, she couldn't help understanding Adriano's words. She was suddenly measuring the fragility of that touristic situation under a borrowed roof, between alien sheets, threatened by railroad timetables, itineraries that carried them into different lives, motives that were unknown and probably antagonistic as always.

"You don't love me the way I love you," Adriano said again, rancorously. "I'm useful to you, I'm useful to you, like a knife or a waiter, nothing else."

"Please," Valentina said. *"Je t'en prie."*

It was so hard to realize why they were no longer happy so few minutes after something that had been like happiness.

"I know very well I'll have to go back," Valentina said without taking her fingers away from Adriano's anxious face. "My son, my job, so many obligations. My son's quite small, quite defenseless."

"I have to go back too," Adriano said, averting his eyes. "I've got a job too, a thousand things."

"So you see."

"No, I don't see. How do you expect me to see? If you make me consider this as just an episode on a trip, you'll take everything away from it, you'll squash it like a bug. I love you, Valentina. Loving is more than remembering or preparing yourself to remember."

"I'm not the one you have to tell that to. No, not me. I'm afraid of time, time is death, its horrible disguise. Don't you realize that we love each other against time, that we have to deny time?"

"Yes," Adriano said, dropping down on his back beside her, "and it so happens that you're leaving for Bologna the day after tomorrow, and a day later I'm going to Lucca."

"Be quiet."

"Why? Your time is Cook's time, even though you try to fill it up with metaphysics. Mine, on the other hand, is decided by my whim, my pleasure, the railroad timetables I accept or reject."

"So you see," Valentina murmured. "You see how we have to give in to the evidence. What else is there?"

"Coming with me. Leaving your famous excursion, let Dora talk about what she doesn't know. Let's leave together."

He's referring to my pictorial enthusiasm; we won't discuss whether he's right or not. In any case, both of them are talking with a mirror in front, a perfect dialogue for a best seller, meant to fill up two pages with nothing in particular. Yes, no, that time . . . Everything was so clear to me, Valentina piuma al vento, neurosis and depression and a double dose of Valium at night, the same old picture of our youthful period. A wager with myself (at this moment I remember it well): of the two evils, Valentina would choose the lesser, me. No problem with me (if she chose me); at the end of the trip good-bye, my dear, it was all so nice and so beautiful, good-bye, good-bye. On the other hand, Adriano . . . Both of us sensed the same thing: you don't fool with Adriano's mouth. Those lips . . . (To think that she let them know every inch of her skin; there are things that are beyond me, of course it's a question of libido, we know we know we know.)

And yet it was easier to kiss him, give in to his strength, slip blandly under the wave of the body that held her; it was easier to give in than to refuse the assent that he, lost in pleasure again, was already forgetting.

Valentina was the first to get up. The water in the shower lashed her for a long time. Putting on a bathrobe, she went back into the bedroom, where Adriano was still on the bed, half sitting up and smiling at her as if from an Etruscan tomb, smoking slowly.

"I want to see night coming on from the balcony."

On the banks of the Arno, the hotel received the last light. The streetlights on the Ponte Vecchio still hadn't gone on, and the river was a purple ribbon with lighter fringes, flown over by small bats hunting invisible insects; higher up the swallows' scissors squeaked. Valentina stretched out in the rocker, breathing in the now cool air. A sweet fatigue overcame her, she could have fallen asleep; maybe she did sleep for a few seconds. But in that hiatus of abandonment she continued thinking about Adriano and time, the monotonous words came back like the chorus of a silly song, time is death, a disguise of death, time is death. She looked at the sky, the swallows playing their neat games, squeaking briefly as if they were shattering the deep blue pottery of sunset. And Adriano was also death.

Curious. After so many false premises suddenly he touches bottom. It might be simpler that way (thinking about it some other day, in other contexts). It's surprising that beings who are so far removed from their own truth (Valentina more than Adriano, that's for sure) hit the mark at times; they don't realize it, of course, and it's

better that way: what follows proves it. (I mean it's
better for me, if you take a good look at it.)

She straightened up, rigid. Adriano was also death. Had she
thought that? Adriano was also death. It didn't make the least
bit of sense, she'd threaded the words together as in a childish
refrain and that absurdity had emerged. She stretched out
once more, relaxing, and she looked at the swallows again.
Maybe it wasn't so absurd; in any case, having thought it was
only good as a metaphor, since denying Adriano would kill
something in her, would pull her out of a momentary part of
herself, would leave her alone with a different Valentina, a
Valentina without Adriano, with Adriano's love, if that bab-
bling for so few days was love, if in herself that furious surrender to a body that dissolved her and returned her as if
exhausted to the abandonment of the sunset was love. In that
way, yes, seen in that way Adriano was death. Everything one
possesses is death because it presages dispossession, it sets up
the emptiness to come. Childish refrains, tra-la-la, but she
couldn't give up her itinerary, remain with Adriano. The
accomplice of death, then, she would let him go to Lucca
simply because it was inevitable sooner or later, there in the
distance Buenos Aires and her son were like the swallows
over the Arno, twittering weakly, plaintive in the nightfall
that was spreading like black wine.

"I'll stay," Valentina murmured. "I love him, I love
him. I'll stay and I'll take him away with me someday."

She knew quite well that it wouldn't be that way, that
Adriano wouldn't change his life for her, Osorno for Buenos
Aires.

How could she know? Everything points in the opposite
direction; it's Valentina who will never exchange Buenos
Aires for Osorno, her established life, her River Plate

> *routines. Underneath I don't think she was thinking*
> *what she's being made to think; it's also certain that*
> *cowardice tends to project one's own responsibility into*
> *others, etc.*

She felt as if she were floating in the air, almost alien to her body, only fear and something like anxiety. She saw a flock of swallows that had bunched together over the middle of the river, flying in great circles. One of the swallows broke away from the rest, losing altitude, coming closer. When it seemed as if it were going to fly up again, something in that marvelous mechanism failed. Like a dull piece of lead, spinning about by itself, it plunged diagonally and with an opaque thud landed on the balcony at Valentina's feet.

Adriano heard the scream and came running. Valentina was covering her face and trembling horribly, taking refuge at the other end of the balcony. Adriano saw the dead swallow and pushed it with his foot. The swallow fell to the street.

"Come inside," he said, taking Valentina by the shoulders. "It's nothing, it's all over. You were scared, poor thing."

Valentina was silent, but when he took her hands away and saw her face he was frightened. He was only reflecting her fear, perhaps the final fear of the swallow as it plunged down out of air that, unfriendly and cruel, had suddenly ceased to sustain it.

Dora liked to chat before going to sleep and she spent half an hour on items about Fiesole and the Piazzale Michelangelo. Valentina listened to her as if from far away, lost in an internal sound that couldn't be confused with meditation. The swallow was dead; it had died in full flight. A presage, an intimation. As if in a strangely lucid half-dream Adriano and the swallow had begun to be confused in her, turning into an almost ferocious desire to escape, break away. She didn't feel guilty of anything but she felt the fault itself, the swallow landing dully at her feet like a fault.

She told Dora in a few words that she was going to change her plans, that she was going directly to Venice.

"You'll meet me there in any case. I'm only moving up two days, I really prefer being alone for a few days."

Dora didn't seem too surprised. Too bad that Valentina would miss Ravenna, Ferrara. In any case, she understood that she preferred going directly and alone to Venice; better to see one city well than two or three badly . . . Valentina was no longer listening to her, lost in her mental flight, in the race that was to take her away from the present, away from a balcony over the Arno.

Here it's almost all true, starting with the mistake, which is ironical and amusing. I accept the business of my not being too surprised and that I performed the necessary lip service to tranquilize Valentina. What isn't known is that my lack of surprise had other roots, Valentina's voice and face as she told me about the balcony episode, so out of proportion unless one felt it as she felt it, a presage beyond all logic and therefore irresistible. And also a delightful, cruel suspicion that Valentina was confusing the reasons for her fear, confusing me with Adriano. Her polite distance that night, her rapid way of getting ready and going to bed without giving me the opportunity of sharing the bathroom mirror, the rites of the shower, le temps d'un sein nu entre deux chemises. Adriano, yes, let's say yes, that Adriano. But why that way of going to bed and turning her back to me, cover-

*ing her face with an arm to suggest that I turn out the
light as soon as possible, that I let her sleep without any
more words, without even a soft good-night kiss between
the two traveling companions?*

On the train she thought about it in a better way, but the fear
was still there. What was she escaping from? It wasn't easy
accepting the solutions of prudence, praising herself for having broken the bond in time. There remained the enigma of
fear, as if Adriano, poor Adriano, were the devil, as if the
temptation of really falling in love with him were the balcony
that opened onto emptiness, the invitation to the irresistible
leap.

Valentina vaguely thought that she was fleeing from herself more than from Adriano. Even the rapidity with which
she'd surrendered in Rome proved her resistance to all seri-
ousness, to all basic new beginnings. The basic had remained
on the other side of the ocean, torn to shreds forever, and
now it was the time of adventure without ties, as with others
already, before and during the trip, the acceptance of circum-
stance without any moral or logical analysis, Dora's episodic
company as the product of a counter at a travel agency,
Adriano at another counter, the time for a cocktail or a city,
moments and pleasures as hazy as the furniture in the hotel
rooms that were being left behind.

*Episodic company, yes. But I would like to believe that
there's more in that reference which would at least equate
Adriano and me as two sides of a triangle where the
third is a counter.*

And yet, Adriano in Florence had advanced toward her with
the demands of the possessor, no longer the fugitive lover

from Rome; worse still, demanding reciprocity, waiting for her and urging her. Maybe the fear was born of that, it was nothing but a dirty, base fear of mundane complications, Buenos Aires/Osorno, people, children, reality installing itself in such a different way in the calendar of that shared life. And maybe not: something else always behind, ungraspable like a swallow in flight. Something that could suddenly have plunged down on her, a dead body hitting her.

> *Hm. Why did nothing go right for her with men? While she thinks the way she's made to think, there's a kind of image of something penned up, besieged: the profound truth, encircled by the lies of an undeniable conformism. Poor thing. Poor thing.*

The first days in Venice were gray and almost cold, but on the third the sun burst through early and it warmed up immediately and with the heat came the tourists who were enthusiastically leaving the hotels and filling the Piazza San Marco and the Merceria in a merry disorder of colors and tongues.

Valentina found it pleasant to let herself be borne along by the rhythmical serpent that went up the Merceria in the direction of the Rialto. Every bend, the Ponte dei Baretieri, San Salvatore, the dark postcard space of the Fondamento dei Tedeschi, received her with that impersonal calm Venice offers its tourists, so different from the convulsive expectation of Naples or the broad opening of the panoramas of Rome. Withdrawn, always secretive, Venice was playing at hiding its true face once more, smiling impersonally at the hope that on a propitious day and hour it will show its real self to the good traveler as recompense for his faithfulness. From the Rialto Valentina looked at the splendors of the Grand Canal and she was surprised at the unexpected distance between her and that luxury of water and gondolas. She penetrated into the alleyways that from *campo* to *campo* led her to churches and museums, went out onto the docks from which she could face the façades of the great palaces corroded by a green and leaden time. She saw everything, she admired everything, knowing, nevertheless, that her reactions were conventional and almost forced, like the repeated praise for the pictures shown us in family albums. Something—blood, anxiety, or just an urge to live—seemed to have remained behind. Valentina suddenly hated the memory of Adriano, found repugnant the petulance of Adriano, who had made the mistake of falling in love with her. His absence made him all the more hateful because his mistake was of the kind that is only punished or pardoned in person. Venice

Having taken a choice, he makes Valentina think the way he wants, but other choices are possible if one keeps in mind the fact that she opted to go to Venice alone. Can exaggerated terms like hate and repugnance really be applied to Adriano? A mere change in the prism and it's not Adriano that Valentina is thinking about as she wanders through Venice. That's why my friendly Florentine faithlessness was necessary: it was necessary to keep on projecting Adriano into the center of an action, which, perhaps in that way, perhaps toward the end of the trip, would return me to that beginning where I had hoped, as I was still capable of hoping.

presented itself to her like an admirable stage without actors, without the sap of participation. Better that way, but also much worse; walking through the alleyways, lingering on the little bridges that cover the dreams of the canals like eyelids, began to seem like a nightmare. To awake, to be awakened by any means, but Valentina felt that only something resembling a whiplash could awaken her. She accepted the offer of a gondolier who proposed taking her to San Marco through the interior canals; sitting in the old easy chair with red cushions, she felt that Venice was beginning to move delicately, to pass by her as she looked at it like an immobile eye obstinately fixed on itself.

"Ca' d'Oro," said the gondolier, breaking a long silence, and he pointed to the façade of the palace. Then, entering the Rio di San Felice, the gondola was swallowed up in a dark and silent labyrinth, smelling of mildew. Like all tourists, Valentina admired the impeccable skill of the oarsman, his way of calculating the bends and avoiding obstacles. She sensed him behind her, invisible but alive, plunging in his oar almost noiselessly, sometimes exchanging a brief phrase in dialect with someone on the bank. She had hardly looked at him when she got in; he seemed to her to be like the majority of gondoliers, tall and thin, his body held in by tight black pants, his jacket vaguely Spanish, his hat made of yellow straw, with a red band. She remembered, rather, his voice, sweet but not low, offering: "Gondola, signorina, gondola, gondola." She had accepted the price and the itinerary, distractedly, but now, when the man called her attention to the Ca' d'Oro and she had to turn to look at him, she noticed the strength of his features, the almost imperious nose and the small, astute eyes; a mixture of pride and calculation, also present in the unexaggerated vigor of his torso and the relative smallness of his head, with something of a viper at the joining with the neck, perhaps in the movements imposed by the rhythmic rowing.

Looking toward the prow again, Valentina saw a small bridge coming up. Already before she had said to herself how delightful the instant of passing under the bridges must be, losing oneself for a moment in the concavity that reeked with mildew, imagining the pedestrians up above, but now she watched the bridge coming up with a vague anguish, as if it were the gigantic cover of a large chest that was going to close over her. She made herself keep her eyes open during the brief transit, but she suffered, and when the narrow strip of bright sky rose up above her again, she made a confused gesture of thanks. The gondolier was pointing out another palace, one of those which only let themselves be seen from the inner canals and which pedestrians have no suspicion of since they only see the service entrances, exactly like so many others. Valentina would have liked to have made a comment, to have become interested in the simple information the gondolier was giving her; suddenly she had to be close to something alive and alien at the same time, to get caught up in a dialogue which would take her away from that absence, from that nothingness which was vitiating the day and things for her. She rose and went to seat herself on a small crosspiece closer to the prow. The gondola wobbled for a moment

If the "absence" was Adriano, I can find no proportion between the preceding conduct on the part of Valentina and this angst that is ruining a ride in a gondola for her, which was not at all cheap. I will never know what her Venetian nights in the hotel were like, the bedroom without words or the day's recounting; maybe Adriano's absence was gaining weight in Valentina, but once again, like the mask of another distance, of another lack she didn't want to or couldn't look in the face. (Wishful thinking, perhaps; but what about that vaunted female intuition? The night we reached for a jar of cream at the same time and my hand came to rest on hers and we

*looked at each other . . . Why didn't I complete the
caress that chance had begun? In some way everything
remained as if suspended in the air between us, and
gondola rides, it is well known, are the exhumers of half-
dreams, nostalgias, and repentant tallies.)*

but the oarsman didn't seem to be surprised at the conduct of
his passenger. And when she asked him, smiling, what he had
said, he repeated his information in greater detail, satisfied
with the interest he was arousing.

"What's on the other side of the island?" Valentina
wanted to know in her rudimentary Italian.

"On the other side, signorina? On the Fondamente
Nuove?"

"If that's what it's called . . . I mean the other side,
where the tourists don't go."

"Yes, the Fondamente Nuove," the gondolier said, rowing very slowly now. "Well, the boats for Burano and Torcello
leave from there."

"I still haven't been to those islands."

"It's very interesting, signorina. The lace factories. But
this side isn't so interesting, because the Fondamente
Nuove—"

"I like to know places that aren't tourist spots," Valentina said, diligently repeating the desire of all tourists. "What
else is there on the Fondamente Nuove?"

"The cemetery is across the way," the gondolier said.
"It's not interesting."

"On an island?"

"Yes, across from the Fondamente Nuove. Look, signorina, ecco Santi Giovanni e Paolo. Bella chiesa, bellissima
. . . Ecco il Colleoni, capolavoro dal Verrocchio . . ."

Tourists, Valentina thought. They and we, the ones to

explain and the others to think we understand. In the end, let's look at your church, let's look at your monument, molto interessante, vero . . .

> *So many cheap tricks, after all. Valentina is made to speak and think when it's a matter of foolishness; otherwise, silence or attributions almost always aimed in the wrong direction. Why don't we hear more of what Valentina might have murmured before falling asleep, why don't we know more about her body in her solitude, about her look when she opened the hotel window every morning?*

The gondola came alongside the Riva degli Schiavoni, by the Piazzetta crowded with strollers. Valentina was hungry and was getting bored in advance thinking that she was going to eat alone. The gondolier helped her ashore, received his payment and tip with a flashing smile.

"If the signorina would like to take another ride, I'm always over there." He pointed to a distant mooring, marked by four poles with lanterns. "My name is Dino," he added, touching the brim of his hat.

"Thank you," Valentina said. She was about to go off, plunge into the human tide of shouts and photographs. There behind her back would remain the only living creature with whom she had exchanged a few words.

"Dino."

"Signorina?"

"Dino . . . where can a person get a good meal?"

The gondolier gave an open laugh, but he was looking at Valentina as if at the same time he understood that the question wasn't a tourist stupidity.

"Does the signorina know the ristoranti over the Canal?" he asked a little by chance, testing.

"Yes," said Valentina, who didn't know them. "I mean a quiet place, without many people."

"Without many people . . . like the signorina?" the man said brutally.

Valentina smiled at him, amused. Dino wasn't stupid at least.

"Without tourists, yes. A place like . . ."

The one where you and your friends eat, she was thinking, but she didn't say it. She felt the man rest his fingers on her elbow, smiling, and he invited her to get into the gondola. She let herself be taken, almost intimidated, but the shadow of boredom was erased immediately, as if dragged away by Dino's gesture as he drove the blade of the oar to the bottom of the lagoon and pushed the gondola along with a clean movement in which one barely noticed the effort.

It was impossible to remember the route. They'd passed under the Ponte dei Sospiri, but then everything became confused. Valentina would close her eyes at times and let herself be carried along by other vague images that paraded by parallel to what she refused to see. The midday sun was raising a foul-smelling vapor off the canals and everything was being repeated, the shouts in the distance, the accepted signals at corners. There were few people on the streets and bridges in that section; Venice was now having lunch. Dino was sculling forcefully and finally he put the gondola into a narrow, straight canal at the end of which the greenish gray of the lagoon could be glimpsed. Valentina said to herself that the Fondamente Nuove must be there, the other bank, the place that wasn't interesting. She was going to turn around and ask when she felt the boat stop alongside some mossy steps. Dino gave a long whistle and a window on the second floor opened noiselessly.

"It's my sister," he said. "We live here. Would you like to eat with us, signorina?"

Valentina's acceptance came ahead of her surprise, her almost irritation. The man's confidence was of the kind that allowed no middle way; Valentina could have refused with the same strength with which she had just accepted. Dino helped her up the steps and left her waiting while he moored the gondola. She heard him singing softly in dialect, in a rather muted voice. She felt a presence behind her and turned; a woman of indeterminate age, poorly dressed in faded pink, was peeping out the door. Dino spoke some unintelligible phrases to her.

"The signorina is a nice lady," he added in Tuscan. "Let her in, Rosa."

And she's going to go in, of course. Anything so long as she can keep on escaping, keep on lying to herself. Life, lie, wasn't it a character in O'Neill who pointed out that life and lie are only separated by one single innocent letter?

They ate in a room with a low ceiling, which surprised Valentina, already used to grand Italian spaces. At the black wooden table there was room for six people. Dino, who had changed his shirt without getting rid of that smell of perspiration, was sitting across from Valentina. Rosa was to her left. On the right the pet cat who, with his dignified beauty, helped them break the ice of the first moments. There was pasta *asciutta*, a large bottle of wine, and fish. Valentina found everything excellent and was almost happy with what her drowsing good sense continued to consider a folly.

"The signorina has a good appetite," said Rosa, who barely spoke. "Have a little cheese."

"Yes, thank you."

Dino was eating avidly, looking more at his plate than at Valentina, but she had the impression that he was observing her in some way, without asking her questions; not even asking her what nationality she was, just the opposite of almost all Italians. In the end, Valentina thought, such an absurd situation has got to explode. What could they say to each other when the last mouthful had been consumed? That terrible moment after a meal among strangers. She petted the cat, gave him a little piece of cheese to taste. Dino was laughing now, his cat ate only fish.

"Have you been a gondolier long?" Valentina asked, looking for an opening.

"Five years, signorina."

"Do you like it?"

"Non si sta male."

"In any case, it doesn't seem to be such hard work."

"No . . . that it isn't."

Then he does other things too, she thought. Rosa served her some more wine, and although she didn't want to have any more, the brother and sister insisted, smiling, and filled the glasses. "The cat doesn't drink," Dino said, looking into her eyes for the first time in a long while. The three laughed.

Rosa left and came back with a plate of small fruits. Then Dino accepted a Camel and said that Italian tobacco was no good. He smoked leaning backward, rolling his eyes; sweat was running down his muscular bronzed neck.

"Is my hotel very far from here?" Valentina asked. "I don't want to bother you any longer."

I really should pay for this lunch, she was thinking, debating the problem and not knowing how to solve it. She named her hotel and Dino said he would take her there. Rosa had left the dining room a moment before. The cat, stretched out in a corner, was dozing in the heat of siesta time. It smelled of canal, old houses.

"Well, you people certainly have been kind," Valentina said, pushing back the rough chair and rising. "I'm sorry I can't say it in good Italian . . . In any case, you understand me."

"Oh, of course," Dino said without moving.

"I'd like to say good-bye to your sister, and . . ."

"Oh, Rosa. She's probably gone out. She always goes out at this time."

Valentina remembered a brief, incomprehensible dialogue in the middle of the lunch. It was the only time they'd spoken in dialect, and Dino had apologized. Without knowing why, she thought that Rosa's leaving had come out of that conversation and she felt a little afraid, and also ashamed at being afraid.

Dino in turn got up. Only then did she notice how tall he was. The little eyes were looking toward the door, the only door. The door opened into a bedroom (the sister had made excuses for having to go through it on their way to the dining room). Valentina picked up her straw hat and purse. He has beautiful hair, she thought. She felt uneasy and at the same time sure of herself, occupied. It was better than the bitter emptiness of that whole morning; now there was something, she was confidently facing somebody.

"I'm so sorry," she said, "I would have liked to have said good-bye to your sister. Thank you for everything."

She held out her hand and he shook it without squeezing, letting go of it immediately. Valentina felt her vague uneasiness disappearing before this unpolished gesture full of timidity. She went toward the door, followed by Dino. She

went into the other room, barely making out the furniture in
the shadows. Wasn't the door that led to the hallway on the
right? Behind her she heard Dino close the dining room door.
Now the room seemed much darker. With an involuntary
gesture she turned to wait for him to precede her. An exhala-
tion of sweat enveloped her a second before Dino's arms enwrapped her brutally. She closed her eyes, barely resisting.
If she could have, she would have killed him right there,
beating him until she caved in his face, breaking that mouth
that was kissing her throat while a hand ran along her con-
tracted body. She tried to get loose and fell suddenly backward onto the shadow of a bed. Dino let himself slip on top of
her, holding down her legs, kissing her full on the mouth
with lips that were damp from wine. Valentina closed her
eyes again. If he'd taken a bath at least, she thought, ceasing
to resist. Dino held her prisoner for a moment, as if aston-
ished at that surrender. Then, murmuring and kissing her,
he got on top of her and with clumsy fingers looked for the
buttons of her blouse.

> *Perfect, Valentina. As Anglo-Saxon* sagesse *teaches, hav-
> ing prevented many deaths by strangulation in that way,
> the only thing to do in such circumstances was the in-
> telligent relax-and-enjoy-it.*

At four o'clock, with the sun still high, the gondola docked by
San Marco. As he did the first time, Dino offered his forearm
for Valentina to lean on, and he stood as if waiting, looking
into her eyes.

"Arrivederci," Valentina said, and started to walk.

"I'll be there tonight," Dino said pointing to the mooring poles. "At ten o'clock."

Valentina went directly to the hotel in search of a hot

bath. Nothing could be more important than that, getting rid of Dino's smell, the contamination of the sweat, the saliva that stained her. With a moan of pleasure she slipped into the steaming tub and for a long time was incapable of reaching out her hand toward the cake of green soap. Afterward, diligently, to the rhythm of her thoughts as they returned little by little, she began to wash.

The memory wasn't painful. Everything sordid about its preparations seemed to be erased by the thing itself. She'd been tricked, drawn into a stupid trap, but she was too smart not to understand that she herself had woven the net. In that confused skein of memories she found Rosa especially repugnant, the evasive figure of the accomplice who now, in light of what had happened, was hard to think of as Dino's sister. His slave, rather, his mistress, willing, out of necessity, in order to keep him for a while longer.

She stretched out in the bath, aching. Dino had conducted himself like what he was, furiously demanding his pleasures with no consideration of any kind. He had possessed her like an animal, over and over, demanding ugly things of her that wouldn't have been ugly if he'd had a minimum of gentleness. And Valentina didn't regret it, didn't regret the stuffy smell of the unmade bed, Dino's panting like a dog, the vague attempt at reconciliation afterward (because Dino was afraid, he was already weighing the possible consequences of his rape of a foreign woman). In reality she regretted nothing except the lack of grace in the adventure. And maybe she didn't even regret that, the brutality had been there like the garlic in common people's stew, the indispensable and tasty requisite.

It amused her, a little hysterically,

No, no. Not hysteria. Only I could see Valentina's expression here the night I told her the story of my fellow student Nancy in Morocco, an identical situation but much uglier, with her rapist Islamically frustrated when he found out that Nancy was in full menstruation, and with blows and whipping making her render him the other route. (I didn't find what I was looking for when I told her, but I saw that her eyes were like a wolf's for an instant before she rejected the theme and sought as always the pretext of fatigue and sleep.) Maybe if Adriano had proceeded like Dino, without the garlic and the sweat, skillful and beautiful. Maybe if I, instead of letting her go to sleep . . .

to think that Dino, while he tried to help her dress with absurdly clumsy hands, had attempted the tenderness of a lover, too grotesque even for himself to believe. Making the date, for example, when he said good-bye to her at San Marco, was ridiculous. Imagining that she could come back to his house, cold-bloodedly give herself to him . . . It didn't make her the least bit upset, she was certain that Dino was an excellent individual in his way, he hadn't added robbery to rape, which would have been easy, and she even admitted that there was a more normal, more logical tone in what had happened than in her encounter with Adriano.

You see, Dora, you see, stupid?

The terrible thing was to realize to what point Dino was far away from her, without the slightest possibility of communication. With the last gesture of pleasure, silence began, upset, the ridiculous comedy. There was one advantage after all: she didn't have to run away from Dino as she did from Adriano. No danger of falling in love; not even he would fall in love, of course. What freedom! With all his filth, the adventure didn't disgust her, especially after she had soaped herself.

Dora arrived from Padua at dinnertime bubbling over with news of Giotto and Altichiero. She found that Valentina was very well and said that Adriano had spoken vaguely about giving up his trip to Lucca, but that afterward she'd lost sight of him. "I'd say that he's fallen in love with you," she dropped in passing, with her oblique laugh. She was enchanted with Venice, of which she hadn't even seen anything, and boasted of being able to guess how wonderful the city was just by the conduct of the waiters and the *facchini.* "Everything so refined, so refined," she repeated, savoring her shrimp.

> *If you'll excuse the word, never in my fucking life have I said a phrase like that. What kind of unknown vengeance lies in this? Or rather (yes, I'm beginning to sense it, believe it), everything is born of a subconscious that has also made Valentina be born, that not knowing her on the surface and being mistaken all the time about her conduct and her motives, hitting the mark without knowing it in deeper waters, there where Valentina hasn't forgotten Rome, the counter at the agency, the acceptance of sharing a room and a trip. In those flashes that are made by fish out of the abyss as they appear for a second over the water, I am deliberately deformed and offended, I become what they make me say.*

There was talk of Venice by night, but Dora was done in by the beaux-arts and returned to the hotel after two turns about the square. Valentina performed the ritual of drinking port at the Florian, and waited for it to be ten o'clock. Mingling with the people who were eating ice cream and taking flash pictures, she spied the quay. There were only two gondolas on that side, with their lanterns lighted. Dino was on the dock, next to a pole. He was waiting.

He really thinks I'm going to go, she thought, almost with surprise. An English-looking couple went over to the gondolier. Valentina saw him take off his hat and offer the gondola. The couple got in almost at once; the small lantern trembled in the night of the lagoon.

Vaguely upset, Valentina returned to the hotel.

The morning light washed away her bad dreams, but without removing a certain feeling of nausea, the pressure at the mouth of the stomach. Dora was waiting for her in the salon for breakfast, and Valentina was pouring herself some tea when a waiter came to the table.

"The signorina's gondolier is outside."

"Gondolier? I haven't asked for any gondola."

"The man indicated the signorina."

Dora was looking at her with curiosity and Valentina felt herself suddenly naked. She made an effort to swallow some tea and got up after hesitating a moment. Amused, Dora thought it would be fun to watch the scene from the window. She saw the gondolier, Valentina going to meet him, the man's curt but decisive greeting. Valentina was speaking to him almost without gestures, but she saw her raise a hand as if begging—of course it couldn't be—for something that the other refused to grant. Then it was he who spoke, moving his arms Italian fashion. Valentina seemed to be waiting for him to go away, but the man insisted, and Dora stayed there long enough to see Valentina look at her wristwatch and make a sign of assent.

"I'd forgotten completely," she explained on returning, "but a gondolier doesn't forget his customers. Aren't you going out?"

"Yes, of course," Dora said. "Are they all as good-looking as the ones you see in the movies?"

"All of them, naturally," Valentina said without smiling. Dino's boldness had left her so stupefied that she was having trouble controlling herself. For a moment she was bothered by the idea that Dora would propose joining the outing; so logical and so Dora. But that would be the solution precisely, she said to herself. Brute that he is, he's not going to feel like raising a row. He's hysterical, that's obvious, but not stupid.

Dora didn't say anything although she was smiling at her with an amiability that seemed vaguely repugnant to Valentina. Without really knowing why, she didn't propose their taking the gondola together. It was extraordinary how during those weeks they did all the important things without knowing why.

> Tu parles, ma fille. *What had seemed incredible to me became simple evidence as soon as they left me out of that little ride. That couldn't have had any importance, of course, just a parenthesis of cheap and energetic consolation without the slightest future risk. But it was the recurrence at a low level of the same verification: Adriano or a gondolier, and I the outsider once more. All that was worth another cup of tea and asking oneself if there still wasn't something to do to perfect the small clockwork I had set in motion—oh, with complete innocence—before leaving Florence.*

Dino took her along the Grand Canal to beyond the Rialto, amiably choosing the longest route. At the Valmarana Palace they went into the Rio dei Santi Apostoli and Valentina, looking obstinately ahead, saw once more, coming one after another, the small, black, swarming bridges. It was hard for her to convince herself that she was in that gondola again, leaning her back against the ancient red cushion. A thread of water ran along the bottom, canal water, Venice water. The famous carnivals. The doge marrying the sea. The famous palaces and carnivals of Venice. I came to look for you because you didn't come to look for me last night. I want to take you out in the gondola. The doge marrying the sea. With perfect cheek. Cheek. And now he was taking her in the gondola, from time to time giving a cry that was somewhere between melancholic and unsociable before turning down an inner canal. In the distance, still very far off, Valentina glimpsed the open, green strip. The Fondamente Nuove again. It was foreseeable, the four mossy steps, she recognized the place. Now he was going to whistle and Rosa would appear at the window.

> *Lyrical and obvious. Missing are the Aspern papers, Baron Corvo, and Tadzio, beautiful Tadzio and the plague. Missing too is a certain telephone call to a hotel near the Teatro La Fenice, although it's nobody's fault (I mean the absence of the detail, not the telephone call).*

But Dino was docking the gondola in silence and waiting. Valentina turned for the first time since she'd gotten in and looked at him. Dino was smiling beautifully. He had stupendous teeth, which, with a little toothpaste, would have been perfect.

I'm lost, Valentina thought, and leaped out onto the first step without taking the forearm he was offering her.

Did she really think that? One must be careful with met-
aphors, rhetorical figures, or whatever they're called.
That's touching bottom too; if I'd known it at that mo-
ment, maybe there wouldn't . . . But I wasn't allowed to
go into time's beyond either.

When she came down to dinner, Dora was waiting with the
news (although she wasn't completely sure) that she'd seen
Adriano among the tourists on the Piazza.

"Very far off, in one of the arcades, you know. I think it
was him because of that light-colored suit, a bit tight. He
probably got in this afternoon . . . Pursuing you, I imagine."

"Oh, come on."

"Why not? This wasn't on his itinerary."

"You're not even sure it's him either," Valentina said
with hostility. The news hadn't shocked her too much, but it
did start up the lamentable machinery of ideas. That again,
she thought. Again. She would run into him, that was certain,
in Venice it's like living in a bottle, everybody ends up meeting on the Piazza or the Rialto. Fleeing again, but why? She
was sick of fleeing from nothing, of not knowing what she was
fleeing from and if she really was fleeing or doing the same
thing as the pigeons there before her eyes, the female pigeons
pretending to avoid the conceited attack of the males, the
better in the end to consent blindly with a leaden ruffling of
feathers.

"Let's have coffee at the Florian," Dora proposed.
"We'll probably meet him, he's such a good boy."

They saw him almost at once, he had his back to the
square under the arches of the arcade, withdrawn in the contemplation of some horrendous Murano crystal. When
Dora's greeting made him turn around, his surprise was so
minimal, so civil, that Valentina felt relieved. Nothing the-

atrical, at least. Adriano greeted Dora with his distant courtesy and shook Valentina's hand.

"Well, this certainly is a small world. No one can escape
the Blue Guide, one day or another."

"Not us, at least."

"Or the ice cream of Venice. May I invite you?"

Dora took over the conversation almost at once. She had
in her possession two or three more cities than they, and naturally she was trying to wrap them up in the catalogue of
everything they'd missed. Valentina might have been wishing
that her themes would never end or that Adriano would finally decide to look straight at her, make her the worst of
reproaches, the eyes that fasten themselves on the face with
something that's always more than an accusation or a reproach. But he was diligently eating his ice cream or smoking
with his head tilted forward—his beautiful South American
head—attentive to every word from Dora. Only Valentina
was observing the slight trembling of the fingers that held the
cigarette.

*Me too, my dear girl, me too. And I didn't like it at all
because that calm hid something that hadn't seemed so
violent to me until now, that tight spring, as if waiting
for the trigger that would release it. So different from
his glacial and matter-of-fact tone on the telephone. For
the moment I was out of the game, I could do nothing to
make things happen as I had hoped they would. Warn
Valentina . . . But it meant revealing everything to her,
going back to the Rome of those nights when she'd slipped
away, going off and leaving the shower and soap free
for me, going to sleep with her back toward me, murmuring that she was so sleepy, that she was already half
asleep.*

The conversation became circular, along came the comparison of museums and small touristic misfortunes, more ice cream and tobacco. There was talk of covering the city together the next morning.

"Maybe," Adriano said, "we'll annoy Valentina, who likes to go alone."

"Why are you including me?" Dora laughed. "Valentina and I understand each other by dint of not understanding each other. She won't share her gondola with anyone, and I've got some little canals that are mine alone. Try reaching an understanding like that with her."

"You can always try," Adriano said. "Well, in any case, I'll come by the hotel at ten thirty, and you people will have decided or will decide."

When they went up (they had rooms on the same floor), Valentina rested a hand on Dora's arm.

It was the last time you touched me. Like that, as always, lightly.

"I want to ask a favor of you."

"Of course."

"Let me go out alone with Adriano tomorrow morning. It will be the only time."

Dora was looking for the key that she'd dropped into the bottom of her purse. It took her a while to find it.

"It would be too long to explain now," Valentina added, "but you'll be doing me a favor."

"Yes, of course," Dora said, opening her door. "You don't want to share him either."

"Him either? If you think . . ."

"Oh, I was only joking. Have a good night's sleep."

*It doesn't matter now, but when I closed the door I could
have dug my nails into my face. No, it doesn't matter
now; but if Valentina had tied the ends together . . .
That "him either" was the end of the skein; she didn't
entirely realize, she let it slip out in the confusion in
which she was living. So much the better for me, naturally, but maybe . . . Finally it really doesn't matter
anymore now; sometimes Valium is enough.*

Valentina waited for him in the lobby and it didn't even
occur to Adriano to ask about Dora's absence; as in Florence
or Rome, he didn't seem too sensitive to her presence. They
walked along Orsolo, scarcely looking at the little inside lake
where the gondolas slept at night, and they headed in the
direction of the Rialto. Valentina went on a little ahead,
wearing a light-colored dress. They hadn't exchanged more
than two or three ritual phrases, but when they went into an
alleyway (they were lost, neither of them had looked at, the
map), Adriano went forward and took her by the arm.

"It's too cruel, you know. There's something swinish
about what you've done."

"Yes, I know. I use worse words."

"Going off like that, shabby. Just because a swallow died
on a balcony. Hysterical."

"You have to recognize," Valentina said, "that the reason, if that's what it is, was poetic."

"Valentina—"

"Oh, enough," she said. "Let's go to some quiet spot and
talk it out once and for all."

"Let's go to my hotel."

"No, not your hotel."

"To a café, then."

"They're full of tourists, you know that. A quiet place

that won't be interesting . . ." She hesitated because the phrase brought out a name. "Let's go to the Fondamente Nuove."

"What's that?"

"The other shore, to the north. Have you got a map? Around here, there it is. Let's go."

Beyond the Malibran theater, alleys without shops, with rows of doors that were always closed, an occasional poorly dressed child playing in a doorway, they reached Fumo and close by now they could see the glimmer of the lagoon. Suddenly they came out of the gray shadows onto a rise dazzling with sunlight, peopled with workers and street vendors. A few evil-looking cafés clung like barnacles to the floating shacks from which the vaporetti left for Burano and the cemetery. Valentina had spotted the cemetery immediately; she remembered Dino's explanation. The small island, its parallelogram surrounded as far as one could see by a reddish wall. The tops of the funereal trees stood out above it like a dark festoon. The landing dock could be seen very clearly, but at that moment the island seemed to contain only the dead; not a ferry, nobody on the marble steps of the landing. And everything was sharply ablaze under the eleven o'clock sun.

Indecisive, Valentina started walking to the right. Adriano followed her morosely, almost without looking around. They crossed a bridge under which one of the inner canals connected with the lagoon. The heat was making itself felt, its invisible flies landing on the face. Another bridge of white stone came up and Valentina stopped at the top of the arch, leaning on the balustrade, looking toward the inner part of the city. If they had to talk someplace, let it be there, so neutral, so devoid of interest, with the cemetery behind and the canal that penetrated deep into Venice, separating the graceless, almost deserted banks.

"I left," Valentina said, "because none of that made any sense. Let me talk. I left because one of us had to leave in any case, and you're making things difficult, knowing quite well that one of us had to leave. What difference does it make except in time? One week sooner or later . . ."

"There's no difference for you," Adriano said. "For you it's exactly the same."

"If I could only explain to you . . . But we'd be left with the words. Why did you follow me? What sense does this make?"

If she really said those things, at least I know she didn't think I had anything to do with Adriano's presence in Venice. Behind it, of course, the usual bitterness: that tendency to ignore me, not even to suspect that there was a third hand shuffling the cards.

"I know it doesn't make any sense," Adriano said. "That's the way it is, that's all."

"You shouldn't have come."

"And you shouldn't have left like that, abandoning me like—"

"No fancy words, please. How can you call something that was nothing but normal after all abandonment? The return to normality, if you prefer."

"Everything is so normal for you," he said furiously. His lips were trembling and he grasped the railing as if to calm himself by the blank and indifferent contact with stone.

Valentina was looking toward the end of the canal, watching a larger than ordinary gondola approaching, still imprecise in the distance. She was afraid to meet Adriano's eyes and her only wish was for him to leave, to shower her with insults if necessary and then leave. But Adriano was still there in the perfect voluptuousness of his suffering, prolonging what they had meant to be an explanation and which didn't go beyond a pair of monologues.

"It's absurd," Valentina finally murmured, still looking at the gondola that was slowly approaching. "Why do I have to be like you? Wasn't it clear that I didn't want to see you anymore?"

"Underneath it all you love me," Adriano said grotesquely. "It can't be that you don't love me."

"Why can't it be?"

"Because you're different from all the others. You didn't give in just like anyone, like a hysterical woman who doesn't know what to do on a trip."

"You're imagining that I gave in, but I could say that it was you who gave in. The same old ideas about women, when . . .

Etc.

But we're not getting anywhere with this, Adriano; it's all so useless. Either leave me alone today, right now, or I'm leaving Venice."

"I'll follow you," he said, almost petulantly.

"We're both being ridiculous. Wouldn't it be better if . . . ?"

Every word of that senseless talk was growing painful to the point of nausea. The façade of a dialogue, a painted hand under which something useless and rotten was stagnating like the waters of the canal. Halfway through the question Valentina realized that the gondola was different from the rest. Broader, like a barge, with four oarsmen standing over the crossbars, where something seemed to rise up like a black and gold catafalque. But it *was* a catafalque, and the oarsmen were dressed in black, without the merry straw hats. The boat had reached the landing alongside a heavy grayish building. There was a dock in front of something that looked like a chapel. The hospital, she thought. The hospital chapel. People were coming out, a man carrying wreaths that he threw carelessly into the boat of death. Others were appearing now with the coffin, and the maneuver of putting it on board began. Even Adriano seemed absorbed by the clear horror of what was taking place under the morning sun in the Venice that wasn't interesting, where tourists weren't supposed to go. Valentina heard him murmur something, or perhaps it was a muffled sob. But she couldn't take her eyes off the boat, the four oarsmen who were waiting with their oars dug in so that the others could put the coffin into the niche with black curtains. In the prow she saw a shiny mass instead of the familiar toothed cutout usually seen on gondolas. It looked like a huge silver owl, a figurehead with something live about it, but when the gondola went forward along the canal (the family of the dead man was on the dock and two boys were supporting an old woman) it could be seen that the owl was a silvery sphere and cross, the only bright and shiny thing on the whole boat. It came toward them; it was going to pass under the bridge, right under their feet. All that was needed was a leap to land in the bow, on top of the coffin. The bridge seemed to be moving slightly toward the boat. ("Then you won't come with me?") Valentina was staring very hard at the gondola, which the oarsmen were slowly moving.

"No, I won't go. Leave me alone, leave me in peace."

She couldn't say anything else among all the things she could have said or not said, now that she felt the trembling of Adriano's arm against hers; she heard him repeat the question and breathe heavily, as if he were panting. But she couldn't look at anything but the boat either, closer and closer to the bridge. It was going to pass under the bridge, almost up against them; it would come out the other side into the open lagoon and cross over like a slow black fish to the isle of the dead, bearing another coffin, piling one more dead body into the silent village behind the red walls. It almost didn't surprise her to see that one of the oarsmen was Dino,

Can that have been for sure, isn't it an abuse of too gratuitous a chance? It's impossible to know now, just as it's impossible to know why Adriano didn't reproach her for her cheap adventure. I think he did, that this dialogue of pure nothing that sustains the scene wasn't the real one, the one that was born of other deeds and led to something that seems inconceivable without it because it's so extreme, so horrible. After all, maybe he kept quiet what he knew so he wouldn't give me away; yes, but what did his giving me away matter if immediately after . . . ? Valentina, Valentina, Valentina, the delight of your reproaching me, insulting me, being here cursing me, being you shouting at me, the consolation of seeing you again, Valentina, of feeling your slaps, your saliva on my face . . . (A whole pill this time. Right away, my girl.)

the tallest one, in the stern, and that Dino had seen her and had seen Adriano beside her, and that he'd stopped rowing to look at her, lifting his astute little eyes to her, full of questions and probably ("Please don't insist") jealous rage. The gondola was a few feet away, every silver-headed nail could be seen, every flower, and the modest iron fittings on the coffin ("You're hurting me, let go"). On her elbow she felt the unbearable pressure of Adriano's fingers and closed her eyes for a second, thinking he was going to hit her. The boat seemed to flee under their feet, and Dino's face (startled, above all, it was comical to think that the poor imbecile had also given himself illusions) slid away suddenly, was lost under the bridge. There I go, Valentina managed to say to herself, there she went in that coffin, beyond Dino, beyond the hand that was brutally squeezing her arm. She felt Adriano making a movement as if taking something out, maybe his cigarettes, with the gesture of someone trying to gain time, to prolong the moment at all cost. Cigarette or whatever it might be, what did it matter since she was already on the black gondola, going toward her island without fear, finally accepting the swallow.

*

THERE
BUT
WHERE,
HOW

*A painting by René Magritte shows
a pipe that occupies the center of
the canvas. At the bottom of the
picture its title:* This is not a pipe.

*TO PACO,
WHO LIKED MY TALES*
(*Dedication of* Bestiario,
1951)

it doesn't depend on will

it's he all of a sudden: now (before beginning to write;
the reason for having begun to write) or yesterday, tomorrow, there's no previous indication, he's there or he's
not; I can't even say that he's come, there's neither arrival nor departure; he's like a pure presence that mani-
fests itself or doesn't in this dirty present, full of echoes
of past and obligations of future

Those of you reading me, hasn't it happened to you, that
thing that starts as a dream and turns into many dreams but

235

isn't that, isn't just a dream? Something that's there but where, how; something that happens in dreaming, of course, nothing but a dream but afterward there too, in a different way because soft and full of holes but there while you brush your teeth, in the bottom of the bathroom glass you keep on seeing it while you spit out the toothpaste or put your face in the cold water, and thinning out already but still sticking to your pajamas, to the root of the tongue while you warm the coffee, there but where, how, stuck to the morning, with its silence that the sounds of the day are already entering, the news on the radio that we turn on because we're awake and up and the world goes on. God damn it, God damn it, how can it be, what's that thing that was, that we were in a dream but is something else, comes back every so often and is there but where, how is it there and where is there? Why tonight again, Paco, now that I'm writing in this same room, beside this same bed where the sheets show the hollow of my body? Doesn't it happen the same way to you as to me with someone who died thirty-one years ago, whom we buried one sunny noon in Chacarita, carrying the coffin on our shoulders with friends from our crowd, with Paco's brothers?

> his small, pale face, his tight jai alai player's body, his eyes like limpid water, his blond hair combed with brilliantine, the part on the side, his gray suit, his black loafers, almost always a blue tie but sometimes in shirt sleeves or in a white terry cloth robe (when he waits for me in his room on the Calle Rivadavia, getting up with effort so I won't realize that he's so sick, sitting on the edge of the bed wrapped in the white bathrobe, asking me for the cigarette he's been forbidden)

I know that what I'm writing can't be written, certain that
it's another of the day's ways of ending the dream's weak
operations; now I'll go to work, I'll find myself among trans-
lators and editors at the conference in Geneva where I've
been for four weeks, I'll read the news from Chile, that other
nightmare that no toothpaste can loosen from my teeth; why
jump from my bed to the typewriter, then, from the house on
the Calle Rivadavia in Buenos Aires where I've just been
with Paco to this typewriter that won't be good for anything
now that I'm awake and know that thirty-one years have gone
by since that October morning, that niche in a cemetery, the
few flowers that almost nobody brought because damn it if
flowers mattered to us while we were burying Paco. I tell you,
those thirty-one years are not what matter, this passage from
dream to words is much worse, the gap between, what still
goes on here but is giving itself over more and more to the
neat rows of things on this side, to the knife blade of the
words I keep writing and which are no longer what follow
there, but when, how. And if I insist it's because I can't help
it, I've known so many times that Paco is alive or that he's
going to die, that he's alive in a different way from our way of
being alive or going to die, that in writing it at least I can
fight against what I can't grasp, I can run the fingers of the
words over the holes of that very slim plot that still binds
me to the bathroom, the toaster, the first cigarette, still there
but where, how; repeating, reiterating formulas of enchantment, really, probably you who are reading me also sometimes try to fix what is getting away from you with some
psalmody, you stupidly repeat a childhood verse, along came
a spider, along came a spider, closing your eyes in order to
concentrate on the capital scene of the frayed dream, rejecting the spider, shrugging off the along-came, the newsboy
knocks on the door, your wife looks at you with a smile and

tells you, Pedrito, you've got cobwebs on your eyes and she's
so right you think, along came a spider, cobwebs, naturally.

> when I dream about Alfredo, about other dead people,
> it can be any one of so many images. options of time and
> life; I can see Alfredo driving his black Ford, playing
> poker, marrying Zulema, leaving the Mariano Acosta
> Normal School with me to go have a vermouth at the
> Perla del Once; afterward, finally, before, any one of
> the days in any one of the years, but not Paco, Paco is
> only the naked and cold room of his house, the iron bed,
> the white terry cloth robe, and if we meet at the café and
> he's wearing his gray suit and blue tie, his face is the
> same, the earthen final mask, the silences of an irrepar-
> able weariness

I'm not going to waste any more time; if I write it's because I
know, even if I can't explain what it is I know and can barely
manage to separate the thickest parts, to put the dreams to
one side and Paco to the other, but it has to be done if one
day, if right now at some moment I can manage to grapple
beyond. I know that I dream about Paco because of logic,
because dead people don't walk the streets and there's an
ocean of water and time between this hotel in Geneva and his
house on the Calle Rivadavia, between his house on the Calle
Rivadavia and him dead thirty-one years ago. So it's obvious
that Paco is alive (in what useless, horrible way do I have to
say it so I can get closer, so I can gain some ground) while I
sleep; what's called dreaming. Every so often, weeks can pass
and even years, I know again while I sleep that he's alive and
is going to die; there's nothing extraordinary in dreaming
about him and seeing him alive, it happens with so many
others in everybody's dreams, I too sometimes find my grand-

mother alive in my dreams, or Alfredo alive in my dreams,
Alfredo, who was one of Paco's friends and died before him.
Anybody can dream about his dead and see them alive, that's
not why I'm writing; if I write it's because I know, even
though I can't explain what it is I know. Look, when I dream
about Alfredo the toothpaste does its job well; the melancholy is left, the recurrence of timeworn memories, then the
day without Alfredo begins. But with Paco it's as if he too
were waking up with me, he can allow himself the luxury of
dissolving the vivid sequences of the night almost immediately and continue on in the present and out of the dream,
denying with a strength that Alfredo, that nobody has in
broad daylight, after shower and newspaper. What does he
care if I can only remember that moment when his brother
Claudio came to get me, to tell me that Paco was very ill, and
that the succeeding scenes, frayed now but still rigorous and
coherent in lack of memory, a little like the hollow of my
body still marked on the sheets, are diluted like all dreams.
What I know, then, is that having dreamed is only a part of
something different, a kind of superimposition, a different
zone, even though the expression might not be right, but I
also have to superimpose or violate words if I want to get
close, if I hope to be there sometime. Broadly, as I feel it now,
Paco is alive even though he's going to die and if I know one
thing it's that there's nothing supernatural in that; I have my
own ideas about ghosts, but Paco isn't a ghost. Paco is a man,
the man he was until thirty-one years ago, my classmate, my
best friend. He hasn't had to come back to my side now and
then, the first dream was enough for me to know that he's
alive on this side or beyond the dream and for sadness to
come over me again as it did those nights on the Calle Rivadavia when I saw him giving ground to an illness that was
eating him up inside, consuming him without haste in the

most perfect of tortures. Every night that I've dreamt about him again it's been the same, the variations on the theme; it isn't the recurrence that could be fooling me, what I know now I already knew the first time, in Paris in the fifties, I think, fifteen years after his death in Buenos Aires. It's true that at that time I tried to be healthy, brush my teeth better; I rejected you, Paco, even though something in me already knew that you weren't there like Alfredo, like my other dead; facing dreams one can be a swine and a coward too, and maybe that's why you came back, not out of vengeance but to prove to me that it was useless, that you were alive and so ill, that you were going to die, that some night or other Claudio would come looking for me in dreams to weep on my shoulder, to tell me that Paco is in bad shape, what can we do, Paco is in such bad shape.

> his earthen and sunless face, not even the moon over the cafés on Eleventh, student night life, a bloodless triangular face, the sky blue water of the eyes, the lips peeled by fever, the sweet smell of Bright's disease, his delicate smile, the voice reduced to a minimum, having to breathe between each phrase, replacing words with a gesture or ironic grimace

You see, that's what I know, it isn't much but it changes everything. Time-space hypotheses bore me, n dimensions, not to mention occultist jargon, astral life, and Gustav Meyrink. I'm not going out searching because I know I'm incapable of illusion or maybe, in the best of cases, of the capacity to enter different territories. I'm simply here and ready, Paco, writing about what one more time we've lived together while I was asleep; if I can help you in anything, it's in knowing that you're not just my dream that there but where, how,

that there you're alive and suffering. About that there I can't
say anything, except what comes to me dreaming and awake,
that it's a there without a handle; because when I see you I'm
sleeping and I don't know how to think, and when I think
I'm awake but I can only think; image or idea, they're always
that there but where, that there but how.

> rereading this means lowering my head, cursing and
> lighting a new cigarette, wondering about the meaning of
> typing on this machine, who for, just tell me, who for
> who won't shrug his shoulders and quickly wrap it up,
> put on a label, and go on to something else, another story

And besides, Paco, why. I leave it for the end but it's the
hardest, it's this rebellion and this disgust at what's happened
to you. You can imagine that I can't think of you in hell, we
would've found that so funny if we could have talked about
it. But there's got to be a why, it isn't true, you yourself have
got to ask yourself why you're alive there where you are since
you're going to die again, since Claudio has to come and get
me again, since, as just a moment ago I'm going to climb the
stairs on the Calle Rivadavia to find you in your sickroom,
with that bloodless face and eyes like water, smiling with
stained, parched lips, giving me a hand that's like a piece of
paper. And your voice, Paco, the voice that I finally recognized in you, precariously articulating the few words of a
greeting or a joke. You're not in the house on the Calle Rivadavia, of course, and I, in Geneva, haven't climbed the stairs
of your house in Buenos Aires, those are the props of the
dream and, as always, on awakening the images become un-
tied and only you are still on this side, you who aren't a
dream, who've been waiting for me in so many dreams but
like someone who makes a date in a neutral place, a station or

a café, the other props that we forget as soon as we've used them.

how can I say it, how can I go on, tearing up reason re-peating that it isn't just a dream, that if I see him in dreams, like any of my dead, he's something else, he's there, inside and out, alive although

what I see of him, what I hear of him: the illness en-circling him, fixes him in that last appearance that's my memory of him thirty-one years ago; that's what he's like now, that's what he is

Why are you alive if you've gotten sick again, if you're going to die again? And when you die, Paco, what's going to happen between the two of us? Am I going to find out that you've died, am I going to dream, since dream is the only zone where I can meet you, that we're burying you again? And after that, am I going to stop dreaming, will I really know that you're dead? Because it's been many years now, Paco, that you've been living there where we meet, but with a useless and withered life, this time your illness lasts interminably longer than the other, weeks or months pass, Paris passes or Quito or Geneva and then Claudio comes and embraces me, Claudio, so young and such a puppy, weeping silently on my shoulder, telling me that you're in bad shape, to go up and see you, sometimes it's a café but almost always you have to go up the narrow staircase of that house that they've already torn down, a year ago from a taxi I looked at that block on Rivadavia and Once and I found out that the house was no longer there or that they'd remodeled it, that the door was missing and the narrow staircase that went up to the second floor, the rooms with high ceilings and yellow stucco, weeks or months pass and I know again that I have to go see you, or I just find you

anywhere or I know that you're anywhere even though I
can't see you, and nothing ends, nothing begins or ends while
I sleep or afterward at the office or here writing, you alive for
what, you alive why, Paco, there but where, old man, where
and until when.

adducing proofs of air, little piles of ash as proofs, se-
curities of a hole; the worst with words, words incapable
of vertigo, labels before the reading, that other final
label

notion of continuous territory, a room next door; time
next door, and at the same time none of that, too easy to
take refuge in the binary; as if everything depended on
me, on a simple key that a gesture or a leap would give
me, and knowing no, that my life locks me up in what I
am, on the very edge but

trying to say it in another way, insisting: out of hope,
looking for the midnight laboratory, an unthinkable al-
chemy, a transmutation

I'm no good for going beyond, trying any of the routes that
others follow in search of their dead, faith or mushrooms or
metaphysics. I know that you're not dead, that three-legged
tables are useless; I won't go consult clairvoyants because
they have their codes too, they'd look at me as if I were de-
mented. I can only believe in what I know, going along my
path like you along yours made small and ill there where you
are, without bothering me, without asking me for anything
but leaning on me in some way so I know you're alive in that
link which ties you to this zone to which you don't belong but
which sustains you who knows why, who knows for what.
And that's why I think, there are moments when you need

me and it's then that Claudio comes or suddenly I find you in
the café where we used to shoot pool or in the room on the
first floor where we played Ravel records and read Federico
and Rilke, and the dazzling happiness it gives me to know
that you're alive is stronger than the paleness of your face and
the cold weakness of your hand; because in the middle of the
dream I'm not fooled the way I'm fooled sometimes when I
see Alfredo or Juan Carlos, the happiness isn't that horrible
deception on awakening and understanding that it had been
dreamed, with you I awaken and nothing changes except that
I've stopped seeing you, I know that you're alive there where
you are, in a land that isn't this land and not an astral sphere
or an abominable limbo; and it's a hard happiness and it's
here while I write and doesn't contradict the sadness of having seen you once more so ill, it's still hope, Paco, if I write
it's because I'm waiting even though it's the same every time,
the stair that leads to your room, the café where between two
pool shots you'll tell me that you'd been sick but that you're
already getting over it, lying to me with a poor smile; the
hope that sometime it will be different, that Claudio won't
have to come and get me and weep embracing me, asking me
to go see you.

> even though it's to be near him again when he's dying,
> as on that October night, the four friends, the cold bulb
> hanging from the ceiling, the last injection of Coramine,
> the bare and frozen chest, the open eyes that one of us
> closed, weeping

And you who read me will think that I'm inventing; it
doesn't matter much, for a long time now people have cred-
ited my imagination for what I've really lived or vice versa.
Look, I have never met Paco in the city I've spoken about

sometimes, a city about which I dream every so often, and like the chamber of an infinitely postponed death, of muddied searches and impossible dates. Nothing could have been more natural than to have seen him there, but I haven't found him there nor do I think I'll find him. He has his own territory, a cat in his marked-out and precise world, the house on the Calle Rivadavia, the poolroom café, some corner on Once. Maybe if I'd found him in the city with the arcades and the canal to the north I would have added him to the machinery of the searches, the interminable rooms in the hotel, the elevators that go off horizontally, the elastic nightmare that returns every so often; it would have been easier to explain the presence, imagine it as part of that scenery which would have impoverished it by polishing it, incorporating it into its clumsy games. But Paco stays in his territory, a solitary cat emerging from a zone all his own and unalloyed; the ones who come to get me are only from his family, it's Claudio or his father, sometimes his older brother. When I awaken after having found him at home or the café, seeing death in his eyes like water, the rest is lost in the noise of awakening, only he remains with me while I brush my teeth and listen to the news before going out; his image no longer perceived with the cruel lenticular precision of the dream (the gray suit, the blue tie, the black loafers) but the certainty that without thinking he's still there and he's suffering.

not even hope in the absurd, knowing him happy again, seeing him in a ball game, in love with those girls he danced with at the club

small gray larva, animula vagula blandula, little monkey trembling with the cold under blankets, holding out a puppet hand to me, why, to what end

I can't have been able to make you live this, I write it just the same for you who read me because it's a way of breaking the encirclement, of asking you to look into yourselves to see if you don't also have one of those cats, those dead you loved and who are in that there which it exasperates me to name with words on paper. I do it for Paco, because this or any other thing might be worth something, might help him be cured or to die, so that Claudio won't come back to get me, simply to feel at last that everything was a trick, that I only dream about Paco and that he, who knows why, grasps my ankles a little tighter than Alfredo, than my other dead. It's what you're probably thinking, what else could you be thinking unless it's happened to you with somebody, but nobody has ever talked to me about things like this, I don't expect it from you either, I simply had to tell it and wait, tell it and go to bed once more like anybody else, doing whatever possible to forget that Paco is still there, that nothing ends because tomorrow or next year I'll wake up knowing as now that Paco is still alive, that he called me because he expected something from me, and that I can't help him because he's ill, because he's dying.

A
CHANGE
OF
LIGHT

On those Thursdays, at dusk, when Lemos would call to me after the rehearsal at Radio Belgrano, I would be forced over two Cinzanos to listen to the projects for new plays with a great urge to go out onto the street and forget all about the radio theater for two or three centuries, but Lemos was the author of the moment and he paid me well for the little I had to do on his programs, rather secondary and generally unsympathetic roles. You've got just the voice, Lemos would say in a friendly way, the listener hears you and hates you, you don't have to betray anybody or kill your mama with strychnine, you just open your mouth and half of Argentina would like to roast your soul over a slow fire.

Not Luciana. On the very same day that our hero, Jorge Fuentes, at the end of *Roses of Infamy*, received two baskets of love letters and a little white lamb sent by a romantic ranch wife from the Tandil region, Shorty Mazza handed me Luciana's first lilac envelope. Used to nothing in so many of its forms, I put it in my pocket before going to the café (we had a week off between the triumph of *Roses* and the beginning of *Bird in the Storm*) and only on the second martini with Juárez Celman and Olive did I remember the color of the envelope and realize that I hadn't read the letter; I didn't want to do it in front of them because bored people are always looking for something to talk about and a lilac envelope is a gold mine. I waited to get to my apartment, where the cat, at least, didn't notice such things. I gave her her milk and her ration of affection; I found Luciana.

I don't need to see a picture of you, Luciana said, I don't care if *Sintonía* and *Antena* publish pictures of Míguez and Jorge Fuentes but never one of you, I don't care because I have your voice, and I don't care either if they say you're unpleasant and a villain, I don't care if your roles fool half the world, just the opposite, because I give myself the illusion of being the only one who knows the truth: you suffer when you play those parts, you put your talent into it but I can tell that you're not really there like Míguez or Raquelita Bailey, you're so different from the cruel prince in *Roses of Infamy*. Thinking that they're hating the prince, they hate you, people get things mixed up and I realized it just last year with my Aunt Poli and other people when you were Vassilis, the murdering smuggler. I felt a little lonely this afternoon and I wanted to tell you this, maybe I'm not the only one who's told you this and I wanted it for you in some way, for you to know that you've got company in spite of everything, but at the same time I'd like to be the only one who knows how to cross over to the other side of your parts and your voice, the one who's sure that she really knows you and admires you more than the ones with the easy parts. It's like with Shakespeare, I never told anybody, but when you played the part, I liked Iago better than Othello. Don't feel obliged to answer me, I'm putting down my address just in case you really want to, but if you don't I'll feel just as happy having written you all this.

Night was falling, the hand was thin and flowing, the cat had fallen asleep after playing with the lilac envelope on the sofa pillow. Since Bruna's irreversible absence there'd been no more dining in my apartment, cans were enough for the cat and me, and cognac and pipe for me especially. During the time off (later I would have to work on the role in *Bird in the Storm*) I reread Luciana's letter with no intention of answering it because in things like that an actor, even if he only receives one letter every three years; my dear Luciana, I answered her before going to the movies Friday night, your words move me and I am not saying this out of courtesy. Of course I wasn't, I was writing as if that woman who I imagined to be rather small and sad and with chestnut hair and blue eyes were sitting right there and I was telling her that her words moved me. The rest came out more conventional because I couldn't find anything to tell her beyond the truth, all that was left was filling up the sheet of paper, two or three phrases of friendship and gratitude, your friend Tito Balcárcel. But there was another piece of truth in the postscript: I am glad that you gave me your address, it would have been sad not to have been able to tell you how I feel.

No one likes to admit it, but when a person's not working he ends up getting a little bored, someone like me, at least. As a youth I used to have a lot of sentimental adventures, during free moments I could cast my line and the fish-

ing was almost always good, but then Bruna arrived and that
lasted four years, at the age of thirty-five life in Buenos Aires
begins to fade and seems to get smaller, at least for someone
who lives alone with a cat and isn't a great reader and doesn't
like to walk much. Not that I feel old, quite the contrary; it
would seem rather that it's the others, things themselves that
are growing old and getting wrinkled; maybe that's why I'd
rather spend my afternoons in the apartment, rehearsing
Bird in the Storm by myself with the cat looking at me, getting my vengeance on those unpleasant parts by raising them
to perfection, making them mine and not Lemos', transform-
ing the simplest sentences into a play of mirrors that multi-
plies the dangerous and fascinating side of the character. And
so at the moment of reading the part on the radio everything
was foreseen, every comma and every inflection of the voice,
slowly increasing the degree of hatred (again it was one of
those characters with certain pardonable traits but who
slowly fell into infamy until there was a chase epilogue up to
the edge of a cliff and a final leap, to the great satisfaction of
the radio audience). When, between two matés, I found Luciana's letter forgotten in the magazine stand and I reread it
out of sheer boredom, it happened that I saw her again; I
have always been visual and it's easy for me to fabricate anything, in the beginning I had seen Luciana as rather small
and my age or near it, most of all with light, almost transparent eyes, and once more I imagined her like that, I saw her
pensive once more before writing me each sentence and then
deciding. Of one thing I was sure, Luciana was not a woman
for rough drafts, certain that she had hesitated before writing
me, but after hearing me in *Roses of Infamy* the sentences
had started coming to her, you felt that the letter was spon-
taneous and at the same time—maybe because of the lilac
paper—it gave me the sensation of a liqueur that has slept in
its flask for a long time.

I even imagined her house by just casting my eyes about; her house must have been one of those with a covered court-yard or at least an inner gallery with plants. Every time I thought about Luciana I would see her in the same place, the gallery finally replacing the courtyard, a closed gallery with skylights of colored glass and screens that let the light pass through, turning it gray, Luciana sitting in a large wicker chair and writing me, you're so different from the cruel prince in *Roses of Infamy*, lifting the pen to her mouth be-fore going on, nobody knows it because you've got so much talent that people hate you, the chestnut hair as if covered by the light of an old photograph, that ash-colored and at the same time clear air of the closed gallery, I would like to be the only one who knows how to cross over to the other side of your parts and your voice.

That evening, before the first performance of *Bird*, it was necessary to eat with Lemos and the others; we rehearsed some of those scenes that Lemos called core and we called bore, a clash of temperaments and theatrical fireworks, Raquelita Bailey fine in the role of Josefina, the haughty girl whom I slowly enveloped in my well-known web of evil, for which Lemos knew no limits. The others fit their parts per-fectly, so damn the difference between this one and the eigh-teen soap operas we had behind us. If I remember the re-hearsal it's Shorty Mazza who brought me the second letter from Luciana and this time I had the urge to read it right away and went to the bathroom for a spell while Angelita and Jorge Fuentes were swearing eternal love at a Fencing Acad-emy ball, those scenarios by Lemos that unchained the en-thusiasm of the fans and gave more strength to the psycho-logical identification with the characters, at least according to Lemos and Freud.

I accepted the simple, beautiful invitation to meet her at a sweet shop on Almagro. There was the monotonous detail of recognition, she in red and I carrying a newspaper folded in four; it could be no other way and the rest was Luciana writing me again in the covered gallery, alone with her mother or perhaps her father, from the beginning I had seen an old man with her in a house meant for a larger family and now full of hollow spaces and inhabited by the mother's melancholy for another daughter dead or absent, because maybe death had passed through the house not so long ago, and if you don't want to or can't I'll understand, it's not my place to take the initiative but I also know—she'd underlined it without emphasis—that someone like you is above so many things. And she added something that I hadn't thought about and which fascinated me, you don't know me except for that other letter, but I've been living your life for three years now, I can sense what you're really like in every new character, I take you out of the play and you're always the same for me when you're not wearing the mask of your role anymore. (That second letter got lost on me, but that's what the phrases were like, that's what they said; on the other hand, I can remember putting the first letter in a book by Moravia I was reading, it must still be there in the bookcase.)

If I had told Lemos about it, it would have given him an idea for another play, certainly the meeting, which would take place, naturally, after a few alternatives of suspense, and then the fellow would discover that Luciana was exactly as he had imagined, a proof of how love precedes love and sight sight, theories that always work at Radio Belgrano. But Luciana was a woman over thirty, years she carried quite well, of course, not quite so small as the woman writing letters in the gallery and with delightful black hair that had a life of its own when she moved her head. I hadn't created a precise image of Luciana's face for myself except for the blue eyes and the sadness; the ones that greeted me with a smile now were brown and not at all sad under that moving hair. I

thought it was nice that she liked whisky, on the Lemos side
almost all romantic meetings started with tea (and with
Bruna it had been café au lait in a railroad car). She didn't
make any excuses for the invitation and I, who sometimes
overreact because I basically don't believe too much in anything that happens to me, felt quite natural and the whisky
wasn't watered for once. We really enjoyed ourselves very
much and it was as if we'd been introduced by chance and
without any implications, the way good relationships begin,
ones where no one has anything to exhibit or cover up; it was
logical that the talk was mainly about me because I was the
one who was known and she was only two letters and Luciana; therefore, without seeming vain, I let her recall me in so
many soap operas, that one where I was tortured to death, the
one about the workers buried in the mine, a few other parts.
Little by little I was readjusting her face and voice, making
an effort to break away from the letters, the closed gallery, the
wicker chair; before we went our separate ways I learned that
she lived in a rather small apartment on the ground floor
and with her Aunt Poli, who had played piano in Pergamino
back in the thirties. Luciana was making her adjustments too,
as always happened with blind dates like that, just about at
the end she told me that she'd imagined me to be taller, with
curly hair and gray eyes; the part about the curly hair surprised me because I'd never thought of myself with curly hair
in any of my parts, but maybe her notion was like a summa-
tion, a piling up of all the villainies and betrayals in Lemos'
plays. I joked about it and Luciana said no, she'd seen the
characters just the way Lemos had painted them but she was
able to ignore them at the same time, to be beautifully alone
with me, with my voice and who knows why with an image of
someone taller, someone with curly hair.

If Bruna had still been in my life, I don't think I would
have fallen in love with Luciana; her absence was still too

present, a hollow in the air that Luciana began to fill without knowing it, probably without expecting it. With her, on the other hand, everything was quicker, it was going from my voice to that other Tito Balcárcel with straight hair and less personality than Lemos' monsters; all those operations lasted barely a month, they took place in two meetings in cafés, a third at my apartment, the cat accepted Luciana's perfume and skin, she fell asleep on her lap, she didn't seem to be in accord with a late afternoon in which suddenly she was in the way, when she had to leap mewing onto the floor. Aunt Poli went to live in Pergamino with a sister, her mission fulfilled, and Luciana moved to my place that week; when I helped her get her things ready I was pained by the lack of the covered gallery, the ash-colored light, I knew that I wasn't going to find them and yet there was something like a lack, a flaw. The afternoon of the move Aunt Poli told me the modest family saga in a sweet way, Luciana's childhood, the fiancé drawn away forever by an offer from the packing plants in Chicago, marriage to a hotel man from Primera Junta, and the breakup six years ago, things I had learned from Luciana but in a different way, as if she hadn't really been speaking about herself now that she seemed to be starting to live because of the presence of someone else, my body against hers, the saucers of milk for the cat, the movies at every moment, love.

I remember that it was more or less around the time of *Blood in the Cornfield* when I asked Luciana to tint her hair a lighter color. At first it seemed to be an actor's whim, I'll buy a wig if you want, she told me laughing, and, by the way, you'd look so nice in one with curly hair, since we're on the subject. But when I insisted a few days later, she said fine, black or chestnut hair didn't really matter to her, it was almost as if she'd realized that in my case change had nothing

to do with my actor's manias but with other things, a covered
gallery, a wicker chair. I didn't have to ask her a second time;
I was pleased that she'd done it for me and I told her so
several times while we made love, while I got lost in her hair
and her breasts and let myself slide with her into another
long sleep mouth to mouth. (Maybe the following morning,
or was it before going out shopping, I don't have it too clear,
I drew her hair together with both hands and tied it at the
back of her neck, I assured her that it looked better that way.
She looked at herself in the mirror and didn't say anything,
although I sensed that she didn't agree and she was right, she
wasn't the kind of woman to tie up her hair, it was impossible
to deny that it looked better on her when she wore it loose
before she lightened it, but I didn't tell her because I liked to
see her that way, to see her in a better way than that afternoon when she'd come into the sweet shop for the first time.)

I'd never liked hearing myself act, I did my job and that
was enough, my colleagues were puzzled by the lack of vanity,
which was so visible in them; they must have thought, maybe
correctly, that the nature of my roles didn't induce me to
remember them too much, and that's why Lemos looked at
me with raised eyebrows when I asked him for the file records
of *Roses of Infamy*, he asked me what I wanted them for and
I gave him some answer or other, problems of diction that I
wanted to solve or something like that. When I got home
with the album of records, Luciana was also a little surprised
because I never talked to her about my work, it was she who
would give me her impressions every so often, would listen to
me on certain afternoons with the cat on her lap. I repeated
what I'd told Lemos but instead of listening to the records in
another room I brought the phonograph into the living room
and asked Luciana to stay with me a while, I made the tea
myself and fixed the lights so she would be comfortable. Why

are you moving that lamp, Luciana asked, it's fine there. It was fine as an object but it gave off a crude, hot light onto the couch where Luciana was sitting, it would be better if only the half-light of the afternoon reached her from the window, a light that was a bit ash-colored and wrapped itself around her skin, her hands, as they busied themselves with the tea. You spoil me too much, Luciana said, everything for me, and you there in a corner without even sitting down.

Naturally, I only put on a few passages from *Roses*, just the time for two cups of tea, a cigarette. It did me good to watch Luciana, intent on the play, raising her head from time to time when she recognized my voice and smiling as if it didn't bother her knowing that poor Carmencita's miserable brother-in-law was beginning his intrigues in order to get hold of the Pardos' fortune, and that the sinister task would continue all through the many episodes until the inevitable triumph of love and justice according to Lemos. In my corner (I had accepted a cup of tea beside her but then I had returned to the back of the room as if I could hear better from there) I felt good, for a moment I was rediscovering something that I had been lacking; I would have liked everything to have been prolonged, for the light of dusk to have kept on resembling that of the covered gallery. It couldn't be, of course, and I turned off the phonograph and we went out onto the balcony after Luciana had put the lamp back in its place, because it really didn't look right where I'd moved it. Did listening to yourself do you any good, she asked me, stroking my hand. Yes, a lot; I talked about breathing problems, vowels, anything that she would accept with respect; the only thing I didn't tell her was that at that perfect moment all that was lacking was the wicker chair and maybe, also, for her to have been sad, like someone looking into space before continuing the paragraph of a letter.

We were coming to the end of *Blood in the Cornfield;* three more weeks and I'd have a vacation. When I got back from the station I would find Luciana reading or playing with the cat in the easy chair I had given her for her birthday along with the matching wicker table. They don't fit this decor at all, Luciana had said half-amused and half-perplexed, but if you like them I do too, it's a beautiful set and so comfortable. It'll be better for you if you have to write letters, I told her. Yes, Luciana admitted, as a matter of fact, I owe Aunt Poli, poor thing. There wasn't much light on the chair in the afternoon (I don't think she'd noticed that I'd changed the bulb in the lamp), so she ended up putting the little table and the chair near the window to knit or to look at magazines, and maybe it was on one of those autumn days, or a little later, that I spent a long time by her side one afternoon; I kissed her for a long time and I told her that never had I loved her as much as at that moment, just as I was seeing her, as I would have wanted to see her forever. She didn't say anything, her hands ran through my hair, mussing it, her head hung over my shoulder and she was quiet, as if absent. Why expect anything else from Luciana, on the edge of dusk like that? She was like the lilac envelopes, like the simple, almost timid phrases of her letters. From now on it would be hard for me to imagine that I'd met her in a sweet shop, that her black hair had swung like a whip at the moment of greeting me, of overcoming the first confusion of the meeting. In the memory of my love there was the covered gallery, the figure in a wicker chair that moved her away from the taller and more vital image that walked about the house in the morning or played with the cat, the image that at dusk would now and then enter into what I had wanted, into what made me love her so much.

Tell her, perhaps. I didn't have time, I think I hesitated

because I preferred keeping her like that, the fulfillment was so great that I didn't want to think about her vague silence, a distraction I hadn't known in her before, a way of looking at me for moments as if searching, something, a quiver of a glance returned immediately to the immediate, to the cat or to a book. That, too, entered into my way of preferring her, it was the melancholy climate of the covered gallery, the lilac envelopes. I know that awakening in the middle of the night sometimes, watching her sleeping against me, I could feel that the time had come to tell her about it, to make her mine again once and for all through a total acceptance of my slowly woven web of love. I didn't do it because Luciana was sleeping, because Luciana was awake, because that Tuesday we were going to the movies, because we were looking for a car for our vacation, because life came in great screenings before and after the dusks where the grayish light seemed to condense her perfection in the pause in the wicker chair. Because she spoke to me so little now, because sometimes she would look at me again as if searching for some lost thing, I held back the obscure necessity to confide the truth to her, to explain at last the chestnut hair, the light in the gallery. I didn't have time, a chance change in schedules brought me downtown one forenoon and I saw her coming out of a hotel, I didn't recognize her when I recognized her, I didn't understand when I understood that she was coming out holding tightly onto the arm of a man who was taller than I, a man who leaned over a little to kiss her on the ear, to brush his curly hair against Luciana's chestnut hair.

THROAT
OF
A
BLACK
KITTEN

Otherwise it was not the first time it had happened to him,
but, in any case, it had always been Lucho who took the initiative, resting his hand almost casually to stroke that of a
blonde or a redhead who pleased him, taking advantage of
the rocking on the curves in the subway, and then there
would be an answer there, a conquest, a small finger that
stayed caught a moment before the look of annoyance or in-
dignation, everything depended on so many things, sometimes it turned out well, ran right along, the rest coming into
play as the stations appeared through the windows of the car,
but that afternoon it was happening in a different way. First,
Lucho was frozen and his hair had been covered with snow

that melted on the platform and slid down his scarf in icy
drops; he'd gotten on the subway at the Rue du Bac station
without thinking about anything, one body stuck in among a
lot of others waiting for the moment of being by the fireplace,
the glass of cognac, the reading of the newspaper before settling down to study German between seven thirty and nine,
the usual thing except for that little black glove on the handrail, among piles of hands and elbows and coats a little black
glove lost on the metal bar and he with his wet brown glove
firmly on the bar so as not to fall on top of the lady with the
packages and the weepy little girl, suddenly the awareness
that a tiny finger was kind of riding horseback on his glove,
that it was coming from a rather worn rabbit-skin sleeve. The
mulatto girl seemed quite young and she was looking down as
if out of it all, one more person swaying in the midst of the
swaying of so many bodies crushed together; to Lucho it
seemed like a rather amusing breaking of the rules, he re-
leased his hand, without responding, imagining that the girl
was distracted, that she hadn't been aware of that gentle
mounting of the damp and quiet horse. He wished he'd had
enough room to take the newspaper out of his pocket and
read the headlines that talked about Biafra, Israel, and soccer
games, but the paper was in his right-hand pocket and in
order to get it out he would have had to let go of the bar,
losing the support necessary for the curves, so that the best
thing to do was hold tight, opening up a small precarious
space in the midst of overcoats and packages so that the little
girl would be less sad and her mother wouldn't keep on talking to her in that tax collector's tone.

He had scarcely looked at the mulatto girl. Now he pic-
tured her mat of curly hair under the hood of her coat and
thought critically that with the heat of the car she might just
as well have thrown the hood back, precisely when the finger

stroked his glove again, first one finger and then two climbing onto the damp horse. The curve before Montparnasse-Bienvenüe pushed the girl against Lucho, her hand slipped off the horse to grasp the bar, so small and silly beside the big stallion who naturally was looking for the tickling with a two-fingered snout, without forcing, amused and still distant and damp. The girl seemed to be suddenly aware (but her previous distraction had also had something sudden and brusque about it), and she moved her hand a little farther away, looking at Lucho from the dark hollow that the hood afforded her to look at her own hand then as if she didn't agree or was studying the distances of good breeding. A lot of people had gotten off at Montparnasse-Bienvenüe and Lucho could now take his newspaper out, except that instead of taking it out he'd remained studying the behavior of the gloved little hand with a somewhat mocking attention, without looking at the girl, who once again had her eyes fixed on her shoes, quite visible now on the dirty floor, where suddenly the crying girl and so many people getting off at the Falguière station were missing. The starting jolt made the two gloves tighten on the bar, separated and each working in its own way, but the train was halted at the Pasteur station when Lucho's fingers sought the black glove, which didn't withdraw as the first time but seemed to loosen on the bar, become even smaller and softer under the pressure of two, three fingers, of the whole hand that was moving along in a slow, delicate possession, without resting on it too much, taking and leaving at the same time, and in the now almost empty car, which was opening its doors at the Volontaires station, the girl, turning little by little on one foot, faced Lucho without raising her face, as if looking at him from the little glove that was covered by Lucho's whole hand, and when she finally looked at him, the pair of them shaken by a hard jolt between Volontaires and Vaugirard, her large eyes in the shadows of the hood were there as if waiting, fixed and grave, without the slightest smile or reproach, with nothing but an interminable waiting that made Lucho vaguely uncomfortable.

"It's always like that," the girl said. "There's just no way with them."

"Ah," Lucho said, accepting the game but wondering why it wasn't funny, why it didn't feel like a game even though it couldn't be anything else, there was no reason to imagine that it was anything else.

"Nothing can be done," the girl repeated. "They don't understand or they don't want to, who can say, but nothing can be done to stop them."

She was talking to the glove, looking at Lucho without seeing him, she was talking to the little black glove that was almost invisible under the large brown glove.

"The same thing happens to me," Lucho said. "They're incorrigible, that's for sure."

"It's not the same thing," the girl said.

"Oh, yes, you saw."

"It's no use talking," she said, lowering her head. "I'm sorry, it was my fault."

It was the game, of course, but why wasn't it funny, why didn't it feel like a game even though it couldn't be anything else, there was no reason to imagine that it was anything else.

"Let's say it was their fault," Lucho said, taking his hand away to mark the plural, to denounce the ones to blame on the bar, the silent distant gloved ones on the bar.

"It's different," the girl said. "It looks the same to you, but it's so different."

"Well, there's always one who starts."

"Yes, there's always one."

It was the game, it was only necessary to follow the rules without imagining that there was anything else, a kind of truth or desperation. Why play dumb instead of following the current if it carried him in that direction.

"You're right," Lucho said. "Something would have to be done about them, not let them have their way."

"It's no use," the girl said.

"That's true, it's just a distraction, you can see."

"Yes," she said. "Even if you're saying it as a joke."

"Oh, no, I'm speaking just as seriously as you. Look at them."

The brown glove was playing at brushing against the motionless little black glove, it passed a finger around its waist, let go of it, went to the other end of the bar and stayed looking at it, waiting. The girl lowered her head all the more and Lucho wondered again why all that wasn't funny now that there was nothing to do but keep on playing.

"If only it were serious," the girl said, but she wasn't speaking to him, she wasn't speaking to anyone in the almost empty car. "If it were serious then probably."

"It is serious," Lucho said, "and nothing can really be done about it."

Now she looked at him in the face, as if waking up; the train was coming into the Convention station.

"People don't understand," the girl said. "When it's the case of a man, of course, he immediately imagines that . . ."

Vulgar, of course, and besides he would have to hurry because there were only three stations left.

"And even worse if it's a woman," the girl was saying. "It's already happened to me and that's why I keep a close watch on them from the moment I get on, all the time, but you can see."

"Of course," Lucho accepted. "That minute when a person is distracted arrives, it's so natural, and then they take advantage."

"Speak for yourself," the girl said. "It's not the same

thing. I'm sorry, it was my fault, I'm getting off at Corentin Celton."

"Of course it's your fault," Lucho mocked. "I should have got off at Vaugirard and look, you've made me go two stations beyond."

The curve threw them against the door, their hands slipped until they came together at the end of the bar. The girl went on saying something, foolishly excusing herself; Lucho again felt the fingers of the black glove as they climbed onto his hand, encircling it. When she let go of him, suddenly murmuring a confused good-bye, there was only one thing to do, follow her along the station platform, come up beside her and look for her hand, which was hanging kind of head down at the end of the sleeve, swaying without any reason.

"No," the girl said. "Please, no. Let me go on alone."

"Of course," Lucho said, without releasing her hand. "But I don't like your going away like that now. If only we'd had more time on the subway . . ."

"What for? What purpose would be served by having more time?"

"We probably would have ended up finding something, together. Something against it, I mean."

"But you don't understand," she said. "You're thinking that . . ."

"Who knows what I'm thinking," Lucho said honestly. "Who knows whether they have good coffee in the café on the corner, or if there is a café on the corner, because I barely know this district."

"There's a café," she said, "but the coffee's no good."

"You can't deny to me that you smiled."

"I don't deny it, but the coffee's no good."

"In any case, there's a café on the corner."

"Yes," she said, and this time she smiled, looking at him.

"There's a café but the coffee's no good, and you believe that I—"

"I don't believe anything," he said, and he was accursedly correct.

"Thank you," the girl said, incredibly. She was breathing as if the stairs had tired her out, and it seemed to Lucho that she was trembling, but once more the little black glove hanging warm inoffensive absent, once more he felt it living between his fingers, twisting, tightening curling bubbling being well being warm being content caressing black little glove fingers two three four five one, fingers seeking fingers and glove on glove, black on brown, finger between finger, one between one and three, two between two and four. It was happening, it was swinging there near their knees, nothing could be done, it was pleasant and nothing could be done or it was unpleasant but, in the same way, nothing could be done, it was happening there and it wasn't Lucho who was playing with the hand that was sticking its fingers between his and curling and wriggling nor was it in any way the girl who was panting as she reached the top of the stairs and was lifting her face up against the drizzle as if she wanted to wash away the stale, hot air of the subway passages.

"I live there," the girl said, pointing to a high window among so many windows among so many identical high buildings across the street. "We could make some Nescafé; it's better than going to a bar, I think."

"Oh, yes," Lucho said, and it was his fingers that were closing slowly over the glove as one squeezes the throat of a black kitten. The apartment was rather large and very hot, with an azalea and a floor lamp and Nina Simone records and a messy bed that the girl embarrassedly and excusing herself made up with some tugs. Lucho helped her set out the cups and spoons on the table near the window, they made some strong and sugary Nescafé, her name was Dina and his was Lucho. Happy, as if relieved, Dina talked about Martinique, Nina Simone, for moments she gave an impression of being barely nubile inside that plain wax-colored dress, the mini-skirt was becoming to her, she worked in a notary's office, broken ankles were painful but skiing in February in the Haute-Savoie, ah. Twice she'd remained looking at him, she'd started to say something with the tone from the subway handrest, but Lucho had cracked a joke, having decided enough now, something else, it was useless to insist and ad-mitting at the same time that Dina was suffering, that it was probably harmful to her to give up the comedy so soon, as if it had the slightest importance. And the third time, when Dina had leaned over to pour the hot water into his cup, murmuring again that it wasn't her fault, that it only hap-pened to her at certain times, that now he could see how it was all different this time, the water and the spoon, the obed-ience of every gesture, then Lucho understood but who knows what, he had suddenly understood and it was differ-ent, it was from the other side, the handrest had its purpose, the game hadn't been a game, broken ankles and skis could go to the devil now that Dina was talking again without his interrupting her or getting her off the track, leaving her alone, sensing her, almost waiting for her, believing because it was absurd, unless it was only because Dina with her sad little face, her small breasts that gave the lie to the Tropics, simply because Dina. I'll probably have to be locked up, Dina had said without emphasis, it happens at any moment, you're you, but other times. Other times what. Other times insults, a slap on the behind, right off to bed, baby, why waste time. But then. Then what. But then, Dina.

"I thought you'd understood," Dina said sullenly. "When I told you that I'd probably have to be locked up."

"Nonsense. But I, at first—"

"I know. It couldn't help happening to you at first. That's just it, at first everybody makes a mistake, it's so logical. So logical, so logical. And locking me up would be logical too."

"No, Dina."

"Yes it would, God damn it. I'm sorry. But it would. It would be better than the other thing, which so many times. Nympho I don't know how many times. Hooker, tart. It would be a lot better in the long run. Or if I cut them off myself with a meat cleaver. But I haven't got a cleaver," Dina said, smiling as if he would therefore forgive her again, so absurd reclining in the easy chair, slipping down fatigued, lost, with her miniskirt higher and higher, forgetting about herself, watching them only taking a cup, putting in the Nescafé, obeying hypocritical industrious tarts hookers nympho I don't know how many times.

"Don't talk nonsense," Lucho repeated, lost in something that he thought could be anything now, desire, mistrust, protection. "I know it isn't normal, you'd have to find the causes, you'd have to. In any case, why go so far? Locking-up or the cleaver, I mean."

"Who knows?" she said. "I'd probably have to go far, right to the very end. It would probably be the only way of getting out."

"What does far mean?" Lucho asked, fatigued. "And what's the very end?"

"I don't know, I don't know anything. I'm only afraid. I'd be impatient too if someone else spoke to me like that, but there are days when. Yes, days. And nights."

"Ah," Lucho said, bringing his match to his cigarette. "Because at night too, of course."

"Yes."

"But not when you're alone."

"When I'm alone too."

"When you're alone too. Ah."

"Understand, I mean that."

"It's fine," Lucho said, drinking his coffee. "It's fine, nice and hot. Just what we needed on a day like this."

"Thanks," she said simply, and Lucho looked at her not because he wanted to please her in anything; he simply felt the recompense of that moment of rest, that the handrest was finally finished.

"And it wasn't bad or disagreeable," Dina said as if guessing. "I don't care if you don't believe me, but for me it wasn't bad or disagreeable, the first time."

"The first time for what?"

"That, that it wasn't bad or disagreeable."

"That they put themselves . . . ?"

"Yes, they put themselves once more and it wasn't bad or disagreeable."

"Were you ever arrested because of it?" Lucho asked, lowering his cup to the saucer with a slow and deliberate movement, guiding his hand so that the cup would land exactly in the middle of the saucer. Contagious, by God.

"No, never, but on the other hand . . . There are other things. I already told you, people who think that it's a proposition and also people who begin, just like you. Or they get furious, like the women, and you have to get off at the first station or run out of the store or the café."

"Don't cry," Lucho said, switching to the familiar form. "We're not going to get anywhere if you start crying."

"I don't want to cry," Dina said. "But I've never been able to talk to anybody like this, after . . . No one believes me, no one can believe me, you yourself don't believe me, you're just good and you don't want to hurt me."

"I believe you now," Lucho said. "Up until two minutes ago I was just like the rest of them. You probably should have laughed instead of crying."

"You see," Dina said, closing her eyes. "You see how useless it is. Not even you, even though you say so, even though you believe. It's too idiotic."

"Have you seen somebody?"

"Yes. You know," she said, going into the familiar form, "tranquilizers and a change of air. You fool yourself for a few days, you think that . . ."

"Yes," Lucho said, offering her a cigarette. "Wait. Like this. Let's see what it does."

Dina's hand took the cigarette with thumb and forefinger, and at the same time the ring finger and the pinky tried to coil around Lucho's fingers as he held his arm out, watching. Free of the cigarette, his five fingers came down until they enwrapped the small dark hand, barely encircling it, beginning a slow caress that slid alone until it was left free, trembling in the air; the cigarette fell into the cup. The hands quickly went up to Dina's face as she doubled over the table, breaking out into a hiccoughing as if she were throwing up.

"Please," Lucho said, lifting up the cup. "Please, no. Don't cry like that, it's so absurd."

"I don't want to cry," Dina said. "There is nothing to cry about, on the contrary, but you can see."

"Drink it, it'll do you good, it's hot; I'll make myself another one, wait till I wash the cup."

"No, let me do it."

They got up at the same time, came together at the edge of the table. Lucho put the dirty cup back down on the tablecloth; their hands hung loose against their bodies; only their lips touched. Lucho looking at her full in the face and Dina with her eyes closed, tears.

"Maybe," Lucho murmured, "maybe this is what we have to do, the only thing we can do, and then."

"No, no, please," Dina said, motionless and without

opening her eyes. "You don't know what . . . No, better not, better not."

Lucho had encircled her shoulders, was slowly squeezing her against him, he felt her breathing against his mouth, a hot breath with the smell of coffee and dark skin. He kissed her fully on the mouth, sinking into her, looking for her teeth and tongue; Dina's body went soft in his arms, forty minutes before her hand had stroked his on the handrail of a subway, forty minutes before a small black glove on a brown glove. He barely heard her resist, repeat the negative in which there had been the beginning of a warning, but everything gave way in her, in the two of them; now Dina's fingers were climbing slowly up Lucho's back, her hair was getting in his eyes, her smell was a smell without words or warnings, the blue blanket against their bodies, the obedient fingers looking for the zippers, scattering clothes, obeying orders, his and Dina's against the skin, between the thighs, the hands like the mouths and knees and now stomachs and waists, a murmured plea, a resisted pressure, a moving back, an instantaneous movement to transfer from the mouth to the fingers and from the fingers to the sexes that hot froth that leveled everything, that in a single movement united their bodies and threw them into the game. When they lighted cigarettes in the darkness (Lucho had tried to put out the lamp and the lamp had fallen onto the floor with a noise of broken glass, Dina had started up as if in terror, refusing the darkness, she'd spoken about lighting a candle at least and going down to buy another bulb, but he'd embraced her again in the darkness and now they were smoking and catching sight of each other every time they inhaled, and they kissed again), it was stubbornly raining outside, the warmed-up room held them naked and lax, rubbing each other with hands and waists and hair they relaxed, they stroked each other interminably, they saw each other with a repeated and damp touch, they smelled each other in the darkness murmuring a happiness of monosyllables and diastoles. At some moment the questions would return, the ones chased away that the darkness was hiding in the corners or under the bed, but when Lucho wanted to know, she leaped on top of him with her wet skin and shut his mouth with kisses, soft bites, only much later, with new cigarettes between their fingers, did she tell him that she lived alone, that nobody lasted long with her, that it was useless, that they never loved her, that there was that illness, everything as if it didn't really matter underneath or was too important for words to be worth anything, or maybe as if it all wasn't going to go beyond that night and didn't need any explanations, something barely started on a subway handrail, something that most of all they had to have some light.

"There's a candle somewhere," she'd insisted monotonously, rejecting his caresses. "It's too late to go down to buy a bulb. Let me look for it, it must be in some drawer. Give me the matches."

"Don't light it yet," Lucho said. "It's so nice like this, not seeing each other."

"I don't want to. It's nice but you know, you know. Sometimes."

"Please," Lucho said, feeling on the floor to find the cigarettes. "For a while we'd forgotten . . . Why are you starting up again? We were fine like this."

"Let me get the candle," Dina repeated.

"Go get it, what difference does it make?" Lucho said, handing her the matches. The flame floated in the stagnant air of the room, outlining the body that was only a little less dark than the shadows, a glow of eyes and nails, darkness again, scratching another match, darkness, scratching another match, the quick movement of the flame that was going out in the back of the room, a short, as if suffocated, run, the weight of the naked body falling across his, hurting his ribs, her panting. He hugged her tightly, kissing her without knowing from what or why he had to calm her down, he murmured words of relief to her, held her against him, under him, possessed her gently and almost without desire from a long fatigue, entered her and rode her feeling her curl and give way and open and now, now, already, now, like that, already, and the ebb tide returning them to a rest face up looking at nothingness, hearing the night throb with the blood of rain outside, the interminable great womb of night guarding them from fears, from subway handrails and broken lamps and matches that Dina's hand had refused to hold, that had folded under to burn itself and burn her, almost like an accident because in the dark space and positions change and a person is clumsy like a child but after the second match was squashed between two fingers, wrathful crab burning itself just so long as the light was destroyed, then Dina had tried to light one last match with the other hand and it had been worse, she couldn't even tell Lucho, who was listening to her out of a vague fear, a dirty cigarette in her hand. Can't you see that they're refusing, there it is again. What again? That. What again? No, nothing, I've got to find the candle. I'll look for it, give me the matches. I dropped them over there, in the corner. Don't move, wait. No, don't go, please don't go. Let go, I'll find them. Let's go together, it's better. No, let me, I'll find them, tell me where the damned candle could be. Over there, in the cupboard, if you lighted a match probably. You can't see anything, let me go. Rejecting her slowly, unknotting the hands that held his waist, getting up little by little. The tug on his sex made him cry out more from surprise than from pain; like a whip he grabbed the fist that bound him to Dina, who was stretched out on her back and moaning, he opened its fingers and pushed it away violently. He heard her call him, ask him to come back, that it wouldn't happen again, that it was his fault for being stubborn. Guiding himself to what he thought was the corner, he crouched beside the thing that might have been the table and felt around for the matches, he seemed to find one but it was too long, maybe a toothpick, and the box wasn't there, the palms of his hands ran over the old rug, he crawled on his knees under the table; he found one match, then another, but not the box; down on the floor it seemed even darker, it smelled of enclosure and of time. He felt the claws running over his back, coming up to the nape of his neck and his hair, he straightened himself with a leap, pushing Dina away as she shouted against him and said something about the light on the landing of the stairs, open the door and the light from the stairs, but of course, why hadn't they thought of that before, where was the door, there opposite, surely not since the table was on that side, under the window, I tell you over there, then you go since you know, let's both go, I don't want to be left alone now, let go of me, you'll hurt me, I can't, I tell you I can't, let go of me or I'll hit you, no, no, let me go. The shove left him alone facing something panting, something that was trembling there alongside, very close; stretching out his arms he went forward looking for a wall, imagining the door; he touched something hot that evaded him with a shout, his other hand closed on Dina's neck as if it were squeezing a glove or the throat of a black kitten, the burning tore his cheek and lips, grazing an eye; he threw himself back to free himself from what was still clutching Dina's throat, fell back onto the rug, dragged himself aside knowing what was going to happen, a hot wind over him, the scratch of nails against his stomach and ribs, I told you, I told you it couldn't be, light the candle, find the door right now, the door. Crawling away from the voice that hung somewhere in the black air, in a hiccough of asphyxia that was repeated and repeated, he came to the wall, moved along it standing up until he felt a frame, a curtain, the other frame, the latch; an icy wind mingled with the blood that filled his lips, he felt for the light switch, behind he heard Dina's running and shriek, her blow against the half-open door, she must have hit her forehead or her nose on the edge, the door closing behind his back just as he pushed the light button. The neighbor who was spying from the door across the way looked at him and with a muffled exclamation went back inside and bolted the door. Lucho naked on the landing cursed him and ran his fingers over his face, which was burning, while everything else was the cold of the landing, the footsteps running up from the first floor, open up, open up at once, for God's sake open up, there's light now, open up there's light now. Inside the silence and a kind of waiting, the old woman wrapped in the purple robe looking from below, a shriek, shameful, at this time of night, pervert, police, they're all the same, Madame Roger, Madame Roger! She's not going to open up for me, Lucho thought, sitting on the first step, wiping the blood from his mouth and eyes; she's been knocked out by the blow and is lying there on the floor, she's not going to open up, always the same, it's cold, it's cold. He began to pound on the door while he heard the voices in the apartment opposite, the running of the old woman going down and calling Madame Roger, the building waking up below him, questions and noises, a moment of waiting, naked and covered with blood, a madman, Madame Roger, open up, Dina, open up, it doesn't matter that it's always been like this but open up, we were something else, Dina, we could have found it together, why are you there on the floor, what did I do to you, why did you bump into the door, Madame

Roger, if you opened up we could find the way out, you've already seen, you saw how everything was going so well, just turning on the light and the two of us continuing to look, but you won't open up for me, you're crying, mewing like an injured cat, I hear you, I hear you, I hear Madame Roger, the police, and you son of a thousand bitches why are you spying on me from that door, open up, Dina, we can still find the candle, we'll wash up, I'm cold, Dina, there they come with a bedspread, it's typical, a naked man is wrapped in a bedspread, I'll have to tell them that you're stretched out there, to bring another bedspread, to knock the door down, to clean up your face, to take care of you and protect you because I won't be there, they'll separate us immediately, you'll see, they'll take us down separately and carry us off far from each other, what hand will you look for, Dina, what face will you scratch while they carry you off so many of them and Madame Roger.

A NOTE ON THE TYPE

This book was set on the Linotype in Bodoni Book, *a type face so called after Giambattista Bodoni, a celebrated printer and type designer of Rome and Parma (1740–1813).* Bodoni Book *as produced by the Linotype Company is not a copy of any one of Bodoni's fonts, but a composite, modern version of the Bodoni manner. Bodoni's innovations in type style included a greater degree of contrast in the "thick and thin" elements of the letters and a sharper and more angular finish of details.*

Composed by Maryland Linotype Composition Company, Inc., Baltimore, Maryland
Printed and bound by The Haddon Craftsmen, Inc., Scranton, Pennsylvania

Designed by Margaret Wagner